BLUENOSE COUNTRY

BY MORTIMER LEVY

 FriesenPress

Suite 300 - 990 Fort St
Victoria, BC, V8V 3K2
Canada

www.friesenpress.com

ISBN
978-1-4602-2125-9 (Hardcover)
978-1-4602-2123-5 (Paperback)
978-1-4602-2124-2 (eBook)

1. Fiction, Coming Of Age

Distributed to the trade by The Ingram Book Company

PROLOGUE

The well known term, Bluenose, has traditionally been associated with the people of Nova Scotia, inhabitants of Canada's most easterly mainland territory. The word was coined in 1785 by a Reverend Jacob Baily, a British Loyalist, to describe the original coarse pioneer colonists of that province. Some maintain it was a description of the natives' noses during the cold winters; others claim it was named for the purplish-blue potatoes of the Annapolis Valley, which most everyone consumed. This popular name was adopted by numerous enterprises, including newspapers, boats and railways. The internationally famous fishing vessel, *BLUENOSE,* was built and launched in Lunenburg in 1921. Her dominance in racing competitions earned her the name, "Queen of the North Atlantic". Lunenburg is now the permanent home of the *BLUENOSE II,* a recently upgraded replica of the original that has become part of Canada's maritime history. It attracts thousands of visitors each year, and its image currently graces the back of the Canadian dime. An extensive renovation of the vessel has just been completed. The town of Lunenburg lies tucked away in a small bay on the southeast coast of Nova Scotia. It's a friendly community of approximately three thousand inhabitants with a two-hundred-and-fifty-year history of shipbuilding and fishing. Its colorful past recounts stories of miraculous progress, mostly by impoverished hard-working immigrants. The patriotism of its citizenry resulted in grievous losses in three wars. It's a place of hardy souls who plied the Newfoundland Grand Banks in small fishing dories, drawing sustenance from an often cruel and begrudging North Atlantic.

***

Author's Note: The story takes place mainly on Canada's east coast. A glossary* appears at the end in alphabetical order.

ONE

"C'mon Jeep, you can make it."

Jim Cabot goaded the old army surplus vehicle up Montague Hill.

"Jeep, whenever I paint you, I fall in love with you all over again. Shoulda' scrapped you years ago."

The red roof of the Cabot House was a welcome sight. The thought of a warm fireplace and a cool beer prompted extra pressure on the gas pedal. The ache in Jim's back and legs was reason enough to cut short his work day at the marina, a day where just about everything had gone wrong. He parked the Jeep but hesitated before getting out. He needed a few extra moments to plan a painless exit.

Jim settled into the verandah couch, rested his feet on the old milking stool and shouted through the screen door,

"Greta, will you please bring me a cold beer and a needle. I've got another bloody splinter."

He suddenly reminded himself that it was the housekeeper's day off.

"Damn, no beer and no fireplace."

The loud bark of a dog startled him.

"Hey Jim, how's the boat coming along, still slaving away at the marina?"

Jim looked up to see his neighbor, Bill Gallant, an Inspector with the Royal Canadian Mounted Police, being pulled across the street by his very large Labrador Retriever.

"Yeah, Bill, but hopefully I'll be in the home stretch in a few more weeks. That dog of yours is going to be disappointed. It's Greta's day off; I'm afraid there's no doggie cookies today."

"That's fine with me, the animal is about twenty pounds overweight."

"Hey, c'mon on up here and I'll get you a beer. How's the crime scene...anything exciting happening?"

"Thanks Bill, but my housekeeper is off today too and I gotta get back to my wife. The crime scene is unusually quiet. Maybe we're becoming more civilized. If this keeps up, I could be out of a job."

"That's probably the best thing that could happen to you. When are you gonna retire?"

"Jim, I think more and more about it these days. I should really spend more time with my wife, and I haven't seen my daughter and grandchildren since Christmas."

Gallant was a stocky, balding, impeccably dressed man. He was a legend in Lunenburg and a familiar face to virtually everyone in town. His spouse was an Alzheimer's victim; he had gone against her doctor's advice suggesting a long-term facility but had decided instead to look after her himself. It was just another reason why the man had garnered Jim's respect and that of just about everyone in the community.

"Bill, how's the wife doing......are you managing O.K.?"

"Everyone asks me the same question. You know Jim, you and I go back a good many years. I remember your wedding like yesterday and I clearly recall what a beautiful couple you and Celia were. I understand how you sympathize with my situation, but think about it. You lost the love of your life but I still have mine. Sure,...she doesn't speak or smile and I don't even know for certain if she sees me. But Jim, I still have her; I can touch her and embrace her,....I can stare at her beautiful face like I did when we were courting. At night I hold her hand and think about the pleasures we shared. Like I said, Jim, don't feel sorry for me, I'm still happily married to my first and only love."

"Bill, you're a special human being. A woman couldn't ask for a better husband and I couldn't ask for a better friend."

***

Jim rose slowly from the couch, his tall, slender figure arched over in discomfort. On the way to the kitchen, he caught a glimpse of himself in the hall mirror and thought, 'Hell, I look as bad as I feel.' Hidden behind the lines of fatigue was a handsome face. His slender features, pale blue eyes and greying hair projected a calm, quiet strength. His profession as an engineer had instilled in him a disciplined and orderly existence.

The short trip to the fridge was a gauntlet of pain. He reached for the beer, moved slowly back to the living room and eased himself into his armchair. The weather channel news was not good. Toronto was digging out of a two-foot snowfall, and all flights were cancelled until at least tomorrow noon. Jim's daughter, Lara, was scheduled to fly into Halifax next evening. He reached for the phone to call her about travel alternatives, but, thinking twice, put down the receiver. Calling her would be perceived as meddling in her personal life. He had offered to pick her up at the airport but she had turned him down, opting instead for a taxi. Jim switched off the TV and lay back on the couch, exhausted after a forgettable day. Designing and building a sailboat with his own two hands was a lifetime dream, but after almost four years there were times when the dream had become a nightmare. It was nearly five years since a fatal stroke had taken his wife, Celia. Jim felt that half of him had been torn away, and he descended into a state of bottomless despair. His physician had coaxed him into the boat project. It may have saved his life, or at least his mind.

Eyes closed, his thoughts wandered and wondered how a beautiful family life had slipped away into oblivion. The panorama of events that followed Celia's passing moved across his field of vision. Lara was living in Halifax doing her final year of an MBA program at St. Mary's University. One day, without any explanation, she quit the faculty and left for Toronto, enrolled at York University and eventually attained her MBA. Jim was now alone. Lara had been close with her mother, but for almost six years there had been only minimal dialogue between him and his only child. "'Celia, Celia, sweet Jesus how I miss you," he murmured as the tears welled up. The late Celia Cabot, tall and slender, beautiful Celia with her glistening auburn hair and piercing dark blue eyes, had commanded attention wherever she went. Strong-willed, clever to the point of brilliant, she was admired and loved. Jim had hoped their first child would be a boy, but later, after Lara was born, they were told that Celia could never conceive again. They were devastated; Jim's dream of sharing the trophy mantelpiece with a son was shattered. Neither was interested in adopting; it had been a difficult period in their marriage. Jim cleared off the sailing and hockey trophies and carried them up to the attic wrapped in paper that was wet with tears. The Cabots poured their resources into their only child. Lara was a top student, an accomplished pianist and a natural athlete. She had inherited her mother's charm, looks and determination, never failing to assert herself in a situation where she felt her opinion was justifiable. Yet her gentle manner and body language were such that her colleagues never felt intimidated. She had many admirers, and her graciousness overcame any question of jealousy from her peers.

The phone startled Jim.

"Oh, Mr. Cabot, it's Hilda, how are you keeping?"

"Fine, Hilda, fine. How's the family? That baby of yours must be a big girl. She's close to three, no?"

"She will be in two months; she's into everything. It's hard to keep track of her."

"Sounds pretty healthy to me. How's Arnie these days? Has he been out fishing, or is it too early?"

She laughed.

"I have trouble keeping track of him too. He goes fishing often, but between you and me, he rarely brings home any fish."

Hilda was married to Arnie Benson, the town womanizer. He was a large hulk of a man with bushy black hair and a pronounced limp. He had a big smile but metamorphosed into an aggressive and violent bully when fueled by alcohol.

"Mr. Cabot, Lara called me from Toronto and said she'd be here tomorrow night. I'm dying to see her. I don't want to disturb your get-together, so please tell her to call me when she has a chance."

Hilda was Lara's closest friend. Each was an only daughter and they grew up like sisters. They had much in common; they were tall, blue-eyed brunettes, very attractive and athletic, with similar tastes. Hilda's family wasn't as fortunate as Lara's. Her younger brother, Danny, was a Down Syndrome victim and their dad, Bert Willis, reacted by drinking himself to an early death leaving the two children and their mother, Mavis, in financial straits. Mavis Willis managed Arnie's Café, a popular bar that attracted both white-collar workers and fishermen. Hilda worked with her mother but she thoroughly detested her job. Fighting off Arnie Benson's advances and listening to his obscenities about the female clientele was a full-time job. Mavis, on the other hand, saw this as an opportunity for a lifetime of security for her daughter. Arnie was about twelve years older than Hilda, but that didn't deter Mavis; she persisted and finally succeeded in getting the couple married. She would later learn that their union was a tragedy of greater magnitude than she could ever imagine. It was also the death knell of a long, unique relationship between her daughter and Lara Cabot.

TWO

Jim recalled the heightened excitement at Lara's high school graduation. The seniors were celebrating a string of athletic achievements. The boys had won both the hockey and basketball championships and the girls were finalists in the provincial junior ladies' volleyball league. Although Lara and Hilda rarely dated, their graduation was considered an exceptional event. Jim tried to push the memories of that evening out of his mind. It was a night that changed so many lives forever.

Hilda and Lara's escorts had picked them up at Lara's home. Although alcohol was always a concern at these celebrations, the girls were licensed to drive and would do so if necessary. The Cabots were confident there would be no problems, although Jim was aware that Lara's date was from a family who were more than social drinkers.

According to tradition Lara wasn't expected home until breakfast, so Jim was surprised when at around 2 a.m., he heard her bedroom door close. He wondered why she was back so early and if perhaps she wasn't feeling well. Later on, when he heard strange sounds from down the hall, he tip-toed to her room, quietly cracked open the door and peeked inside. A full moon had illuminated the room, and Jim could distinguish two nude female figures entwined in a white symmetrical mass. Their torsos pulsated, timed to the sounds of rhythmic, labored breathing. Jim reeled back, fumbled for the doorknob and pulled the door shut. He pressed his hands against the wall for support; his chest tightened as he fought for air. He moved slowly back to his room praying his knees would hold out long enough for him to reach the bed. He lay in the dark, staring up at nothing; he wondered how he was going to tell Celia. She lay beside him, breathing quietly, deep in a peaceful sleep that he felt certain he would never experience again. The night was endless. He finally dozed off around 6 a.m. and slept until Celia prodded him awake for breakfast.

"Hi, how come you slept so late? You're the early bird in the family."

Jim shook his head as he recalled the bedroom scene. He felt a sick sensation in his stomach. It was more than a nightmare; it was a sudden awakening to a shocking reality. He lumbered into the bathroom and stared at his drawn image in the mirror. It reflected exactly how he felt. The orderly life he took for granted had been abruptly torn away. He couldn't bring himself to shower or shave. He slumped into a kitchen chair, mentally and physically exhausted.

"Don't just sit there, Jim, have your juice and pills, but before you read the paper, tell me about your night."

He swallowed his medication but remained silent, oblivious to the food in front of him.

"Jim, c'mon now, you're acting really strange. Are you feeling ill? What's up?"

"Listen Celia, Lara came home around 2 a.m. I didn't expect her till much later and thought she was ill. I went to her room and looked in."

"Was everything O.K.?"

"Dammit no!, Shit no!, everything wasn't O.K. Christ, I can't believe this is happening to us!"

"Don't tell me you went in without knocking."

"Bloody right I did. How did I know she wasn't alone?"

"Jim, if it's what I think it is, I guess it's time you found out."

"Jesus, don't tell me you knew about this and never told me."

"My loving husband, what good would it have done had I told you? I've known for two years. I caught them together in the shower when they were sixteen. They're inseparable; they always have been. They love each other. If they don't sleep here, they'll sleep at Hilda's place.

"Celia, I'm having trouble handling this. I'm going back to bed."

She moved quickly and placed her hands on his shoulders.

"Sit down Jim, and listen..... for God's sake, hear me out. We're living in a different world today. People don't hide these things anymore. Just keep in mind that we, you and I, made her what she is."

"Celia!, ..what the hell kind of reasoning is that?"

"Jim, it's a biological thing. It's rare, but it's not abnormal. You've got to get it into your head that she's like everyone else, with one exception. Are you willing to lose our only child by condemning one aspect of her life?"

"Christ, you don't understand, you should have seen what they were doing."

"Believe me, I know exactly what they were doing." She leaned over and buried her cheek in his hair. "Is it any different from what we did together?"

Jim rose abruptly; she reached out, but he broke away and stalked out of the room. She felt dizzy, dropped back into her chair and wiped the tears from her eyes. Soon after, the girls walked in.

"Hi mom, what's with dad? He passed us on the stairs and didn't even say good morning. Hey, are you O.K.? Your face is all red; is your pressure up again?"

"I'm fine, sweetheart. Dad will be O.K. I guess he had a bit of a surprise during the night. He didn't expect that you'd both be home."

"Mrs. Cabot, I'm sorry. Am I causing a problem here?"

"Not at all, Hilda," she replied, but Lara interrupted.

"Wait a minute, how did he know Hilda was here? Gawd, don't tell me he came into my room!"

"Sit down girls, and we'll have a girl-to-girl talk. Let's start out by saying that Mr. Cabot peeked in at a very inopportune moment."

Hilda jumped up. "Oh my God. I'm going home."

"Mom, that's not fair. Why didn't he knock?"

"Calm down, girls. Keep in mind Lara, that dad still thinks you're his little girl. I guess he hasn't learned to knock."

"Mom, I'm eighteen, old enough to vote and drive an army tank; In two months, I'll be able to buy beer. Aren't we entitled to some privacy? We're eighteen!"

"I fully agree, girls. If you recall, I didn't dispute your right to 'privacy' when you were sixteen, and according to Canada's ridiculous laws, just a few years ago you could have even had your 'privacy' when you were fourteen."*·

The remark drew a prolonged silence and the discussion ended.

---

* *The 'Age of Consent' in Canada was revised in 2008 from fourteen to sixteen years of age.*

THREE

And now, years later, Jim Cabot stood in the darkened living room, face pressed against the window, watching the corner intersection for a sign of a taxi. The red, yellow and green blotches of the traffic lights reflected off the wet pavement. He counted the light changes until he lost track and then started over again. Lara had visited each Christmas since moving away four years ago, but this visit was ten months early. Jim didn't dare question her about returning so soon, but he knew his daughter.......she rarely made a decision without a good reason. It was her timing that was troubling. Jim was acquainted with Lara's partner, Frances, whom he had met on a previous visit. Although they co-owned a condo in Toronto, Lara's recent e-mails never mentioned her; Jim was now speculating on other possibilities. Lara had college friends in Australia and New Zealand, and he worried that perhaps she was entertaining plans to join them.

He followed the progress of a private car as it moved up the street, unexpectedly turning and proceeding up the driveway, its headlights momentarily blinding him. Lara Cabot flung open the car door; her head covered with a magazine, she dashed through the rain and climbed the porch steps two at a time. Jim moved quickly to the door and was greeted by an outstretched hand grasp, but, as usual, no embrace.

'Things haven't changed,' he thought to himself.

"Hello dad, how are you?"

"Fine, fine, thank you. I was expecting you in a cab. Is that a rental you've got?"

"Yes, I may be staying longer than usual and I'll need a car."

"Great, that's great news. I'll run down and get your bags. Go inside and pour yourself something hot."

"Dad, I thought about staying at a hotel while I'm here."

Jim was taken aback. Lara continued, "It would really be more convenient if I stayed downtown."

Jim hesitated and then countered, "It's up to you, but if you're going to stay a while, why not live here? I'm away almost every day and you'll have the house to yourself. Greta won't bother you. She's glued to the basement TV most of the time. The Toyota is in the garage and I hardly ever use it. I'd really like to spend some time with you."

At this point, Jim stopped short; listening to his own voice, he realized he was begging. He stared at her dark hair; little ringlets of curls, soaking wet and shining, clung to her forehead. Her blue eyes were bluer then he had ever seen, and yet he knew he had seen them before. Tiny rivulets of water streamed down her face. He looked at her full lips, slightly parted and showing the whiteness of her teeth. His legs suddenly felt like rubber, and he reached out for the arm of the chair for support. 'My God,' he thought, 'is that you, Celia, or is it our daughter?'

He was thankful that at that moment, Lara's attention was elsewhere among the family photos on the wall. She turned to him.

"Dad, don't trouble yourself, I'm dressed for the rain. I'll get my stuff out of the car and size up the situation tomorrow."

Jim was grateful that she left the room for a few moments. He went to the kitchen, splashed cold water on his face and ran his wet hands through his hair. He filled the kettle and placed a dish of Greta's cookies on the table together with a couple of green tea bags. Lara strode in and sat down facing her father. They spoke at the same time, then laughed in embarrassment.

"I'm sorry, Lara, what were you going to say?"

"Well, I was wondering how you're managing."

"Actually, I'm doing O.K. I can't believe it's nearly five years. I still expect to see mother's face in the morning when I wake up. I guess these things don't pass easily. I really think I'm doing better, both mentally and physically. Doc Wilson says my sugar and cholesterol are under control and I'll probably live till eighty." He stared down at the table, a faint smile on his face. "Frankly, I think that's too long, especially in an empty house."

"Dad, you're only sixty-one and you have a long way to go. I can tell you though, it's not good to be alone."

Lara immediately regretted the remark, but Jim caught the inference.

"Are you speaking from recent experience?"

Lara remained silent and just stared at her father. Jim sensed her uneasiness; for the first time in years, he felt that he dominated the conversation and it was his daughter on the defensive.

"Dad, Frances and I are no longer together. We agreed to disagree and we had a fairly amiable separation."

She turned her head away as she spoke. Lara could never face her dad when she told a lie. She forced a smile.

"Actually, I'm not alone, I bought myself a little Schnauzer for company. He's in a kennel, and I hope he's O.K. till I get back."

"Well, how is the job going? Is it keeping you busy?"

"You know, it's become routine. My boss claims I've developed my own technique for solving problems and that I've become bored. I think it's an oblique compliment. She doesn't want to lose me so she's looking around for some bigger challenges. Looks like I may ruffle a few feathers in the men's department if I decide to stay."

Jim was surprised; could this be his Lara speaking, the strong-willed young woman, opinionated and so sure of herself? Could this be the same person, now so thoughtful and indecisive? Jim felt confident enough to steer the conversation. Perhaps their relationship could be revitalized, and the barrier that had separated them for years would finally come down.

"Lara, I recall that top execs in my firm took sabbaticals when the work became uncomfortable. I would have done the same, but when mom got sick, I decided on early retirement."

'It's going well', Jim thought; time to push his luck.

"I'd love to have you back here. Lunenburg is a good place to recharge your batteries after four years in Toronto."

There was a lengthy, uneasy silence. Jim decided to go for broke.

"Lara, I miss you."

He could control his thoughts, but not the tears. For the first time in years, there was no sign of hostility from his daughter, either in her attitude or her voice. He reached for a napkin and wiped his eyes. Lara slid her hand across the table and placed it on top of his. She held it tightly, never taking her gaze off her father's face.

FOUR

Danny Willis, Hilda's fifteen-year-old brother and a Down Syndrome child, pedaled his bike against the icy wind and stinging rain. He parked at the rear of Arnie's Café and pushed open the heavy door to the storeroom. As he hung up his wet clothes and put on a work apron, he was startled by the sound of loud snoring. He was surprised to see Arnie Benson asleep in a chair, his enormous bulk covered by a heavy blanket. Danny went out front and gave mother Mavis his usual warm hug.

"Mommy, the boss is asleep in the back!"

"I know, I know, Danny. Hilda has already phoned. Arnie never came home last night. He walked in here about an hour ago, shivering and looking like a wasted tomcat."

"Gee mommy, that was a bad thing the boss did."

"That's right, son, sometimes people do bad things to each other. Better get into the kitchen and start in on those dishes; they're piling up."

Mavis was serving at the bar and in spite of the early hour was already admonishing some of the local rowdies, urging them to calm down. Arnie's was a colorful, noisy place with a warm and friendly atmosphere. It attracted a cross-section of the town's citizenry; fisherman and office executives rubbed elbows at the bar. The lunchtime office crowd enjoyed the throbbing music, the seafaring decor and above all the repartee between Mavis and the clients. She laughed, joked, cajoled and delivered her inimitable words of wisdom non-stop to an admiring clientele. She was a small, extremely attractive woman, with a strong, commanding voice. Mavis could stare down an abusive client with her stunning green eyes, and no one doubted that she was in command. Her flaming red hair and longshoreman's vocabulary, delivered in an exaggerated Newfoundland accent, rendered her a Lunenburg legend.

Ned Hill, a fellow Newfoundlander, a jolly, grey-haired veteran who'd fished the Grand Banks for over half a century, raised his tankard to Mavis and shouted,

"Mavis, my darlin', if I ever saw ye naked, I'd die happy."

Mavis's response time was like the speed of light.

"Ned, my darlin', if I ever saw ye naked, I'd die laughing."

Danny walked into the kitchen and received his usual warm welcome. Georgie, the chef, tussled Danny's hair and gave him a warm hug.

"Good morning, Danny boy. Grab a towel, son, I'm running out of plates. This lousy weather is bringing them in off the streets. We're busy as hell."

The warm water felt good on Danny's cold hands. The slow, deliberate ways of Down Syndrome victims served him well. The dishes were spotlessly cleaned and carefully wiped. Georgie could never recall a plate or a cup slipping out of the boy's grasp. Georgie, a widower himself, treated the fifteen-year-old like a son, and when there was a lull, they would sit and converse. Georgie's daughter Alma was a high school senior and part-time waitress at Arnie's. She and Hilda were close, their friendship something of a big-sister–little-sister relationship. When Hilda's baby, Jennie, was born, Alma stepped in and took over, helping Danny with his schoolwork and shopping.

Arnie awoke around one in the afternoon and lurched into the kitchen.

"Hey Georgie, I smell fish; make me a plate. I'm going out front to talk to Mavis."

"Have a seat, boss, and relax. I'll bring it out in five minutes."

Arnie went behind the bar, opened the cash register, counted out a handful of bills and stuffed them in his pocket.

"We've had a busy morning," Mavis whispered, "why don't you go home? Hilda and the baby are expecting you."

He helped himself to a beer and looked around to see if anyone was within earshot. Turning to Mavis, he gave her a glaring look.

"Christ, Mavis, your Hilda couldn't care less if I came home or not. And you know something, I don't give a shit either."

Mavis grabbed him by the arm.

"Stop behaving like an idiot: you've got a three-year-old daughter who's crazy for you, and don't ask me why. You're almost never home."

He brushed her aside and settled at his table near the kitchen. Georgie brought out the meal and sat down.

"You O.K., Arnie?"

"Yeah, yeah Georgie, I'm O.K. Mavis is forever down my neck. I just don't get no peace. On top of that, my wife pisses me off. Between you and me, I needed a woman like your Alma. She's got a great little body and is probably a real fire-cracker compared to my cold fish."

Georgie rose abruptly, put his hands on the table and leaned forward, his head almost touching Arnie's.

"Listen, you asshole, I'm the best goddamned chef in Lunenburg and you know it. I like this town and I make good money for both of us. Now lemme tell you something; you mention my daughter's name together with yours one more time, and she and I are outta here. O.K.?"

Georgie stormed back into the kitchen in a fit of rage. The loud noise of banging pots and pans competed with the raucous music out front. Arnie's head was still pounding from the hangover. He buried his face in his hands, avoiding the stares of the customers. He picked at his food but eventually pushed the plate aside and motioned Mavis into the back storeroom.

"Mavis, I've got business in Halifax. If there's anything important, get me on my cell. I won't be back till Monday or Tuesday."

She gave him an icy look.

"Go home and rest up, Arnie. You look like hell and you probably feel even worse."

Mavis shuddered at the thought of him stumbling into the house and letting out his anger on her daughter and the baby.

***

Georgie sat on a wooden stool in the far corner of the kitchen, his hands trembling as he put a lighted match to a cigarette.

"Danny boy, would you please pour me some tea."

Danny brought the teacup over and stood in the opposite corner, eyes glued on Georgie's shaking hands, expecting him to drop the cup at any moment.

"Gee Georgie, the boss really makes people mad. He's always shouting at Hilda when I go over to play with the baby. I think he's really mean. Once I even saw her crying and holding some ice on her face. I wanted to tell my mother, but I was afraid she would have a fight with Arnie and quit."

Georgie thought, 'This fifteen-year-old kid with the brain of a nine-year-old has got more sense than most of those guys sitting around the bar.'

The Friday office crowd finished early, and by four p.m. Arnie's was standing room only. Alma and Danny worked as a team. She served the beer and he picked up the empty mugs. The boy enjoyed working out front when the place was busy. He surprised the clients with his memory for names and addressed them politely as Mister or Miss, managing a smile for everyone. He listened to their jokes and joined in occasionally for some singing. Alma was fascinating to watch. She served four mugs at a time and wove her way seamlessly in and out of the crowd. She moved quickly and spoke very little, but she could break in with a dry-witted remark when necessary. Baby Face Romeo, a regular client with one hand permanently attached to a beer bottle, often taunted Alma with inappropriate, lewd remarks. As she walked by, both hands burdened with beer mugs, he reached out and grabbed her apron. She gave him a cold stare.

"It's time you went home, Romeo; you've had more than enough for today."

He leaned over and said in a loud whisper,

"I never get enough, baby; d'ya think you'll ever have sex with me?"

She was taken aback, but, never at a loss for words, shot back,

"Romeo, I wouldn't even have a diet soda with you."

But Romeo was undaunted and shouted over to Mavis,

"Hey Mavis, did you hear about the Newfie* woman who bought a scarf and then returned it 'cause it was too tight?"

Mavis shot back, "Romeo, weren't you expelled from third grade public school when they found beer in your lunchbox? I heard they had to take you back 'cause you were legal drinking age."

Mavis always managed to have the last word.

FIVE

Hilda always tensed up when she heard Arnie's car in the driveway. As he strode into the kitchen, baby Jennie ran over to greet him.

"Daddy, daddy," and wrapped her arms around his leg. Arnie leaned over and pushed her aside.

"Jennie, don't touch me with those sticky fingers, dammit. Shit, Hilda, why the hell don't you wash her hands? She'll get my clothes all mucked up."

During Hilda's pregnancy, Arnie spoke incessantly about having a son. He made no secret of his disappointment when Jennie was born. Hilda had become accustomed to Arnie's rejection of Jennie, but she could never get used to the look of sadness on the child's face whenever her father shooed her away like a bothersome insect.

"Arnie, the way your clothes look today, no one would notice the difference."

"Shut your fuckin' mouth, I'm too tired to get into a fight. I want to get going to Halifax. Did Drifter show up for the envelope?

"Yup, he showed up alright, and he smelled like he'd fallen into a barrel of whiskey."

"Well, it's Friday today. He starts his weekend drinking on Fridays."

Hilda laughed. "Arnie, every day is Friday with your friend. Tell me, while we're on the subject, I never looked inside any of those envelopes you give him. I wonder what he's costing you every week."

Arnie glared at her.

"None of your fuckin' business. You got enough to eat? You got a nice house? Your mother and that dummy brother of yours have jobs? None of you are doin' too bad with ol' Arnie."

Hilda would never debate her husband's rants. It was common knowledge that if Mavis opened a bar across the street, Arnie would go broke in a month.

He shouted, "I gotta get outta here, I've an appointment at five in Halifax. I gotta' leave soon or I'll get screwed in the traffic."

"Can't you watch your language in front of Jennie? The nursery school teacher gave me hell. Your daughter has been repeating some of the stuff she picks up at home. She's the only one in class who knows a whole pile of four-lettered words. The other children are learning from her."

Arnie laughed. "Well great, at least they'll learn something in that fancy school of yours. Shit, what a waste of money. It's a great setup for women too fuckin' lazy to look after their own kids."

Arnie had a preconceived, unshakeable opinion on just about every subject. Hilda cut the discussion short. She always recalled something she had learned from her dad:

"Never argue with a fool, because after a while, the audience can't tell who's who"

"Arnie, do you want some lunch?"

She was glad he was sober. At least he'd keep his hands off her.

"Never mind, I ate at the bar. If Drifter calls, tell him I'll see him on Monday or Tuesday."

He filled his overnight bag and walked out without a further word to Hilda or the baby. Hilda listened as he pulled out of the driveway. She scooped Jennie up in her arms, gave her a close hug and breathed a sigh of relief.

SIX

Jim reached down for the newspaper, shielding his eyes from the morning sun. He settled into the verandah couch, leaned back and took several deep breaths of the crisp morning air. The weather had finally improved and the heat on his legs felt good. He wondered what Lara was planning and if it included him. In any case, it was an ideal day for catching up on the boat work. A quiet tranquility enveloped him, a feeling he had almost forgotten….the sound of Greta and Lara's voices, the warmth of the morning sun and the smell of brewing coffee. The screen door swung open and Lara appeared with the food tray.

"Good morning, breakfast is served. Almost like old times, eh dad?"

"Almost, Lara. Come here and sit beside me. You know, we live our lives remembering the good and brushing aside the unpleasant. I guess it's a defense mechanism that keeps us from going insane."

"Dad, five years is a long time to be alone. Why don't you do something about it? It seems to me that you wandered away from your friends after mom died."

"Yeah, maybe you're right, but I felt like a fifth wheel whenever I was invited out. I actually got phone calls from some very bright and attractive women, but I never felt I was ready. I guess they eventually gave up."

Jim paused and fidgeted; Lara knew he was carefully measuring the next sentence.

"I allowed the boat project to push almost everything else out of my life. I was counting on taking her offshore to God knows where. I spent years on the design and construction but never considered how I was going to manage her alone. I thought of advertising for a cook, a young guy with sailing experience, but the newspapers don't allow gender preference in ads. I was afraid I'd get a whole bunch of women applying. Remember Josh Elder, the guy who owned the hardware store? He was an old bachelor and a great sailor. He placed an ad in the papers and only heard from women. He took a fancy to one of them and they sailed off to the Mediterranean. Believe it or not, they're still together."

"Dad, you just answered your own question. I remember Mr. Elder. I never saw the man smile. I'll bet he's a different person now."

Jim chuckled. "Don't tell me I'm becoming an old grouch."

"Not yet," her blue eyes sparkled, "but you never know!"

Shortly after Jim left for the marina, Lara headed for the shower but was interrupted by the phone.

"Hi, it's me. Am I calling too early?"

"Hi Hilda, not at all. Are we going to see each other today?"

"I'm counting on it. I've lots to tell you."

"Me too. By the way, how's Jennie?"

"Oh Lara, she's a little angel. She's in bed with me right now, all warm and cuddly. Arnie never lets her sleep with us when he's home, but when he leaves town for a few days, Jennie knows it's O.K. to spend the night with mommy. I don't know what I'd do without this child."

"Hilda, I've got to get to the bank this morning, but I can pick you up for lunch. I rented a car at the airport. I may be staying a bit longer than usual."

"Super! Don't pick me up. I'll drop the baby at Alma's place. She's off till tonight. I can meet you outside the bank at about eleven this morning."

"Sounds good. See you soon."

SEVEN

Lara parked in the Maritime Bank parking lot, but didn't go inside. Instead, she walked down the block toward St. Christopher's Church, crossed to the rear of the building and climbed the steps to the rectory. As she reached for the bell, the door opened unexpectedly and Father James McCrory, SJ, appeared carrying an umbrella, his pipe hanging from his mouth.

"Good morning, Father. How are you?"

The priest, startled, looked over his glasses.

"Well for the love of Jesus, look who's here. Lara, my little girl, you back so soon? I wasn't expecting you till Christmas. Is everything alright? Is there a problem with your dad?"

"No Father, everything is fine. We're all in good health. I took a chance on finding you in; I guess I should have phoned ahead. If you're busy, I can see you later today or tomorrow."

"My angel, I take one look at your face and I know that my morning walk can wait. I'd rather hear what's on your mind; not many people visit me at the rectory."

He turned about, slowly manipulating his cane into position for support. He seemed more frail since Lara's visit last Christmas.

"Come into my study, my dear; my aching back would prefer my old chair over a morning walk."

Lara had always been fascinated by this room. Dark oak wall paneling surrounded a massive, carved mahogany table. It stood in the centre of the room, flanked by high-backed, brick-red upholstered chairs that appeared like sentinels on guard. The shelves lining the walls held numerous leather-bound editions; the room had a quiet dignity and an ambience that encouraged subdued conversation. Lara almost felt compelled to remove her shoes and speak in whispers. Father McCrory motioned her to sit next to him.

"Better sit here, my dear, my hearing is not what it was."

He settled into an old leather armchair which, over the years, had adapted to his shape; when he sat, the chair seemed to absorb him and diminish him in size.

"Well, young lady, you can start whenever you like."

"Father, aren't you ever going to light that pipe of yours? I love the smell of pipe tobacco. It reminds me of my dad when I was a youngster."

He smiled mischievously,

"Lara, haven't you heard, smoking can be very unhealthy. My doctor ordered me to stop years ago. I managed to quit, but I could never detach myself from the feel of the pipe. So tell me, my dear, what's up?"

"It's about Frances, my companion in Toronto. I mentioned her when I was here at Christmas. We felt we were in a lifetime relationship. We both loved children, so after a couple of years, the subject of taking on the responsibility of parenthood seemed quite natural. As a matter of fact, we agreed on it almost immediately. We never considered possible complications. The nature of our relationship was such that I would carry the child."

Father McCrory removed his pipe and leaned forward abruptly.

"Am I hearing correctly? You are considering parenthood but not adopting? Do you intend to have a child out of wedlock?"

"Father, wedlock is not the issue. You see, I'm already pregnant. I was impregnated 'in vitro' in a hospital laboratory. I know all about the father, but I never met him, nor do I know his name."

The priest removed his pipe, shook his head and stared at Lara. The silence seemed interminable.

"Father . . ."

"Wait dear, hear me out. Your mother and I spoke about your lifestyle years ago. The reason for these things happening is still a matter of debate, but let's not dwell on a subject which will make me lose the rest of my hair. The important thing now is to look ahead. Obviously something is troubling you. Do you regret your decision to carry the child?"

She thought to herself,

'This priest is a mind reader.'

"Father, you certainly come straight to the point, don't you."

"When I see that tight little smile of yours, I know there's a problem."

"I only found out I was pregnant when I got back to Toronto after the New Year. I was overjoyed. I was walking on air, making all kinds of plans and hoping for a boy that would look like dad. I was alone that week, but I wasn't really alone. It was just baby and me. It was the happiest time of my life. Frances was traveling in the Pacific and I couldn't wait for her to return. When she walked through the door, I pounced on her and hugged her. I laughed and cried with joy. Father, she pushed me away and sat me down. She said she was really happy for me but the trip gave her time to rethink her future. She said she wasn't ready to handle the added responsibilities of a family and felt that at her age she still had a lot of traveling to do before settling down. My God, it was more than a shock, I was frozen; I felt abandoned and deceived. I locked myself in the bedroom and didn't come out for almost two days. Would you believe I never saw her again? She left a note in the kitchen telling me it was my choice whether to either stay or sell the condo. Either way, I was to send her back her portion as soon as I was able and to mail the documents to her mother's address. When the movers came, I showed them her things and walked out. I came back to the apartment after they left."

The priest shook his head, leaned over and held her hand tightly.

"Lara, for the baby's sake and yours, it's better that it happened now than later."

"You know Father, I came here to ask your advice. Given the circumstances of the pregnancy, being unnatural in the eyes of the church and the fact that I'm unattached and alone, I thought perhaps you would understand a decision to terminate. I'm not naive enough to expect your full approval but I guess I was hoping for some sympathy and moral support."

"I'll always be here for you when you're in need, Lara, but let's think about this for a moment. A decision to end the pregnancy would be tantamount to declaring Frances's wellbeing more important than both the baby and you. You haven't changed.....only Frances has. Why alter your plans on account of her? The child will have a loving mother and grandfather, and thankfully you have the means to assure the baby a good life."

She looked at him apprehensively.

"The grandfather doesn't know that he's going to be a grandfather."

"My dear, when you make the announcement to your dad, I'm betting on a positive reaction."

He placed his cane firmly on the floor and pressed down, slowly lifting himself from the armchair. Lara rose to help, but he quickly straightened out, smiled and wrapped his arms around her. He kissed her lightly on the forehead and stepped back, locking his steel-blue eyes on her face. Putting aside his cane, he placed both hands gently on her head and in a strong clear voice,

"May the Lord Jesus Christ bless you and the child within you. May He shield you both from all harm and may He make His face to shine upon you and bring you everlasting peace."

EIGHT

Father McCrory's voice echoed inside Lara's head, smothering the din of the traffic. She went into the bank and waited outside the manager's office, unable to recall the walk from St. Christopher's. The priest's words were more than an answer to her dilemma. They pushed her to the next level of reality. These were new challenges. This wasn't the playing field or the corporate boardroom. This was about a human life, a flesh and blood responsibility.

Jake Allen, the bank manager, called out from his office.

"Lara, is that you? C'mere and let me give you a hug. You never mentioned making another visit so soon. Is your dad O.K.? We haven't spoken for a while."

"Dad's fine, but he's still working away at the marina. It seems endless. You know him, Jake, he's a perfectionist."

"Lara, I offered him a bank loan to finance the sailboat of his dreams, but he insisted on building it himself. I dropped down to the marina just after New Years to see how he was doing. It was a cold, miserable day, but there he was, working like a guy half his age. For his sake, I'm anxious to see it finished and to attend the launching. I'm buying the champagne."

"Jake, everyone keeps asking him how the boat's coming along. I think he's feeling pressure from the neighbors at this point. From what I gather, though, it should be ready in a month or two if the weather permits. Geez, I gotta comment on your appearance. The diet you wrote about is really working. My God, you look real slim."

"Had to,....doctor's orders. Too many business luncheons, too many Mooseheads* and not enough exercise. He showed me some test result numbers that really scared the hell out of me."

"You promised to stop smoking but I still see ashtrays all over the place."

"That's my next project. Mustn't do too much at a time" he laughed, "my body may not withstand the shock."

Whenever Lara visited with Jake Allen, she felt a certain closeness, yet the feeling wasn't altogether positive. She well understood the nature of it but always pushed it to the back of her mind.

She thought, 'Someday I'll have to confront this.'

Jake was a tall, handsome man with shining black hair, a wonderful sense of humor and a smile that seemed engraved on his face. His trademark was a black suit and an elegant black mustache. People joked that he looked like Gable in 'Gone With the Wind.' But Lara had heard rumors he had suffered a period of depression when her mother chose her dad instead of him. There could be some truth to it because Jake had never married.

"Jake, I need a favor. It's about the mortgage for my half of the condo. Unexpected events have put me in a situation where I have to buy out my partner's half. Do you think I can qualify?"

He gave her a surprised look and reached into the filing cabinet for her dossier.

"If I recall, didn't you gave a substantial down payment for your half of the property. I tell you what, I believe I can double the current mortgage without any extra cash."

"But that would make my monthly payments sky high."

"Not necessarily. First of all, I can now offer a lower interest rate, and if you prefer, we can extend the mortgage to twenty years instead of the current one of fifteen. I recall that you're in a good location. Your condo is probably worth substantially more now than when you bought it. By the way, is this breakup with your partner a clean one, or could there be legal entanglements?"

"Not a problem, Jake. It's clean, very sudden and very unexpected. I'll tell you about it some day. In the meantime, I don't know how to thank you. You've unburdened my mind. You know, when I was little, didn't I call you Uncle Jake?"

"That's right. It seems like yesterday. And now that I'm a bank manager, you can call me your rich Uncle Jake!" He laughed and stood up.

"Lara, I've got a few clients waiting for me. I"ll need to see you again before you go back. I'll prepare the documents and call you."

He rose, gave her a hug and kissed her on both cheeks.

"Uncle Jake, please look after yourself. I worry about you. Next time around, I don't want to see any ashtrays."

"You know, I guess I'm just plain lucky. Each time you visit, you warn me about my unhealthy habits. I hope you keep it up. How many old bachelors have a beautiful young woman to worry over them?"

His eyes remained glued to her as she left the office. All kinds of thoughts whirled about in his mind as his brain churned through events from the distant past. He shook his head, turned to his secretary and motioned to send in the next client.

NINE

Lara relaxed on a bench outside the bank, closed her eyes and turned her face toward the warm morning sun. She was back home in Lunenburg; she was on familiar ground...the easy laughter, the "good mornings" from strangers and friends alike.

A voice above the din of the traffic shouted her name. Hilda rushed up, threw her arms around her and held on tightly.

"Oh God, Lara, it's good to see you. I can't believe you're back so soon. What a treat!"

They clung to each other for a long moment. Hilda felt a familiar tingling throughout her body.

"Let's have a bite at the café. I want my mom and Danny to see you."

As they rounded the corner to Arnie's, Hilda exclaimed,

"I'm not walking, I'm floating on air."

Lara gave her arm a knowing squeeze.

"Yeah, I remember, we always said that to each other."

"Lara, I don't know about you, but it's never changed for me."

"Hey, you've got a husband and a child. Hilda, you're into another life."

"I've gotta be honest with you. I feel like a single mom. I have a child, but as far as a husband is concerned, I might as well be just another one of his women. There's lots more I want to tell you, but I'll save it for later."

They walked into Arnie's in the midst of the noon rush. Mavis spotted them and hurried over.

"Lara, is it really you? Welcome home!" She shouted to Danny,

"C'mon over here and see Lara."

Danny, surprised but very cool as usual, put down a tray of beer mugs and walked over. Lara reached out and held him close, pressing her face to his. She pulled a Kleenex from her pocket and wiped her eyes. There was no doubt about it; this was home.

Lara and Hilda found a quiet table near the kitchen and sipped slowly from their mugs. Moments like this were to be enjoyed, savored and not rushed. They stared at each other for a while without uttering a word. Lara reached for Hilda's hand.

"Tell me what's going on at home. Sounds like you've got a full plate."

"Lara, let me say that it was never any good, right from the start. Maybe it was partially my fault because of the way I'm made, but it's become worse as the months and years go by. I may not be perfect, but I don't deserve the abuse I'm getting. The happiest time for me is when Arnie's out of town. He left yesterday for Halifax and won't be back for three days, and frankly I'm not going to be lonesome. Lately he goes quite often."

"I don't like the word 'abuse' . . . are we talking mental or physical?"

"Both. I even have the bruises to show for it. Let's go a bit further, how about sexual abuse?"

Lara felt a shiver throughout her body.

"Jesus, don't tell me we're going there."

"Listen, according to the law, I could have had him arrested dozens of times for marital rape. But once you lodge a formal complaint, your life is in danger. I can't expect the police to protect me twenty-four hours a day. Remember that old adage, "If rape is inevitable, relax and enjoy it'? Well, let me tell you, you can't relax, and the only enjoyment is when he stops."

Lara suddenly burst into tears. Hilda was taken aback.

"Hey, I'm sorry, I shouldn't have told you. I didn't mean to shake you up. I guess I'm so used to all this that I'm starting to be able to talk about it. But believe me, you're the first one I've ever mentioned this to."

Lara was silent for a moment. Her mind flashed back to another place and another time.

"I'm crying for you and for me."

"Really? What's that supposed to mean?"

"Hilda, I'm no stranger to rape. I survived one four years ago. But it only happened once to me; it's happened often to you, in your own home and with your child close by. I feel sick."

"You feel sick? Shit, I'm devastated. Why didn't you tell me? Why? You kept this inside all this time? You went through it all by yourself, alone, with no one to share it? Jesus, I'm torn apart. Who did this to you? Tell me who. I would have done something. I don't know what, but something."

"I kept silent for the same reason you do. I knew the person well, but had I reported it to the police, it would have destroyed other people who are very dear to me."

Hilda persisted,

"Well, what about later on? Did you discuss it with Frances?"

"No, not at all. I tried not to think about it. I had to get professional help. I needed things to occupy my mind, so I took the toughest courses available at university. Now let's talk about you. There must be a way of getting you out of this mess; it can destroy you and the baby. You say he often goes to Halifax; does he have someone there?"

Hilda laughed.

"Probably, but he doesn't need a woman in Halifax,… he's got a few of them right here in town. If he doesn't kill himself driving drunk, some jealous boyfriend or husband may do it for him."

She reached out for Lara's hand,

"How is your job coming along, and how is Frances?"

She thought about the question, looked at Hilda and finally said,

"You have no husband, and I have no friend. Looks like we're back to square one and perhaps a lot wiser. Let me tell you what happened since Christmas."

She ran through the events that she had shared with Father McCrory. As expected, Hilda was shocked. They clutched each other's hands in silence. Hilda whispered,

"I can't believe all this. I just saw you a couple of months ago. My God, you're going to have a baby. God bless you. Please tell me you're happy, because I'm ecstatic."

"I am, I am, and honestly, the priest was a great help. Although he never condoned my lifestyle, his words of advice were supportive and I see things a bit differently now; he made me feel more positive about the future."

Their hands and eyes locked together.

"Hilda, I'm going to need your help. I know nothing about raising kids."

They ate a light lunch and reminisced about the intervening years. Were they worthwhile, or were they just lost in time? They had experienced so much, but there was so much pain mixed in with their learning. Real happiness still eluded them. Hilda whispered,

"Let's go back to my place. Alma will bring the baby back later, and I'd like you to see her. We really must talk more about what's happening to us."

They parked the cars in Hilda's driveway and went inside. As they walked into the living room, Hilda turned to Lara.

"Let me hold you again. I can't believe we're here together.

"They embraced and clung to one another.

"Lara, I never stopped loving you; I never forgot what we were to each other."

Their tears wet each other's faces as they kissed and moved over to the couch. It was a déja vu experience. Dormant feelings began to reappear as they caressed each other. Their old passions resurfaced and soon began to overwhelm.

"Lara, I have a full heart and an empty bed."

"You're a mind reader; I'm glad we still need each other."

That afternoon, they became as one. It was clear to them both that this was the way it should have been from the beginning. By the end of the day, an understanding was reached. They would make their own decisions about the future. No one, absolutely no one, would ever direct their lives again.

TEN

The shrouds* that support the mast of the sailboat arrived at the marina just before noon. Jim wondered if they would be the proper length. He'd be disappointed if they weren't, but not surprised. He was always puzzled by the way the manufacturer would receive exact measurements and yet somehow send back a final product that required adjustments The weather was perfect and Jim was anxious to finish up the varnish work on the deck and interior. His next job would be to thread the mast with the electric wiring and the halyards.*

Friends and neighbors dropped by continuously, commenting on his progress and asking endless questions. Handling the friendly onlookers was becoming uncomfortable, and he occasionally ignored them, even though it felt impolite. But the conversations deprived him of much needed time and concentration.

Today, however, for the first time, Jim felt the end was in sight. He had installed the electronics during the bad weather, although they had yet to be tested in a sea trial. The major remaining tasks were installing the rudder and aligning the engine and propellor shaft. If the weather held out, perhaps ten days of solid work would bring him to the point of launching. With the mast properly prepared, he would need less than a day to step* it. The new sails were expected any day now, but he might need extra time to adjust them. Now that Lara was in town, Jim hoped they could witness the launch together.

The renewed relationship with his only child and the anticipation of seeing his project finished were exhilarating. Jim couldn't recall the last time he had felt so confident.

A voice from outside startled him.

"Jim, where the hell are you hiding? I'll bet you haven't eaten yet. I'm down here, man, and no way will you get me to climb up that ladder."

Jim peered over the gunwale.

"Jake, what are you doing here? You're gonna dirty that funeral suit of yours."

"No problem, I've got a half dozen more at home. How about dropping the paint brush and grabbing a sandwich with me? I see a SUBWAY has opened down the street. Aren't you hungry? Hell, I'll bet you haven't eaten and it's almost two o'clock."

"O.K., O.K., sounds good. Lemme clean up a bit. I'm coming right down."

As they crossed the street, Jim grabbed Jake's arm and wondered out loud,

"O.K. friend, tell me what's on your mind. You don't visit me in the middle of a banking day unless you want to talk about stuff that has nothing to do with boats."

"Well, you have a point. You must be happy to have Lara back for a while. I spotted her this morning talking to Hilda outside the bank."

They bought their food and took a quiet table at the rear.

"Jim, this may surprise you, but I want to talk a little about Hilda Benson and her family. In a moment or two you'll understand why. Hilda's late dad and myself were pretty close. As you know, Bert Willis couldn't accept his Danny being a Down victim and drank himself to death. I wonder if you recall that I was both Hilda's and Danny's godfather. When I worked at our downtown branch in St. John's, Mavis was a part-time employee of mine while she was a student. She was a whiz with numbers and had great managerial potential. She nearly completed her MBA degree at Memorial* but she met and married Bert Willis, became pregnant and quit school. She soon gave birth to Hilda, and a few years later, after they had moved to Lunenburg, she had Danny. I was transferred here and Mavis worked part time for me for a couple of years. When Bert passed away, she took that job running Arnie Benson's café. I was really surprised at her decision to work in a place like that, but evidently he paid her extremely well and she was badly in need of money; Bert had left her with a lot of debt. Now, I'm also aware that Mavis was instrumental in getting Hilda married to Arnie."

"You're probably wondering why I'm telling you all this. Here's the bottom line. Arnie approached me last week and asked for a sizable loan. He wants to expand the restaurant and wanted a mortgage to acquire the property next door. That sounded pretty reasonable.

When it came around to personal references, he gave me two or three names, among which was yours. Now if that surprises you, listen to this. Last week I'm at Arnie's having a beer with your Mountie neighbor, Bill Gallant. Bill pokes me and says,

"Jake, do you see that little guy who just walked in, the one with the grey hair done up in a ponytail?"

"I answered that I had seen him around but didn't know who he was."

"His name is Drifter" he says, "an ex-con who did time at Dorchester prison for that armored car robbery at Halifax airport. Time sure flies; I can't believe he's already out. I wonder what the hell he's doing in Lunenburg."

"Jim, we watched the little man knock down a few whiskeys and then leave. The interesting thing though is he didn't pay for them; he just got up, said goodbye to Mavis and walked out. Mavis didn't react at all. Now when we were leaving, I went over to her and discreetly asked if the ponytail guy left without paying. She said he's Arnie's friend. He usually takes two or three shots of whiskey and comes in about twice a week. Now if you don't mind me asking, Jim, did your Lara ever mention anything to you about Hilda's marriage to Arnie?"

"Hell, Jake, you know as well as I that Arnie is his own best bar customer and the town skirt-chaser. Somehow I don't see Hilda going to Sunday mass thanking God for bestowing him upon her."

"You know Jim, womanizing is one thing, but with this ex-con Drifter on the scene, we're talking about criminal association; we're into a different ball game."

"Jake, did Gallant speculate about the relationship between Arnie and Drifter?"

"No, but he says he's going to check the RCMP records of both men and let me know. Arnie was born here in Lunenburg but was gone for about fifteen years before he came back to take over the family café. That long absence could be interesting. If he has a criminal record, Mavis was obviously unaware of it; he'd be the last person in the world she'd have as a son-in-law."

Jim climbed the boat ladder and continued working, but after about an hour, he gave up. More work today was out of the question. Jake's words were haunting him. Why would Arnie even consider him as a reference? Was he taking advantage of his wife Hilda's friendship with Lara? Jim was in no mood to support Arnie, and yet if he refused, would it compromise Lara and Hilda's relationship?

ELEVEN

Jim called out from the top of the staircase, "Greta, I'm home."

The woman was absorbed in her television soap opera, but after a second try she acknowledged him and came upstairs. Greta was in her early seventies but appeared more like fifty. Slender and spry with sparkling blue eyes, she wore her grey hair in two pigtails. She had a kindly face and spoke with a soft German accent. She had been Celia's caregiver after her first stroke but became so involved in their lives that Jim decided to keep her on as housekeeper after his wife's fatal attack.

"Hi Greta, did you hear from Lara today? Will she be home for supper?"

"She just called before you came in, Mr. Cabot, and said she was at Hilda's. She'll have supper there but will be home early."

He regretted that Lara would miss the wiener schnitzel. No one made it like Greta. After supper,

Greta washed the dishes and Jim dried them, their usual routine.

"Mr. Cabot, if you don't mind me saying, it's nice to see Lara calm and friendly. I think she misses Lunenburg."

"I'm keeping my fingers crossed. I hope she misses Lunenburg as much as I miss her."

They continued a light conversation and around nine o'clock, Greta bade him good-night and retired. Jim turned on the TV but kept glancing at his watch. He was anxious to hear about Lara's day. Shortly after ten, he heard her come up the driveway. She walked in with a smile on her face that brought back memories of years ago.

"Hi dad, it's nice to see you so relaxed. Today was gorgeous. You must have worked like a slave."

"Not really, sweetheart, but it wasn't a bad day. I made some progress on the varnishing, plus a few other details, and left a bit early. How about some tea before bed?"

"Good idea, let me prepare it this time. Any of Greta's cookies left over?" Without waiting for an answer, she continued.

"Dad, I've got some important news. I think it's good news, and I'm really hoping you agree."

They sat facing one another. Lara reached over and gently covered his hands with her own.

"Dad, I started to tell you last night that I was now alone, but it was only part of the story."

She went into detail explaining the parting with Frances, the in-vitro pregnancy and her morning encounter with Father McCrory. As expected, Jim sat back and shook his head, stunned.

"I'm speechless. This is like a bombshell."

There was a long silence, and for a seemingly endless moment, they stared at their entwined hands. Finally, he said,

"Lara, I'm sitting here listening to your voice and looking at your face. I've never seen you so happy in years. You have the courage of your convictions. You are truly Celia's daughter. What can I say? I'm overjoyed with the thought of being a grandpa, even though it'll probably make me feel older than I already do. I'm stunned and surprised, but I must admit, I'm excited enough for both of us."

She rose abruptly and came around the table. She stood behind him and placed her arms around his neck, snuggled her face in his hair and whispered,

"I love you."

Jim felt an electric tremor run the length of his body. It arose from the depths of his memory. He had never forgotten the feeling, and the embrace was so familiar. In his mind he heard himself whisper,

"Celia, I love you too."

***

The following morning, Greta served breakfast on the porch. It was another beautiful day, and they sat back and enjoyed the warm sun on their faces.

"Lara, it's been years since I've felt this good. I lay in bed last night feeling guilty about not being able to share it with your mother."

"Dad, if you can believe that mom is watching you, then you can believe she's happy for you."

"Yeah, I guess it's a question of faith, something to lean on when very little else makes sense."

"Listen dad, I paid Jake a visit yesterday morning. I explained I needed to buy out Frances's share and he went along immediately. Not only that, but my monthly payments are almost the same as before."

"Well, as a matter of fact, Lara, Jake came down to the boat yesterday and we had lunch. He told me he spotted you talking to Hilda. I guess you can trust Jake to keep your things confidential. He never mentioned you were in his office. Lara, Jake doesn't usually take time off for social visits during business hours. I think you should be aware of why he came to see me. It seems that Arnie went to see him for a rather large loan. When he asked Arnie for character references, Arnie mentioned a few names and, surprisingly, I was one of them."

Lara was startled. "Are you serious? You're acquainted, but certainly not friends. What's happening here?"

"I wish I knew. Jake told him that he'd give him an answer in about a week or ten days. Now this may not mean anything but have you ever heard of a chap named Drifter? Evidently he's a friend of Arnie's and walks around sporting a ponytail. Has Hilda ever mentioned him? Does she know where he lives or what he does for a living?"

"I didn't know his name but I think I know who you mean. One evening at Hilda's, last Christmas, he rang the doorbell. Hilda didn't look too pleased to see him, and she made him wait in the vestibule while she got something for him. Later I asked who he was, and she told me he's an old friend of Arnie's. I believe she said he lived on a boat in the harbor. He does a lot of fishing and a lot of drinking, but that's all he does. He's not commercial. She was kinda reluctant to talk about him, so I didn't question her any further. I remember him because it was the first time I ever saw a grey-haired guy with a ponytail."

"Lara, Jake is naturally concerned about this man's relationship with Arnie, for two reasons. First, it seems that Drifter has done hard time in Dorchester prison. Jake will know more in a couple of days from RCMP files. Secondly, as you are well aware, Jake's pretty close to Mavis Willis and the family. He's curious about where Drifter fits in."

Lara was visibly shaken.

"If this Drifter guy is involved with Arnie in any shenanigans, people I'm close with could suffer."

She stared at her father. Jim understood the look.

"Lara, something's bothering you, isn't it?"

"Dad, when I was with Hilda yesterday afternoon, she showed me things which devastated me. I saw bruises on her back and arms. When Arnie's sober, it's mental abuse, but when he's drunk it's physical. Dad, would you believe that this has been going on since they were married, and she never breathed a word to anyone?"

A feeling of revulsion clawed at Jim's stomach as she spoke. He had never liked Arnie. He was a loud-mouthed bully and a drunk. And now this.

"Lara, I'm shocked and yet not surprised. I tell you what, Jake and Inspector Gallant are delving into this whole affair. Let's all hang in for a couple of days and see what develops."

"Dad, I'm not going to let anything bad happen to Hilda ever, ever again. I mean it, dad. I mean it with all my heart."

Jim listened to her words. They were more than a promise, they were a firm commitment. He replayed her voice over and over in his mind and soon realized this was a turning back of the clock, a rebirth of an almost-forgotten relationship between two people who truly loved one another.

TWELVE

The afternoon Lara spent with Hilda together with the conversation with her dad put all kinds of thoughts into her head. She finally dozed off around 2 a.m. Early next morning, a phone call from Hilda jolted her awake.

"It's me, and you sound like I woke you."

"Yeah, and I'm glad you did. I couldn't fall asleep until very late. How are you?"

"I'm really O.K., I'm much better. Just being with you and holding you has rejuvenated me."

"Hilda, I was awake and thinking a good part of the night. We really have to get together and talk. I'm concerned about you and Jennie."

"Look, I don't think Arnie is coming back until tomorrow or perhaps even Tuesday. I'd love to spend some time with you. I'm embarrassed to tell you about the thoughts and feelings that resurfaced after all these years."

"Hilda, it's nothing to be embarrassed about. It was always very special with us."

"Well, I can't get enough of you. When we're together I feel safe. Look, I can ask Alma to pick up the baby and sit for me today. She may have some free time. What do you think?"

"I've a better idea. I'll pick you and Jennie up. I really enjoy her. How about if I get there about noon and we go to Mario's for a quiet lunch?"

Lara went down to the kitchen, drank her coffee, took a quick shower and drove over to Hilda's. The Benson house stood out from the others on the block. It was almost a hundred years old and painted a bright red. There was a widow's watch surrounding the second floor and a large verandah with carved wooden railings that gave the house a unique and traditional appearance. Hilda had put much effort into renovating it, but the only thanks she received from Arnie were a never-ending stream of complaints about the cost. Hilda and Jennie ran up to the car, and Lara scooped the baby up in her arms.

"Lara, let's take my car, it's got the kiddie seat. You can play with her in the back while I drive."

Mario's was a good choice. The lunch menu was excellent, and Mario's wife hovered over Jennie like a mother hen. Lara reached for Hilda's hand.

"The situation you're in can't continue. Arnie is never going to change and I simply can't accept you living in that environment. Believe me, he's going to grind you down until you're nothing. I've given it a lot of thought and I'd like you to consider living with me in Toronto. I have an excellent job and we could be a great family. In a few months, I'm going to need your motherly advice. It could be an ideal situation."

"Lara, slow down! I knew you'd be shocked and sympathetic when you saw the bruises, because that's the way you are. But now you're talking about changing your lifestyle and jeopardizing a career, all on account of me. You're right, I'd love to break away from Arnie, but he's so unpredictable it's impossible to know how he'd react. His feelings for the baby are ambivalent. I don't know if he would even miss Jennie. But he's such a vindictive person, I doubt if he'd readily agree to a separation."

"Hilda, whatever it takes, something has to be done. I just can't leave you alone with him. It tears me apart when I see those bruises."

"Lara, I love you too much to be a burden. If I were to leave him, he'd try to cut me and the baby off completely."

"Maybe he would and maybe he wouldn't. Don't forget you've got your mother in your corner. The café would go under without her. And besides, Uncle Jake once told me he wouldn't mind having Mavis back in the bank. He claims she's the best manager material he's ever seen."

"Lara, this is all too new to me. It's so unexpected, it's too much to digest, it's crazy."

"You're right, it's crazy, and you'll become crazy if you stay on. Hilda, for the love of God, your child needs you. If Arnie destroys you, what becomes of Jennie? Listen, let me make you aware of something. I don't know much about Arnie's background, but I can tell you that his friend Drifter is a bad apple. He's done time in Dorchester prison. My mom always used to say,

"Tell me who your friends are and I'll tell you who you are"

Hilda reached out for Lara's hand.

"Lara, I know this will shock you; just after Jennie was born, Arnie opened up and told me his whole story. My head was in a turmoil for weeks. I know all about Drifter; guess who his prison cellmate was, none other than my husband."

"Arnie, in prison?" Lara was stunned.

"How did this happen? How did these two people come together?"

"Lara, listen to this. Arnie was in Canadian Special Forces. It didn't take long for the trouble to start. He was fine when sober, but on two occasions he wrecked army vehicles while drunk. The second time, the truck rolled over and he ended up in the hospital for three months. His souvenir from the accident was a permanent limp. They gave him a general discharge, which is nothing to brag about, plus a modest pension. A couple of months after he left the army, he got into a fight in a hotel bar. It involved a married couple, and when it was over, her husband was a vegetable and she ended up in the hospital with a miscarriage. Arnie got a five-year sentence but wangled an early release. Lara, you're the only one I've ever mentioned this to. I couldn't bring myself to tell my mom. She brought Arnie and me together. If she knew what she had done, it would kill her."

Lara was at a loss for words.

"Lara, years ago, there was an armored car robbery at Halifax airport, and Drifter was involved. Arnie met Drifter in prison. He told me he was more than Drifter's cellmate, but his bodyguard too. They never found the stolen money and I'm sure it's the reason Arnie stays close to Drifter. I know that he shelled out eighteen thousand dollars for the boat that Drifter lives on. She reached over for Lara's hand and smiled.

"And that, my beautiful lover, is the background of Arnold Benson, the man I married, the guy who never came across a brand of whiskey or a woman he didn't like."

THIRTEEN

Jim Cabot awoke to a beautiful red sunrise. He parted the curtains, opened the window and breathed the fragrant air blowing in from the garden.

'Red sky in the morning, sailor take warning', he recalled. He decided to go down to the boat and put in some work before the weather deteriorated. Lara was still asleep but Greta was up and had prepared a hot breakfast. About an hour after climbing aboard the boat, he put down the varnishing brush and answered his cell phone.

"Jim, it's Jake; how about a little lunch with me and Bill Gallant? We'll eat at Mario's. It's quieter than Arnie's. Our Inspector has acquired some interesting stuff that you'll want to hear. I promise I won't keep you long."

Jim knew Jake wouldn't call on any trivial matter. After a couple of hours of work, he drove over to Mario's. Mrs. Mario greeted him and directed him to Jake's table.

"Hi guys, what's up?"

Jake reached out.

"Sit down, my friend, we've got an interesting story for you. Jim, you may be surprised who a couple of your fellow Lunenburgers are."

The businessman's lunch at Mario's was usually well attended. Small professional and commercial groups seeking a quiet getaway for private discourse appreciated Mario's ambience and tranquil atmosphere. Gallant removed a folder from his briefcase and placed it on the table.

"Gentlemen, the boys down at Halifax headquarters opened their files and gave me both an earful and an eyeful. Keep in mind that what I'm revealing today is in the public domain. Now I've got to go back a little in time. After Arnie lost his parents in a car accident, he went to live with one of his late father's brothers in Moncton. Another brother, Jed, came back to Lunenburg to take over the café. Now Arnie was a big kid, a bully and forever in trouble. He was in and out of juvenile court. When he was about twenty-one, the family convinced him to join the army, hoping he'd get a little discipline. His size and brute strength made him an ideal candidate for Special Forces. But he had a severe drinking problem that got him into a lot of trouble. After seven or eight years he was tossed out with a general discharge and a permanent limp from a DUI accident that was entirely his fault. A few months later, he was in a hotel sports bar and, according to witnesses, he assaulted a female client. Her husband was alerted by her screams, came running and shot a hard right to Arnie's nose; but the guy was a lightweight and didn't stand a chance. In a few seconds, he was on the floor and Arnie was stomping on his head. The poor fellow ended up in a coma, and from what we know, after more than six years, he's still a vegetable. His name is Maitland, and our records indicate he was a board member and a VP at Campbell's Brewery in P.E.I.* His wife was a former Miss Nova Scotia and a Miss Canada runner-up. I heard she was pregnant at the time, and I believe she lost her baby after the incident. Arnie went to trial, and the charges and plea bargains flew around the courtroom like a flock of seagulls at a beach picnic. In the end he was sentenced to five years but got out in about four. He got off easy mainly because he was a veteran and was well liked in prison by the staff."

"Now, before this all happened, you may recall an armored car robbery at Halifax airport. Three guys were involved. They eventually caught two of them, and both were sentenced to hard time in Dorchester prison. That's where they ran into Arnie. One of them, Roger Beck, had planned the whole operation. The other guy was a former employee at the airport, none other than our little friend Drifter. It was Drifter who had set up the logistics for the robbery. Now, Drifter and Roger Beck were cellmates. The warden kept them together and wired their cell for sound because the stolen cash and gold were never recovered. Roger Beck blamed Drifter for screwing up and causing their eventual capture. He never forgave him and treated him like dirt. Drifter, being a little guy, couldn't defend himself. Roger got money and drugs from the other inmates by forcing Drifter into prostitution and humiliating him in every way. The guy was sodomized on a regular basis and was a mental and physical wreck. Now it took a year to find the third guy. His name was Schmidt; they finally arrested him at his mother's house in Ontario, and he went to prison in Kingston."

"One evening, at dinner, Arnie broke up a fight between some inmates and beat the hell out of two of the trouble-makers. Drifter was a witness to this and decided to ask Arnie for help. Arnie had years of commando training and the guards liked him because he kept the lid from blowing from time to time when prisoners acted up. Now Arnie didn't become Drifter's protector out of the goodness of his heart. We believe Drifter promised him some of the stolen money after their release. But maybe, just maybe, Arnie got a little greedy, and one winter afternoon, Arnie and Roger Beck were shoveling snow off the prison roof. They were alone except for the guard who was watching them from his sentry shack. As fate would have it, Roger fell five stories and died of internal injuries including a broken neck. Both Arnie and the guard said it was an accident, but rumors persisted that Arnie had shoved him off the roof while the guard was grabbing a smoke. Drifter then asked the warden to allow Arnie to be his cellmate. Arnie moved in with Drifter, but although the cell was wired, the police never learned anything further about the missing money. Both the armored car and the insurance companies claimed the loss was two million. We think it was much higher because they offered half a million as a reward. You don't offer that kind of money for a two-million-dollar robbery. These armored car people try to minimize their losses for PR purposes."

Jake chimed in,

"I knew Arnie came in to take over when his uncle Jed died, but I had no inkling of his background. It puts a different slant on things as far as the bank is concerned."

Jim exclaimed, "What a story! By the way, can I buy the beer?"

"We're not retired like you, Jim, no drinking on the job."

***

Inspector Bill Gallant was an icon in Lunenburg. With his dark business suit and serious manner, he could easily be mistaken for a banker or an accountant. He had turned down several prestigious positions, preferring instead to be out in the field. His manner was efficient and business-like. He had solved cold cases that had been on the books for years....just by dogged persistence. He would gnaw away at a problem until he found a solution. That was a culture that Jim appreciated. He ruminated over his own life. So many disappointments, so many things gone wrong and yet you get back on your feet and start over again.

And that's what made Jim go back to the boat, day after day, sweating in the heat of the summer, freezing and coughing under a winter cover in the middle of January.

'Who knows,' he wondered, 'maybe in a few more weeks, there'll be a bottle of Jake's champagne breaking over the bow of *Lunenburg Lady*. Lara will kiss me, and I'll whisper in her ear, 'hey, I did it!'"

FOURTEEN

Arnie parked his van at the extreme end of the marina where Drifter's boat, *Easy Time*, was tied up. He took his fishing gear and walked down the dock. Drifter was sitting in the cockpit holding a glass of whiskey.

"Hey Arnie, you change your mind about fishing today? The weather looks good. You told me you just wanted to talk."

"Yeah, yeah, but let's go out anyhow, we can do both."

The boat, an older, twenty-six-foot cabin cruiser was Drifter's floating home. In winter, when it was on dry land, he lived on board with a couple of electric heaters. Officially, the boat belonged to Arnie; he also subsidized Drifter's way of life, mainly fishing and drinking. About a mile offshore, they threw in their lines, sat back and filled their glasses.

"Drifter, I finally got some good news. I got a contact who can move both the cash and the gold for us. After all this time, things have cooled down enough that we can go ahead on a deal."

"Who are these people anyhow? Where did you meet them?"

"I've been talking to a lawyer in Halifax who has some connections. I feel pretty good about him 'cause he's part of a respectable law firm. We're close to an agreement on the deal and I'm supposed to go into town again over the weekend. I've got to move the stuff to a location where they can pick it up. Storing it in your aunt's cellar was a good idea, but we're lucky they haven't searched the place yet."

"Arnie, maybe they went in without a warrant. They could have jimmied the cellar door lock and we didn't know about it. The phony chimney base I built could have fooled them."

"Well, maybe they have and maybe they haven't; all the more reason it's time we made a move. Now listen, these people are going to take a percentage off the top, but we're gonna have to accept it. It would be stupid to start shopping around. The less people who know about this, the safer I feel."

"What about Charlie Schmidt? He's getting out any day now. When I saw him in Kingston at Christmas, he was fuckin' anxious to get his hands on the dough. He doesn't know about you and me and he's expecting a fifty-fifty split."

"Why do you keep bringing up this guy Schmidt's name? He's your fuckin' problem. You never even mentioned him when we made our deal. He brought you and Roger into the airport and then drove you guys out. He was only the driver in the heist. What the hell does he expect? You and Roger put the deal together. You guys tied up the guards and then you brought the stuff out. You took all the risk. You could have been killed. Schmidt just sat behind the wheel. Do I have to go over this again? I don't even want to hear Schmidt's name again, O.K? I risked my ass and saved yours by getting rid of Roger. That was strictly for you and me. I did it for a fifty-fifty split, and now you pop up again with this Schmidt crap. Now stop being an asshole; when I shoved Roger off the fuckin' roof, you were excited as hell that you were going to split his share. So when did you decide to bring Schmidt back in? What the hell is going on in that fuckin' head of yours?"

"Arnie, even if I give him half of mine, he'll still want more. He knows Roger is dead, but he thinks it was an accident. He doesn't have a clue about you. How can I hide your share?"

Arnie didn't reply; he got a sudden sick feeling in his stomach. Drifter was punching holes in his watertight plans. 'Oh no,' he thought, 'this is no good, this is no good at all.'

Arnie sat back in the chair, but his thoughts were not about fishing. The more he thought about Drifter's dilemma, the more he realized it had become his own. The gnawing feeling in his stomach got worse. Drifter was a weak character and a liar: he was liable to cave in to Schmidt and reveal everything to him, if he hadn't already done so. Arnie decided then and there that he needed a new approach. He had invested a lot of time and money in this risky caper. 'No way is Schmidt or Drifter going to throw a monkey wrench into this deal,' he thought. 'There's only one way to break the connection.'

FIFTEEN

On Friday afternoon, Drifter called Arnie's cell from a public phone.

"Hello, Arnie. Yeah, it's me. Where the fuck are you anyway? You told me you'd be at the café this morning. I'm still not happy about things. I gotta talk to you."

"I'm in Halifax, Drifter. What the hell is bugging you?"

"Shit man, how come you didn't take me along? You know I wanna go visit my ma in the nursing home."

"Goddammit, I'm not making a social visit. Remember our talk on the boat? Well, I'm here for a meeting with that lawyer. I'll tell you about it when I get back. O.K.? Do you understand? I can't talk now, I'm late for the appointment."

"Go fuck yourself," Drifter shouted and slammed down the receiver.

Arnie thought, 'The same to you, my little friend. I won't be putting up with you much longer.'

***

Arnie drove into the Ritz Hotel parking lot and went directly to the bar. His lawyer connection, Tony Manolo, awaited him at a corner table. He stood up as Arnie approached.

"Hello, Arnold. Don't bother sitting down. Let's go into the men's room, it's quieter."

Tony was a tall, lanky, awkward-looking man. One shoulder was visibly lower than the other, and his shiny black hair hung down on his forehead. He kept pushing it away from his black horn-rimmed glasses. His eyes blinked constantly and he had a nervous twitch and a permanent grimace around the left side of his mouth. His dark suit and grey tie reminded Arnie of a funeral director. He wondered if he was on drugs and was overdue for a fix. Tony used the urinal and then checked all the booths.

"O.K. Arnold, here's the arrangement. We get the money back in U.S. funds. There'll be a delay with the gold. They keep twenty percent to launder the cash and twenty-five percent for fencing the gold. Now that may sound like a lot, but in Europe it can go as high as fifty. I get five percent. These guys don't want to know you or even meet with you. You just have to make the stuff available and they'll pick it up. The place for the transfer will be a quiet indoor parking lot downtown. I'll tell you where when you're ready. You said there were seven plastic containers, each weighing around forty pounds. Right? The transfer can be done in about fifteen minutes, and if no one else is around, it should go smoothly. The garage doesn't have any video surveillance and we do it on a weekend when it's quiet. You'll get your money in about ten days. It may be in big bills, but don't worry. I guarantee you they're clean. Arnold, I want to warn you now; all of your bills that are bigger than hundreds can be traced and my people will burn them. You'll get the rest of the money after they melt the gold and fence it."

Tony glanced furtively from side to side. Although they were alone, he spoke in whispers. His blinking and twitching worked on Arnie's nerves. Arnie reached for some paper towels and wiped the perspiration from the back of his neck. The heat was oppressive, and he longed for some fresh air.

"Tony, let's go outside and walk a little. I'm dying with the fuckin' heat in here."

"I can't leave now. I've got a full afternoon ahead of me. Now, when do you think the stuff will be available?"

"I've got a detail or two to look after, but I'm anxious to move it. I'm gonna call you soon, maybe tomorrow or the day after."

"That's sooner than I expected, but that's great. Like I said, the weekend is quiet. It should go smooth."

Tony's departing words were not comforting.

"There's one more thing I want to make clear, Arnold. If anything goes wrong, you never, ever point a finger at me. Remember, my guys are major-league international, and they'll protect me. They'll get to you no matter where you are. They'll erase you without thinking twice."

Arnie reached out and grabbed Tony's hand in a vice-like grip and twisted. Tony bent over and howled in pain, but Arnie held on.

"Now you listen to me, my little friend, don't you fuckin' well threaten me. I'm giving you guys all this stuff not knowing if I'll hear about it again. So now let me tell you something. If anything goes wrong at your end, I'll get to you sooner than your friends get to me. I promise you."

Arnie stared him down and slowly released his grip.

"Shit, Arnold, control yourself, we're on the same side."

"Right on, Tony, and don't you forget it."

Arnie hurried out without a word and headed for the bar, his head spinning, his shirt stuck to his back. The whiskey glass quivered in his hand. His mind was in high gear and moving too fast. He wasn't thinking straight.

'Relax, Arnie, relax,' he thought. 'Stay in control, tonight's a big night.' He had done his share of risk-taking in the past twenty years, but this evening's plans were different. This time it was more than money. If anything went wrong, he could spend forever in prison.

'Gotta be calm. Cool it, Arnie, cool it.'

SIXTEEN

Madge Cullen, Arnie's current lover, reached over to answer her cell.

"Hi Madge, I'm here at the Ritz. I reserved our room for the night."

"Sounds great, Arnie. What time you want me there?"

"Make it right after five this afternoon. I'm celebrating a little deal I'm putting through. But Madge, do me a favor. Don't forget to park in the mall parking lot behind the hotel as usual. Remember, come in by the back entrance door. They don't tow cars at the mall, and if you get an overnight parking ticket, I'll cover it."

"Fine. I'll bring you something I baked today—dark chocolate brownies, your favorite."

Arnie drove into the Ritz parking and purposely left the front passenger window open about ten inches. He opened the trunk and took out a bottle of White Label single malt whiskey and a bottle of Shiraz wine he had bought for the occasion and paid for with cash. He placed them in a large leather shoulder bag together with a pair of leather kid gloves. He got out of the car and and locked the doors with the remote. He then reached through the open passenger window and purposely dropped the remote key on the car floor. He shouted to the garage attendant,

"Joe, I just blew it,... I locked my remote keys in the car. Try to jimmy the door if you can. But don't worry if you can't get to them, I'll get one of my employees to bring me an extra key tomorrow morning. I won't need the car tonight anyhow."

"I'll give it a try later, Mr. Benson. Those new recessed door locks are hard to fool with."

Arnie checked in and went up to his room, took a hot shower and relaxed. He pulled a small bottle of clear liquid from his pocket and doctored up both the wine and the whiskey. He returned the whiskey to his leather bag and went over his plan again.

"It must be perfect. Nothing must go wrong," he muttered.

Madge arrived around 5:30.

"Well, lover boy, what's the big occasion? I've got the baked goodies for you."

"Listen Madge, I'm in the middle of a deal and it looks like it's going pretty well. Here, I got you a bottle of your favorite wine."

Arnie ordered a room service meal for one person. He took a couple of small whiskeys for himself from the fridge bar and served the doctored wine to Madge. They fooled around in bed for a couple of hours until Madge complained of fatigue and fell asleep. He poked her a few times, but there was no response. He rinsed out the glass and the wine bottle and placed them in his shoulder bag. Arnie dressed quickly, reached into

Madge's purse and took her car keys and registration. He left the toilet seat up to see if she got up while he was away. He hung the 'Do Not Disturb' sign on the door, took the stairway down to street level and left by the rear entrance. He crossed the street to Madge's car, donned his gloves and noted that the vehicle was parked directly beneath a street lamp.

Arnie drove cautiously to Lunenburg. As he neared the harbor, he turned into a wooded area, and parked. He hadn't figured on a full moon, so he waited patiently and scanned the area, making certain there was no movement near the marina. He remembered to dim down the interior lights so they wouldn't show when he opened the car door. He took his bag and walked through the bushes and along the main dock to the slip where *EasyTime* was tied up. The red porthole light moved about as the boat gently tugged at the dock lines. He climbed aboard and knocked on the cabin door. There was no response, but after a few moments, just as he was about to force it open, Drifter called out.

"Who's there?"

"It's me, open up."

The door opened slowly, and Drifter stood there wavering, barely able to stand. He was very drunk. He held onto the door frame, swaying with the boat from side to side.

"What the fuck you doin' here? You're supposed to be in Halifax. I still think you're a shit for not takin' me. I ain't seen my ma in over a month."

"Listen to me, for Christ's sake, this is a special celebration. It looks like our deal is going through. Here, look, I got you a bottle of eighteen-year-old booze. Stop your fuckin' complaining and drink up."

"Shit man, single malt White Label! That stuff's like gold. Pour me a big one."

In less than ten minutes, the little man had emptied three shot glasses.

"Drifter, they're ready for the stuff any time. I'm gonna meet them at a pre-arranged place in town and make a quick transfer from my van."

Drifter's head weaved from side to side. Through half-closed eyes he muttered,

"O.K., when do we leave?"

"There's no 'we'. They don't want anyone around when the transfer is made. I need the padlock key to get into the cellar. Where did you hide it."

"Fuck you, man, you ain't going without me."

"Drifter, I'm not gonna let you screw this deal up."

Arnie got up and grabbed the little man in a headlock; with his free hand, he held him in a half-nelson and began twisting. Drifter howled in pain.

"You crazy bastard, you're breakin' my arm!"

"Yeah, you little creep, and if I have to smash that cellar padlock, I'll smash your arm first."

Drifter gasped in pain, but Arnie kept twisting.

"Now give me the fuckin' key, or I'll tear your arm off."

The tears rolled down Drifter's face. The pain was excruciating, and he finally relented.

"O.K., O.K., let go you bastard, it's under the front bilge board."

Arnie unscrewed the floor panel, turned it over and found the key taped to the underside.

"Now pour yourself another drink, Drifter, calm down, and let's not argue anymore."

He sat back and watched as the little man reached over to seize the bottle. Arnie grabbed it from his shaking hand and filled the glass. Drifter took a large gulp, looked at Arnie with glazed eyes and blurted,

"Aren't you gonna have some?......I gotta take a leak, help me up."

"I can't drink now, I'm driving back to Halifax."

Arnie dragged Drifter to the toilet, pulled down his trousers and left him sitting there. A few minutes later, he went back. Drifter was out cold. Arnie tried to wake him, but to no avail. The doctored whiskey had done its work. He poured the rest of the bottle over Drifter's clothes and down his neck. He shut the cabin light, picked the little man up in his arms and carried him out of the cabin into the cockpit. Arnie looked around the harbor for any sign of life and then lifted Drifter over the gunwale onto the dock. He knelt down and listened to make certain he was still breathing. He held him firmly by his jacket and rolled him carefully off the edge of the dock. Drifter stirred at the shock of the cold water, but Arnie had no trouble holding the little man's head under the surface. In just a few minutes, Drifter was still. Arnie pushed him firmly away from the dock. He went back into the cabin, turned on the light and looked around, making certain there were no signs of a struggle. He filled both the whiskey bottle and the empty wine bottle with water, climbed back into the cockpit and pitched the bottles and the glasses far out into the harbor. All seemed quiet, the rippling of the waves against the hull of the boat being the only sound. He detached the stern line of the boat and let it hang overboard, leaving the vessel secured only at the bow. He then walked quickly to the car.

Arnie drove cautiously back to Halifax, his mind replaying every detail of the evening's events. He pulled into the mall parking lot at about 1:30 a.m. and parked the car exactly where he had found it. He crossed over to the hotel's rear entrance and waited in the shadow of the doorway for the overnight parking monitor to appear. He knew the lot was patrolled at 8:00 p.m. and then again around 2:00 a.m. Sure enough, the traffic cop showed up on time, laid his ticket pad on the hood of Madge's car and began writing by the light of the streetlamp. Arnie turned and went into the hotel. So far, so good. The overnight parking alibi was in place. He took the stairs up to the room, placed the keys and the wallet back into Madge's purse and returned his gloves to the overnight bag. He poked Madge a couple of times, but she was still in a deep sleep. He went into the bathroom and saw that the toilet seat was still up. I le lay awake for hours.

'I pulled it off, shit, I pulled it off! Drifter's gone, and I've got a bullet-proof alibi. Arnie, you're a fuckin' genius.'

SEVENTEEN

Several months earlier, on a cold and stormy Saturday morning in January, Mavis and her son Danny were about to leave for the café when they heard a scratching sound at the back door. Mavis opened it and was met by a small, shivering white dog that could barely stand. The animal moved slowly across the kitchen floor, eyes half open, and collapsed. Its dirty white hair glistened with tiny ice pellets. It lay there whimpering, its gaze fixed upon Danny.

"Danny, give the poor thing some milk and dry him off with a towel. We'll drop him off at the SPCA."

Danny held the dog in his lap in the back seat of the car and covered it with a blanket. Traffic was barely moving, and Mavis became impatient. Snowbound parked cars had narrowed the streets down to one lane.

"Listen Danny, we're late, and I can't stand being late. When we get to work, put the dog in a box in the storeroom. We'll get Alma to take it to the pound after the noon rush."

When they arrived at Arnie's, the dog awoke, alerted by the smell of food.

"Hey Mavis, what have you got there, a live animal? Since when?"

"Good morning, Georgie. Yup, we had a visitor this morning. Came in unannounced. He's a live animal alright, even though he looks half dead."

"Geez! Couldn't you come up with something better than a skinny mongrel? You intend keeping him?"

"No way. Alma can take him over to the dog pound after lunch."

Danny remained silent and gave Georgie a hurt look. He was glad the snow storm kept the crowds to a minimum, it allowed him to visit the storeroom every few minutes and pamper the dog. When the noon rush was over, Danny couldn't contain himself any longer.

"Mommy, can I talk to you in the kitchen?"

"Sure Danny, what's up?"

"I want to keep the dog. Mommy, please don't let Alma take him. He won't mess up, I promise. He scratched on the door twice to go pee outside. He's a clean dog, please, mommy."

Tears rolled down Danny's face. Obviously moved, she thought,

'My God, he hardly ever cries.'

Mavis and Georgie looked at each other in silence.

Georgie shook his head and smiled. Mavis put her arms around her son.

"He's not at all like the Boxer I promised you for your sixteenth birthday."

"Mommy, I'm calling him Boxer. He's my birthday present. He's a good dog. You'll see, you'll get to like him."

Mavis rolled her eyes in dismay.

"O.K., son, we'll try him for a week and see what happens. If it doesn't work, out he goes."

It was now April, and Boxer was part of the family. His gentle nature and endless tail-wagging ingratiated him to everyone. Boxer observed Danny's every move. His eyes followed the boy each moment they were together.

It was bedtime on a Friday evening. Danny undressed, brushed his teeth and climbed into the shower. His mental impediment hardly affected his physical movements. They were calculated and precise. His dresser was spotlessly neat, and his drawers were tidy and organized. Boxer waited patiently outside the shower stall for Danny. They curled up in front of the TV, and around 9:30 p.m., the dog scratched on the front door to be let out. Danny had forgotten to walk the animal but didn't feel like dressing again. He opened the front door and was greeted by a cold gust of wind blowing up from the bay. He opted to let Boxer out on his own, certain that the brisk weather would encourage him to return promptly. Around 10:30 p.m., Danny realized he had made a mistake. The dog failed to show up. The boy phoned Mavis at the café.

"Mommy, Boxer ran away, and I want to go and look for him; can I go? Please let me go."

"Danny, it's no night to be out. Where do you think you can find him at this hour?"

"He may have gone down to the harbor. When it's windy, he can smell the fish. I'm sure he's there."

"Listen carefully. Arnie left for Halifax for the weekend, and I have to close up tonight. I won't be home until late. Promise me you'll phone as soon as you get back. If you can't find him in an hour, come right home. You'd better dress warm, it's cold out there."

The boy threw on his clothes, jumped on his bike and headed down to the harbor. A full moon lit up the marina, and sparkles of moonlight reflected off the little wavelets. The creaking docks moved about in the breeze as he walked cautiously by each slip. He kept calling the dog's name in a loud whisper, but to no avail. The marina was dark and Danny was worried he'd wake someone. Although it was early in the season, there was always the possibility that people were asleep on their boats. Danny spotted *Easy Time* tied to a slip at the end of the marina property. He noticed a red light shining through the cabin porthole but decided he'd take a chance that Boxer wasn't there. He remembered Drifter from the café and always had an uneasy feeling about him. He opted not to intrude, especially at this hour. Suddenly the red cabin light went out, and almost immediately the door opened. Danny could make out the silhouette of a tall, heavyset man emerging and carrying something that Danny was certain was a body. Both the man and his limp were familiar.

'Geez, it's the boss. What's he doing here? Mommy said he was in Halifax.'

The boy crouched behind a deck box and watched the drowning scenario unfold in front of his eyes. Between the shock and horror of what he witnessed and the cold wind that pummeled his face and body, he was soon shivering beyond control. Anxious to get back and call Mavis, he ran quickly to his bike, glancing fearfully over his shoulder, and sped home. He bounded up the steps to find Boxer waiting on the porch. The dog slithered on his stomach, begging forgiveness but Danny didn't bother with a reprimand. Both he and the dog were shaking. He scooped up the animal, went quickly into the house, threw off his clothes and jumped into bed, hugging Boxer so tightly the poor animal squirmed in pain.

He thought again about telling his mother but knew that a confrontation with Arnie could mean the end of everything. He was thoroughly confused and his chest felt like a pounding drum. Danny couldn't control his tears. Perhaps it was all a dream. Perhaps it never really happened. Mavis arrived earlier than expected, but the boy feigned sleep when she looked in on him. The image of Arnie kneeling over a body, rolling it into the water and then lying on the dock as he pressed it below the surface horrified him. Sleep was out of the question.

EIGHTEEN

Arnie had a restless night. He finished off the whiskey samplers and finally fell asleep around 4:00 a.m. He awoke with a start around 8:30 a.m. when a phone call came in from the hotel parking level.

"Mr. Benson, this is Joe in the garage. I noticed your passenger window was partially open. We're in luck. I managed to get my arm inside and open the door. I found your keys on the floor. Don't bother sending home for another set."

Arnie hung up and laughed to himself.

'Arnie Benson, you're on a roll.'

The phone had awakened Madge.

"Hi Arnie, what kind of a night did you have? I slept right through, but my head is pounding like a drum and I feel like puking. Geez, what the hell was in that wine? Excuse me, I've gotta pee. My bladder is busting."

"I'll order you up some bacon and eggs and a pot of coffee. I've got a busy morning and have to be outta' here by ten."

"Arnie, I feel dizzy and I've got a migraine or something. I can't eat a damned thing."

"Listen, the food should help, but if you really feel sick, take a cab home and pick up your car later. Don't worry. I'll cover everything. Go home and rest up. I'll call you tonight."

He made his usual TV checkout, and they left the hotel through separate exits.

Arnie drove to the edge of town, close to Drifter's aunt's house. It was raining lightly, and he hoped the weather hadn't changed her Saturday morning routine of visiting her sister in the nursing home. The house was located in a wooded area just off the highway. He scouted around and parked at a public phone. To assure himself no one was home, he dialed the aunt's phone number. No answer. He waited in the van for half an hour and then dialed her again. Still no answer. He drove back and parked behind the house, obscured from the highway traffic.

Arnie put on his gloves, took his flashlight, opened the padlock and pushed open the cellar door. He was met with a rush of cold, damp air and an overpowering odor of mold. He listened for a few moments for any sounds of activity on the floor above, but all seemed quiet. Arnie took the axe that Drifter had purposely left when he built the false chimney, and swung it at the enclosure surrounding the base of the chimney. In a few minutes, bricks lay scattered over the cellar floor revealing the seven green plastic containers. They were heavy, and by the time he finished loading the van, he was exhausted. He drove to a nearby public phone and called Tony's cell.

"Tony, I'm ready. Where do I go?"

"Good, Arnold, it's sooner than I expected. Do you know the Ryan Hotel?"

"No, but I'm in town. I'm driving a white Caddy Escalade van."

"Okay, it's a small place on the corner of Coronation and Fenton. It's below-ground parking. Drive in, pick up a ticket from the machine and park at the bottom level facing a wall. It's nearly empty on the weekend. Lock the van but leave the key behind the left front tire.. Go upstairs to the lounge and stay there for at least an hour. Ask the barmaid to validate your ticket for free parking. There's no surveillance camera. Don't worry about the stuff. It'll be out of your van in less than an hour. It's slow on the weekend and the concierge goes down to the garage only if there's an unusual problem. That's it, Arnold. Nice and simple. Call my cell from a pay phone anytime and bring me up to date. Good luck."

Arnie turned into the Ryan parking and proceeded to the lowest level. It was three floors down, and sure enough, he was alone. He followed Tony's instructions and then went upstairs to the lounge. He ordered a double and tried to relax, but it was useless.

"What if they don't pick up the stuff?" he wondered.

After a very long hour, he took the elevator down to his parking level and looked inside the van. It was empty. He picked up the key and came back to the bar; he ordered a sandwich and parked himself in front of the TV. Arnie sat back, relaxed and felt the tension slowly drain away.

"Arnie boy," he muttered, "you always dreamed of being fuckin' rich, and now it's gonna happen."

NINETEEN

At 7:00 a.m. on that same Saturday morning, Mavis called Danny to breakfast. After several minutes of no response, she went to his bedroom to fetch him. She found him seated on the toilet, his head in his hands.

"Danny, what's happening? Are you O.K.?"

"Mommy, I don't feel like work today. My stomach hurts and I have diarrhea. It won't stop. I'm freezing."

The boy was pale and trembling.

"Honey, you don't look too good. Get dressed and try to eat a bit. I don't want to leave you alone, but I have to open up the place. Come with me, and if you're too sick to work I'll get Alma to take you to the clinic and stay with you."

They arrived at the bar and Danny headed for the washroom. After a while, he joined Georgie in the kitchen.

"Good morning, Danny."

Georgie gave him his usual hug.

"Hey kid, you look a little peaked. Don't tell me you've got a hangover."

"Georgie, I had nightmares all night and couldn't sleep."

"Sounds exciting, do you want to tell me about them?"

"No, I can't."

"I see. You and I always talked about your nightmares. Are these different? Why can't we talk about them?"

"This time it's different. It's too scary."

"Uh huh. Were you ever in danger?"

"No. Maybe." He stopped and thought for a moment. "Maybe other people are too."

"Is this about your family?"

"I don't know, maybe."

"Well, when you feel like talking about it, kid, I'm ready to listen. In the meantime, make yourself some dry toast and a cup of tea."

Just before noon, Mavis ran into the kitchen, visibly shaken.

"Jesus, Georgie, a customer just told me the eleven o'clock news reported an unidentified body washed up in the harbor. Now I just got a phone call from Sam, the harbormaster. He says it was Drifter. I've got to call Arnie. I don't believe this."

"Mavis, take it easy, calm down. Did Sam have any details?"

"He said he probably fell into the water while tying up his boat. He thinks Drifter was drunk. The coast guard said he smelled booze when they hauled him out."

Danny listened and realized that his nightmare was more than a dream. He was carrying an armful of dirty plates when he suddenly felt faint. He dropped the dishes and fell forward against the sink. Georgie grabbed him and lowered him to the floor as the boy started convulsing. Georgie screamed at Mavis,

"Shit, what the hell's happening? Get a doctor, the kid's dying!"

"Georgie, just try to keep him calm; hold him down gently. I'm calling 911."

Visions of the past reappeared. It was always Mavis Willis carrying her young son in her arms into an ambulance. Time and time again she witnessed his struggle against the monster that enveloped her little boy's brain. Danny would win battles but never the war. The beast would inevitably attack again. As the boy grew older, Mavis fought a valiant but lonely campaign while her husband, Bert, basked in the comfort of self-pity, caressing his bottle of whiskey. Around 2:00 in the afternoon, Mavis reached Arnie on his cell phone.

"Listen, can you get back here? We've got all kinds of stuff going on. Danny had a bad attack and we rushed him to the hospital. I'm here now with Hilda and Lara. They've got him in the ER and he's still convulsing. On top of that, I hope you're sitting down, Drifter is dead. The Coast Guard pulled him out of the water this morning."

There was a moment or two of silence.

"Arnie, are you there, do you hear me?"

"I hear you, I hear you. O.K., I'm coming back. I should be there by four or five."

Arnie immediately phoned Madge.

"Listen baby, there's a change of plans for tonight. I just got a call from home. My mother-in-law's kid was rushed to the hospital. I've got to go into work. I'll call you on Monday or Tuesday. If you have to speak with me, call me on my cell from a public phone

TWENTY

Arnie walked into the café around 4:00 p.m. and went directly to the kitchen.

"Georgie, what the hell is going on? How did it happen? Are they sure it's him?" Arnie felt so secure with his alibis, he surprised himself with his performance.

"Boss, I only know what the harbormaster told Mavis. The Coast Guard has the body. They said they smelled booze on his clothing. He was probably drunk and fell off the dock. I guess you know that Danny's in the hospital."

Arnie replied off-handedly,

"Yeah, Mavis mentioned it. It's nothing new, he's had those attacks before. Georgie, I'm gonna run down to the marina and talk to Sam. I should be back in an hour."

Arnie hummed a tune as he drove to the harbor. He was surprised at the number of cars in the parking lot. The sailing season didn't start for about another month, yet some boat owners had launched and others were fixing and painting. He headed over to *Easy Time,* where a knot of people were gathered, conversing and speculating about the drowning. He climbed aboard but was confronted by a padlock on the cabin door. He walked back to see Sam at his shack. The harbormaster saw him coming and came out to meet him.

"Geez Arnie, sorry about your friend. I know you two guys were pretty close. When I got here this morning, I saw something floating near the shore. It looked like a body, but from a distance, I couldn't be sure. I called the Coast Guard and they came and fished him out. When I saw it was Drifter, I almost keeled over. Here, take the padlock key."

"Thanks, Sam. Shit, you never know from one day to the next. Why did you lock up the boat?"

"I had to. The cops came around, got aboard and went inside without my permission. I tried to explain you're the owner and they'll need your O.K. They marked your name down in a book. They didn't stay long,..by the time I got there they were already leaving. They asked me if anyone was on the boat today. I told them no, but that I found the stern untied early this morning. The same guy marked everything down in his little book while the other guy opened a bag and showed me some empty whiskey bottles and a couple of glasses. He said they had to check them out. I asked him why. He told me to figure it out for myself. When they left, I decided to lock up the boat. There's always curious people snooping around."

Arnie put on his gloves and went aboard to check out the cabin. Except for what the RCMP had removed, everything seemed to be as he had left it the night before. He closed up the boat and headed back to the café.

"Arnie, did you find out anything?"

"Yeah, Georgie, you were right. He was probably drunk and fell off the dock."

TWENTY ONE

Mavis and Hilda sat in Dr. Evan Patrick's office at Lunenburg General awaiting news about Danny's condition. The doctor was chief of pediatrics and had treated Danny from birth. He came in carrying a thick folder and spread it open on his desk. Mavis looked warily at his face. Today, he wasn't wearing his usual smile.

"Ladies, Danny's attack seems to be different this tIme. We've made some progress. The convulsions have stopped. He's semi-conscious but his speech is fragmented, and I'm a little mystified about what he's saying. He seems to be in shock and continues to relive a particular experience like a bad nightmare. There's been no other change in five or six hours. My gut feeling is that all of this was brought on by a very recent event. There appears to be a lot of anxiety, which is probably a reaction to something, real or imagined. Can you describe Danny's recent behavior?"

The women looked to each other for support. Mavis responded.

"Doctor, things have been nice and smooth lately, both at home and at school. Danny puts in time at the café and the customers like him. He hasn't experienced any harassment from his schoolmates and they respect him. His teacher says he's well liked and takes a keen interest in the goings-on. When he's not working at the café, he's into his books and his dog. He's behaving responsibly. His dog strayed last night and the boy was worried, so he went looking for it around 10 o'clock. The animal came back by himself but not before Danny spent a couple of hours searching down by the harbor. He woke up this morning very agitated and with a sick stomach. His bed was a pool of perspiration and I doubt if he slept much."

"Mavis, I'm going to try to talk to him again. Why don't you and Hilda grab some supper in the cafeteria and then come and see me later."

Evan Patrick had a reputation as one of the finest diagnosticians in Nova Scotia. He was a teaching professor at Dalhousie and child psychology was a subspecialty that interested him greatly. The human body was a challenge, but the human mind even more so. He pulled up a chair next to Danny's bed and reached over to touch the boy. Danny opened his eyes and stared at the doctor.

"Hi son, how are you feeling tonight?"

The boy responded in a whisper.

"I had a bad, bad dream."

"Danny, I'm here to help, and after all these years I'm sure you know I'm your friend. How about sharing your dream with me?"

The boy looked away and shook his head.

"It's too dangerous, Doctor, it's scary."

"It's probably not dangerous for me. Besides, sometimes it helps to share something bad with someone."

"You wouldn't want to know this, Doctor."

"On the contrary, it'll be a big help in making you better. You were fine before this morning. Did something happen during the night that upset you?"

Danny turned away abruptly.

"No, no, I don't want to talk about it."

"Your mom said you went down to the harbor last night to look for your dog."

"No, no, I didn't see anything at the harbor. There was nothing in the water."

"Well, did you look in the water for your dog?"

"I don't want to talk about the water. Please, no more water."

"There was something in the water that you don't want to talk about, is that it?"

"Please don't ask me what was in the water, please. I didn't see anything."

"O.K., son. If you feel like telling me more tomorrow, you know I'm always ready to listen. Goodnight now, and try to sleep a little."

Dr. Patrick went back to the waiting room. Mavis was pacing the floor, and Hilda was on the phone with Lara. He called Mavis aside.

"In my opinion, the boy is hiding something he's finding difficult to wrap his brain around. It may have something to do with the harbor last night. I believe he saw something that really shook him up. Why don't you go home and rest. He'll fall asleep soon, and if not, we'll sedate him again. Perhaps he'll have more to tell us in the morning."

`Mavis drove Hilda home.

"Mom, this has been a rough day for you. Lara's been here and babysitting for hours. I brought her here in my car, and I'll let her drive it home. She's probably dead tired. Never mind giving her a lift, just go straight home."

"O.K., but I have to go back to the café first and close up."

"Take it easy tonight, the kid will be fine. You should be used to this by now."

"You never get used to something like this. For some reason, though, this time seems different."

***

Dr. Patrick went to the physician's lounge, scrubbed up and changed his clothes. He got into the car anticipating a hot shower after a grueling day. The ten o'clock news was on.

> *"Good evening, and thank you for joining us. This morning, the body of an adult male was taken from the water by the Canadian Coast Guard near the entrance to Lunenburg harbor. Identification is being withheld pending notification of next of kin. The Coast Guard believes the person may have fallen from a boat during the night. Police are asking the public to come forward if they were near the harbor*

last evening and witnessed any unusual activity. We should have more on this report by tomorrow. The budget in Ottawa is being debated. . ."

"Well, I'll be damned. I wonder, I just wonder."

He was home but remained in the driveway, resting his head on the steering wheel. He pondered,

'If the kid saw something, why didn't he tell his mother or call the police? If he saw the man fall in, why didn't he report it or get help? Why is he so frightened? Why did he keep saying it was dangerous to talk about it?'

Dr. Patrick walked into the house and put a finger over his lips, politely ignoring his wife's greeting. He reached for the phone and dialed Police Chief Harry Collins's cell number.

"Harry, it's Evan Patrick. Sorry to call so late. Can you tell me more about the fellow they pulled out of the harbor this morning?"

"Doc, he must have fallen off the dock or off his boat during the night. There was no one around to help him. The poor bugger smelled like a brewery. He was probably drunk when it happened."

"Was there any evidence of foul play, any trauma?"

"Doesn't look like it. The RCMP checked his boat and found nothing unusual except plenty of whiskey bottles. He was alive when he hit the water. The coroner says that as of now, it appears to be an accidental drowning."

But the doctor's curiosity had captured his mind. He finally dozed off around 2:00 a.m.

***

Dr. Patrick walked into Danny's room at around 8:00 the next morning. Mavis and Hilda were already at his bedside.

"Good morning, ladies, the nurse tells me Danny had a quiet night."

"Good morning, Doctor. Danny spoke to me a little and said he felt better. As a matter of fact, he asked for some food. I guess it's a good sign."

Dr. Patrick reached over and took Danny's hand.

"You're going to be fine, lad. Just rest up, and we'll have you on your feet in a couple of days. Remember what I told you last night. I'm always available when you feel like talking."

He motioned the women to the waiting room. Mavis spoke first.

"Doctor, something is really bothering you, isn't it? Is it something we should know? Maybe I can help."

"What's bothering me is trying to find out what's bothering your son. I think we'll have some news by the end of the day. I've got a full schedule coming up, but you take it easy and we'll speak again this evening."

Evan Patrick walked into his office and called his secretary on the intercom.

"Emma, get the coroner on the line for me, will you?"

Evan took the call in his office behind a closed door.

"Good morning, John, it's me, Evan. How are things?"

"Evan, when things are lively with me, it's dead serious."

"You and your gallows humor, you'll never change. Listen, something a bit perplexing has come up.

It's about that body they found floating in the harbor yesterday morning. I've got a young lad in the hospital who seems to be suffering from anxiety and shock. He's a Down Syndrome victim, but very bright and observant. He was at the harbor late Friday night. The following morning, when he heard the news about a body being found in the water, he passed out and started convulsing. Later on I questioned him. John, I've got a hunch he saw something, but the mystery is why he's keeping it to himself. He keeps begging me not to ask him because he says it's dangerous. I haven't been able to pry anything further out of him."

"Sounds strange indeed. What can I do?"

"What are the chances of ordering a post-mortem? I have a gut feeling that there's more to be learned about the incident."

At about 3:00 in the afternoon, Evan answered a call from the coroner.

"Evan, you son of a gun. The RCMP just called. They told me their lab found Rohypnol in your guy's blood sample. By the way, he had a blood alcohol above 0.20, and he was just a little guy. Frankly, I don't know if we can learn anything further from an autopsy."

"John, if he was drugged as well as drunk, wouldn't you agree he needed help to take that midnight dip?"

"Yup, and it could probably merit an investigation. Anything new from the young kid?"

"Not yet, but we're hoping he'll open up a bit by tonight or tomorrow."

TWENTY TWO

By Wednesday, the warm, sunny weather had turned to rain. Mavis held fast to her umbrella against a challenging wind. As she entered Danny's hospital room, she ran into Evan Patrick. He motioned her to the waiting room.

"Mavis, it's been almost five days now, and Danny's keeping everything to himself. You can take him home today; hopefully he'll be more talkative with you."

Mavis reached out for the doctor's arm.

"Evan, last night he told me he's not working at the café anymore. He said he was never going to his sister's house again and not to count on him to babysit. I don't know what's come over him. He's crazy about Hilda and Jennie, and everyone at Arnie's loves him. Something's really gone wrong."

"Look, I think it's all part of a pattern. It's all related. There's a common thread there, but I don't know enough about your personal lives to come to any conclusion."

***

Mavis brought Danny home in the afternoon. The boy went straight to his room and into his schoolbooks. Around 4:00 p.m., Hilda called to ask about him.

"Danny, Hilda wants to talk to you."

The boy came quickly to the phone.

"Hello, Hilda. I'm home and I'm O.K."

"Oh Danny, that's great, we're going to visit you after supper."

"Who's coming?"

"Why, just me and Jennie, Arnie's working tonight."

"Good. You and Jennie and Lara are O.K. No one else. That's good."

Mavis took back the phone and waited for Danny to return to his room.

"Hilda, did you hear that? He said 'no one else', it's not like him."

"Mom, I wonder if it has something to do with Arnie. You told me Danny wants to quit work, and now you tell me he doesn't want to come over to visit me anymore."

"Hilda, you've just put a thought in my head. I'm going to talk to Danny again this evening. I'll call you in the morning."

Later that night, Mavis walked into Danny's room, but the boy was in the shower. She returned to the darkened living room and sat by the window. This was her favorite spot. She cherished the dark. The thoughts that crossed her mind were clearer; the colors of the images were saturated. Alone in the dark, she was in full control. The voices spoke when she wanted them to. She could either listen or simply brush them aside if they were uncomfortable. There were no bright lights or noises to compete with the meanderings of her mind. Events became more orderly, problems became more focused and solutions seemed easier. Awhile later, Mavis looked in on Danny. The boy was lying in bed staring up at the ceiling.

"Hi son, how was your shower? You must have enjoyed it, you were in there a long time."

"Mommy, I really liked it a lot."

"Well, that's good. Everyone should take more time, slow down and think. The world goes too fast. Sometimes I feel I can't catch up. Before I can figure things out, something new comes along."

Mavis sat quietly by his bed and held his hand. She gave it a little squeeze and enjoyed a wave of pleasure when he responded in similar fashion.

"Danny, have you thought some more about working at the café? The customers love you and we can certainly use your help."

"Mommy, I can't go there, I can't."

"Danny, you're always truthful with me. Has this something to do with Arnie? I know he doesn't treat you nicely, but he's really not there that often."

The boy turned away and stared at the wall. Mavis thought that perhaps the conversation had gone far enough. She leaned over to kiss him goodnight, but he suddenly turned to face her and blurted out,

"Mommy, he's a very bad man. You don't know how bad he is. I saw him do some bad things. He doesn't know I saw him, and if he found out, he'd hurt me."

Anyone who ever walked into Arnie's could tell you that Mavis Willis was never, ever at a loss for words.

But now, as she stood there leaning over her son, she was suddenly fighting for air. Her throat tightened, and when she tried to speak, no sound emanated from her mouth, at least nothing that sounded like her own voice.

"Mommy, are you O.K.? Are you O.K.?"

"Yes Danny, yes, I'm fine."

Mavis stood up and walked about the room, her hands clasped to her chest. Danny followed her every move. The tense, silent scenario was stifling; it was too much for Mavis to handle.

"Son, I'll let you sleep now and we can talk in the morning. I want to help you, and you have to help me. What do you say we speak about all this in the morning?"

"Yes, mommy. Goodnight, I love you."

Mavis turned out the light and walked back to the living room. Her body shook as she reached out for support. She felt cold and took the woolen shawl from the chair, threw it over her shoulders and settled in again by the window. She finally fell asleep around 2:00 a.m.

★★★

At 7:00 a.m., the dark shadows in the room had melted away and Mavis was awakened by a bright beam of sunshine that squeezed through a narrow opening in the drapes. She had fallen asleep in an awkward position, and every movement of her back and legs drew pain. Anticipating the next conversation with Danny brought on a tightness in her chest and a wave of nausea.

'Mavis, what the hell have you done?' she asked herself. 'You intimidated your daughter into a marriage the girl didn't want. You rationalized away the negatives and the warnings, opted for family security and placed it ahead of everything else. What kind of a person did you force upon your child? Dear Christ, strike me dead. My child was never meant to live with a man. I went against my own knowledge and against God's will. Hilda, Hilda my angel, can you ever forgive me? Lord God in heaven, can You ever forgive me?'

She sobbed uncontrollably. Talking further to Danny at this moment was out of the question. She decided to leave the house before he awoke. The thought of him revealing things impossible for her to accept was overwhelming. Her fear was palpable. This fiery-tongued, red-headed extrovert that confronted the meanest and toughest clientele from Cape Breton to Maine was running and hiding. Mavis was rocked by 'déjà vu' images as she recalled a certain encounter years ago; it was a series of tragic events that she couldn't handle, events which changed her life and career.

TWENTY THREE

"Jennie, you sit quiet in the car while mommy takes the groceries inside. I'll only be a moment."

The kitchen phone was ringing.

"Oh hi, Lara. Listen, I'm just putting stuff away and the baby's in the car. Can I call you back?"

"Fine; Hilda, I'm free this afternoon, let's get together for a few hours. Please bring the baby up to my place. It's Greta's day off and we'll have the house to ourselves. Dad is overnight in Halifax on boat business."

Hilda felt that warm inner feeling again. The anticipation of being with Lara, the way they clung to each other, enjoying each moment as if it were their last and yet, in some way, hoping it would continue forever. As Hilda drove up, Lara was waiting on the porch. She scooped Jennie up in her arms.

"You are the most delicious child in the world," she exclaimed.

"Auntie Lara, what is 'delicious'? Why am I delicious?"

The women embraced for a moment and went upstairs.

"Lara, Jennie hasn't had her nap. I brought her favorite doll. She'll cuddle up with it and fall asleep in no time. I've had a busy morning, and I could use a hot shower. Is that O.K. with you?"

"Fine, but lemme play with her and tuck her in; I need the practice."

***

Lara watched Hilda ease herself out of the shower stall, her youthful body draped in a blue bath towel. She reached over, took her hand, and pulled her gently down on the bed.

"Lara, why is it that when I'm with you, the excitement is endless?"

"It works both ways, sweetheart. By the way, have you noticed I'm starting to show? Looks like I'll soon need a new wardrobe."

"There'll just be more of you to love," she whispered.

They fell asleep in each other's arms

***

A couple of hours later, Jennie awoke and climbed into Lara's bed, squeezing herself between the two women. Hilda awoke and reached out.

"Lara, my love, I leave reluctantly; my duty is now to my child."

"Hilda, I've got a suggestion. Let's order in chicken for supper and have a little feast without worrying about dirty dishes. I've been doing some thinking, and I'd like to speak more about your situation."

Later in the evening, after a hearty meal and with Jennie sound asleep, they sat back and relaxed in the living room.

"Hilda, I've given a lot of thought about you coming to Toronto on a permanent basis. You have your mom and Danny here, and perhaps I was being selfish when I suggested it. But listen, you really merit a separation from Arnie. He doesn't deserve either you or Jennie. If you were legally apart, any future decisions you make would be easier and not made under stress. I know you're worried about how he'll react, but listen carefully. I can't go into details just now, but if you allow me to get involved, then trust me, I think we can swing it quietly and discreetly without any real threats from him. I know a good attorney in Halifax. Don't worry about the legal fees. I can help. If I didn't think this thing was possible, I wouldn't bring it up. By the way, is your house in your name?"

"Whoa, Lara, whoa. Let me catch up. I can't absorb all what you're saying. You're full of surprises. I wish I had your courage. I wish I had your strength to deal with this."

"Hilda, marriage is like a business partnership. If the parties are incompatible, why prolong the relationship, especially if abuse and injury are involved? Abusive people don't change. Arnie was always a bully, even as a child. He hasn't changed, and he never will."

"Yeah, but there's other people involved, other relationships. It's a complicated situation."

"Hilda, if Arnie came home tonight and demanded a separation, what would you do?"

"I'd probably jump for joy, providing of course he wouldn't put Jennie and me on starvation diets and try to take the house away."

"Fine, don't worry about starving. Let's see what we can work out, but first you must agree to go ahead with this. There's an attorney I know. His name is Jeff Segal. He's a kind man and specializes in family matters. He's married to my former roommate from school. Do you know if Arnie will be at work tomorrow morning?"

"Yeah, he should be, but I'm never sure. Why do you want to know? Lara, you're up to something. What is it?"

"Leave it to me and trust me on this. I want to speak with him before we contact the lawyer. I promise to fill you in very soon."

Lara carried the baby and walked Hilda to her car.

"Hilda, what's happening with Danny and how is he feeling?"

"That's another problem. He's still having nightmares, and mom refuses to press him for more details. They're going over to see Evan Patrick tomorrow morning at the hospital. Listen Lara, I'm afraid. What are you planning with Arnie tomorrow?"

"Please don't fret. I promise there's nothing to worry about. Sleep tight, my love."

TWENTY FOUR

"Good morning, Mavis, and a good morning to you too, Danny."

Dr. Patrick's secretary put her arm around Danny. She was a large woman, her kind face and gentle manner ideally suited for a pediatric practice.

"Hello, Emma, how's the family?" asked Mavis.

"We're all fine and getting excited. My daughter's getting her medical degree next month, and the whole family is flying over to St. John's for convocation. Dr. Patrick is already in. I don't think you'll have to wait long; we're not terribly busy today."

Evan Patrick came in shortly after and greeted them.

"Hello, Mavis. What do you say if Danny and I have a man-to-man talk, just the two of us? Wait out here. We shouldn't be too long. Is that O.K. with you, son?"

"O.K., Doctor, a man-to-man talk is O.K. with me."

Evan Patrick winked at Mavis, put his arm around Danny and disappeared into the examining room. Mavis was relieved. She wasn't looking forward to hearing things she simply couldn't handle.

Dr. Patrick placed a hand on Danny's shoulder.

"Tell me, son, how are you sleeping these nights? Still having those bad dreams?"

"Not so much as before, but they still wake me up."

"Just between you and me, Danny, are they always about the same thing? Do you dream about other things too?"

"Just between you and me, Doctor, there are two dreams that keep coming back."

"Tell me, is there a person in your dreams?"

"Yes, yes, and I get scared when I see what he's doing."

"Why do you think he's doing bad things?"

"Well, I think they're bad because you wouldn't do them. A good person wouldn't do them."

"Danny, again between you and me, could you give me an example?"

"Well, I saw this man punch my sister on the head. I could see his underwear. I once saw somebody do that in a movie. He was hurting her, because she was moaning real loud and trying to push him away. He was pushing something against her face, and she was shaking her head."

"Where did this happen, and how come you were there?"

"It was in my sister's house, on the living room floor. I was on my way home from the library and came to borrow a movie."

"What did you do then, Danny?"

The boy hesitated for a while and then looked sheepishly at the doctor. "I ran out."

"Do you know who this man was?"

"Sure, Doctor, he's my boss. He's married to my sister."

"Danny, did you see anyone you knew at the harbor that night?"

The boy hesitated, but then, with a determined look, replied.

"Yes, I saw my boss. I saw him on Mr. Drifter's boat, and then I saw him push somebody into the water and hold his head down till he floated away."

The doctor had heard many incredible stories in his practice, but this one startled and shocked him.

"Did you see Mr. Drifter that night?"

"No, all I saw was my boss and that person in the water."

"Then tell me, now that we've talked about it, do you feel a little better after sharing this with me?"

"I guess so. But please don't tell my mommy."

"I promise you I won't. I'm just going to ask your mom to phone me tomorrow and tell me how well you slept during the night. O.K.?"

"O.K. You're a good man, Doctor, I wish you were my boss."

"Before you go, I have a good friend, Inspector Bill Gallant. I'm sure you've seen him at the café. I'd like you to meet with him, and I want you to understand that no harm will come to you by talking to him just as you've spoken to me. How do you feel about that?"

"If you say so, it's O.K. with me. But please don't tell my mommy."

Dr. Patrick ushered Danny back into the waiting room and motioned to Mavis to come out in the corridor.

"Mavis, your son witnessed some things which are causing his current condition. I don't want to alarm you, but they may be important enough for the police to know about."

"Evan, are you serious? How on earth could Danny be involved?"

"Danny is not involved in any way, except he may have witnessed something important, so important, as a matter of fact, that it's caused him a tremendous amount of anxiety."

"How can I help?"

"I want you to allow me to have Danny meet Bill Gallant. Please understand, it would be in my presence and here in the hospital. Danny is in no danger whatsoever, and I assure you that in his current improved mental condition, he's going to handle this thing very well."

After Mavis and Danny left, Evan Patrick went over to his assistant's desk.

"Emma, try to get in touch with Mavis's daughter, Hilda. If you recall, she was here with Mavis when Danny was admitted last week. I'd like to speak with her tomorrow if possible, and I wouldn't want anyone, including her mother, to know about our meeting."

TWENTY FIVE

That same morning, Lara walked into Arnie's café. She made a point of coming in before the noon rush and took a table in a quiet corner. She ordered a coffee and asked Alma to call Arnie over. Mavis wasn't due in for a while, and that made things less complicated. Arnie sauntered over with a surprised look.

"Well, look who's here," he said, lowering his voice, "my favorite dyke. To what do I owe this visit?"

"Sit down, Arnie. If you don't sit now, you'll want to lie down later."

"Wow, sounds serious. What have I done?" He looked down at her with a sarcastic grin.

"You've done plenty, and it's all been bad. Now you'll have a chance to do some good for a change."

He pulled up a chair, sat down and leaned over with elbows on the table, his massive grinning face supported by two clenched fists.

"Jesus, Lara, you're still beautiful. What a waste of woman. O.K., fire away."

"In about ten days, you're going to be served with separation papers from an attorney representing Hilda. She's tired of being your punching bag. She wants a little peace and quiet for her and Jennie. Maybe she's just running out of tears."

Arnie leaned back in his chair and opened his mouth wide in a mocking, bored yawn.

"Are you serious, bitch? Is that what she sent you here to tell me? If this is her idea, she'll need the emergency room at the hospital when I get home tonight."

"Relax, Arnie, now I'm going to tell you the important part of the story. Do you know what DNA is?"

He sat there with the same bored grin.

"Answer me, Arnie."

"Of course I do, you bitch. That's how they pin murders on people."

"Right, and it's also how they pin charges of rape using semen samples. Semen is very stable stuff, it keeps for years. After you raped me, I drove to the Sexual Assault Centre in Halifax. They kept me overnight and treated my cuts and bruises. You also ripped my insides apart with that well-practiced weapon of yours. It's all in the hospital records. They kept samples of your semen and tested your DNA. The hospital put pressure on me to reveal your name, but I didn't lay charges against you because my father would have killed you, and I didn't want him sitting in jail for ten years for the likes of you. There's a statute of limitations where you can't lay charges after a certain period of time. It doesn't apply to sexual assault."

The arrogant grin gradually faded as Arnie sat up in his chair.

"You threatening me with blackmail, you bitch? If you were a man, I'd break your fuckin' neck and toss you out on the sidewalk."

Lara stared him down and responded calmly.

"Arnie, man or woman, since when did it make any difference to you who you were beating up? And yes, you're right, I'm a fucking blackmailer, and you're a fucking rapist. Now before you break my neck, let me tell you about your son."

Arnie's eyes widened. He struggled to get his words out.

"My son? Shit, you're really crazy."

He reared back in his chair, picked up a napkin from the table and wiped the spittle from his lips.

"Yes, Arnie. I couldn't stay here after that night, so I quit university, went to Toronto and soon found out I was pregnant. When I had the abortion, I had already contracted for DNA testing. It matched with the sample in Halifax. It's all in the record. Your son ended up in the hospital garburator."

She stopped, sat back and let It all sink in.

Arnie sat there stupefied. His complexion turned reddish-purple, his eyes bulged. After what seemed an eternity, he spoke almost incoherently.

"You fuckin' bitch, he was your son too!"

"No, Arnie, no way. I could never have a son of yours. I couldn't live for nine months with your poison in my belly."

"Why are you telling me all this, what the hell do you want?"

Lara felt completely devoid of any emotion or fear. She spoke slowly, confidently and defiantly.

"For starters, you're never going to physically or mentally abuse Hilda or the baby again. You're going to give her an uncontested legal separation and a divorce with a reasonable amount of financial support. You're going to move out of her house and never harass her again. You'll be a genuine bachelor, Arnie. You'll be able to stop lying about your marital status to all those women you've been screwing."

He sat there in a daze, staring and speechless. She waited while her words took hold.

"I've grown up and learned a lot in the past few years, Arnie. I could blow the whistle on you today. And furthermore, if you fight me on this, you'll be back in prison for at least five years. With your record, maybe even longer. My dad and I have more credibility in this town than you'll ever have. The scandal alone would destroy you. When it comes to violence, Arnie, you never learned your lesson."

Her eyes never left his as she pushed back slowly from the table, got up and left. She stepped out into the street and took a deep breath. It was a clear, crisp morning, and as she walked toward the parking lot, her mind caught an image of her late mother. The way she had spoken to Arnie reminded her of her late mother, Celia. Celia, the strong-willed, courageous person who never minced words but rarely offended. Celia, whose decisions were always translated into action. Whether it was the school, the church or the hospital, she was always there, talking, leading, helping and moving ahead. No doubt about it, her mother would have pursued the same path. It reinforced her decision about what had to be done to turn her life and Hilda's in a new direction. She was definitely Celia's daughter.

Lara dialed Hilda's cell phone.

"Hi, it's me. Well, I just left Arnie at the bar. We had a great conversation, but I must admit, I did most of the talking."

"Jesus, Lara, you scare me, what happened? What did you tell him? I don't understand any of this."

"I gave him some food for thought. I'll fill you in a little when I see you."

"Now I'm really frightened. I'm thinking about what happens when he gets home tonight."

"Relax, it's too soon to guess his long-term decision. One thing I can pretty well guarantee is that he won't lay a finger on you anymore. I honestly believe we'll get some positive news within a couple of days. As soon as we do, we'll get in touch with the lawyer."

"Listen Lara, I just got an unexpected call from Dr. Patrick. He wants to see me later today. It has to do with Danny, but for some reason he doesn't want Mavis there. I'm worried that something's gone wrong."

"Don't worry before you have to. If you want to leave Jennie with me, that's fine."

"No thank you, sweetheart. I'll manage O.K. I have to go now, she's howling for her lunch. I'll call you tonight, that's if I'm still alive after Arnie gets to me."

TWENTY SIX

Hilda and Jennie arrived at the hospital near the end of the afternoon. Emma greeted them.

"Dr. Patrick's almost through. He'll be out in a few moments."

Jennie made a beeline for the toys and bumped into the doctor as he was entering the room..

"Hilda, thanks for coming down on such short notice. I see you didn't have time to get a babysitter. I apologize. Your Jennie seems to be coming along beautifully."

"Well, she's in the hands of a great doctor."

"Arguable, but nevertheless appreciated."

The doctor sat back and reached over for Hilda's hand.

"I had a serious talk with Danny. He confided several things to me, but before I go into that, I'd like to ask you a couple of questions. I hesitate because of their personal nature. Hilda, this whole affair is not only about Danny's welfare, but the welfare, ...well, maybe it's not a strong enough word, let's say the safety of other people close to you."

The remark was unexpected, and she hesitated.

"Dr. Patrick, I feel comfortable speaking with you. If there's something that I should be aware of regarding Danny, please tell me. I'll tell you all I know."

"I really need some further information, but it's on a subject I must discuss with you alone and without anyone's knowledge for the time being. On a scale of one to ten, how happy are you in your marriage?"

Evan Patrick expected her to be surprised by the query, and he wasn't disappointed. Hilda was startled.

"Doctor, you're aware that Danny lives with my mother; what would he have to do with my marriage?"

"True, but Danny has recounted an incident he witnessed quite by accident. He never told anyone until this morning when I met with him. It was a one-on-one discussion, just Danny and me. I must tell you, though, that if there's any truth to it, and personally I think there is, it could be profoundly important for everyone."

She felt her stomach tighten up and a sudden throbbing in her head. She tried to respond but couldn't find the words.

"Hilda, we're talking about a possible rape that took place in your home a few years ago. Danny witnessed it one night when he came by unexpectedly. He told me the perpetrator was your husband and that you were the victim. As you know, rape is rape, whether you're married or not. My professional concern may be misplaced in discussing this private matter with you, but since Danny is my patient and I'm really concerned about his mental state, I felt I had to get involved. Now Hilda, there's more. There are certain other things which I cannot reveal at present but that Danny witnessed which are causing him great mental stress, so much so that he had to be hospitalized. Unfortunately, the resolution of these problems could affect you and your family."

Hilda was visibly shaken. She felt a tinge of nausea.

"Doctor, give me a moment or two. I really have to think about this. Could I please trouble you for a glass of water? My throat is parched."

"Take your time. These are difficult questions."

Her hand shook as she lifted the glass to her lips.

"Doctor Patrick, you asked about a scale of happiness regarding my marriage. Well I'll tell you honestly, it's closer to zero than it is to one, let alone a scale of one to ten. What's more, I've been married over four years and have been subjected to marital rape on numerous occasions along with other physical abuses and mental torments. So without going into any further detail, if you're wondering if Danny's imagination was working overtime, well it wasn't. He's a reliable witness in spite of his handicap."

"Hilda, I've known you and your family for many years. Naturally I'm shocked at these revelations, but what I wonder is how and why you tolerated this situation."

"Dr. Patrick, it's not how I tolerated it, it's why I continue to do so. I'm living a complicated life involving other people. I'm hoping that things will turn around for me and my family in the near future."

"Well, you have my sympathy. Whatever relief you're expecting, I hope it happens soon. I wish there was a way I could help. You know of course I'm here for you at any time. In any case, don't worry about Danny.

There's been a marked improvement in the past few days. With all he's been through in his short life, he's become a pretty tough young man."

TWENTY SEVEN

Hilda turned into the street from the parking lot and shielded her eyes from the dazzling orange sunset. She was driving on autopilot, her whole attention on her thoughts. She went over Evan Patrick's words again and again. And then she asked herself, 'how could Danny have possibly witnessed the rape that he recounted to the doctor? The boy would never, ever come upstairs to our bedroom, especially at night. My God, did he stumble on something that happened downstairs? None of this makes sense.'

And then it struck her like a bolt of lightning. Danny had told the doctor only what he perceived and not what had really happened. A tragedy had taken place that Hilda had completely overlooked.

"Jesus, dear Jesus, that wasn't me, it could only have been Lara! Lara, Lara, my God, why didn't you tell me?"

Her throat seized up and she gasped for air. Her body trembled in disbelief. This was incredible. This was a confirmation that the man she had married was the epitome of evil. No longer would she fear him. She would fight with every ounce of strength she could muster. She would unburden herself at any price from this monster with whom she had shared a life and a bed for over four years. She grabbed her cell phone, dialed and left a voice mail.

"Lara, I must talk to you. I just can't talk now. I'm driving with the baby, so please come over."

She hung up and drove home, her face wet with tears, her teeth chattering; her arms and hands shook.

"Mommy, mommy, you're crying!"

"Just sit tight, my angel, we'll be home soon."

She stopped abruptly in the driveway, grabbed the baby and ran up the stairs. A voice mail from Mavis awaited her.

"Hilda, what the hell is going on with Arnie? I've been trying to reach you since four o'clock. Call me as soon as you get in. I hope you're O.K."

Hilda dialed Mavis immediately.

"Hello mom, are you O.K.?"

"No, I'm not O.K. What's going on between you and Arnie? He took off for Halifax this afternoon and told me he's moving out of the house. Is this for real?"

Oh my God, momma, did he say that? Oh my God, thank you Lara, thank you, I love you, I love you."

She burst into tears again, her speech almost incoherent.

"Hilda, for God's sake control yourself, what's going on? Is Lara there with you? I'm coming right over."

"No, momma, no. I'm O.K. Believe me. Stay where you are. Lara'll be here soon. I've lots to tell you when I see you. If what Arnie said is true, I'm so happy, I'm so happy. You'll see, momma, we'll all be happy now. I'll come over in the morning."

Jennie tugged at her mother's coat.

"Mommy, why are you crying?"

"Jennie angel, mommy's crying because she's happy."

Hilda splashed cold water on her face and tried to regain her composure. She snatched the baby up in her arms, hugging, squeezing and kissing. She fed and bathed her, and thankfully the child went to sleep almost immediately. Hilda needed Lara all to herself.

A short while later, she heard Lara's car in the driveway. She greeted her at the door and they held each other tightly.

"Hilda, why are your eyes all red, what's happening?"

"Arnie's leaving! Arnie's leaving! Let's go inside. I have lots to tell you.

Lara seated herself on the sofa; Hilda approached, fell to her knees sobbing, and laid her head in Lara's lap.

"Hey, this is no time for tears, we should be having a drink and celebrating."

"Lara, the tears are for you, not for me. Today I've learned what true love is all about. My ego and my stupidity made me think you left for Toronto because you resented my marriage."

Lara leaned forward and lifted Hilda's head with both hands. She stared down at her, their eyes focused on each other. Hilda continued,

"The night you babysat, I called your house after I got home. Your father told me you were spending the night in the hospital in Halifax because you weren't feeling well. He said that you forbade him to come and see you there. You called me the next afternoon and said you'd drop by in a couple of days. I couldn't get through to you by phone, and when I spoke to your dad, he said you'd left for Toronto. He sounded as confused as I. It didn't make sense that you dropped out of school and took off on a day's notice. A week later you e-mailed me from Toronto saying that you were going back to university, and then all I got were occasional messages. Lara, everything fell into place this afternoon. I know what happened when Arnie came home that night. When I got in from work, I found him half naked and in a drunken stupor. No one but you knows how much you suffered because of me. You love me so much, you hid everything."

Lara looked down and caressed her hair.

"Hilda, sometimes people have no choice. You were two months pregnant. Had I known that Arnie was assaulting you at the time, perhaps I would have acted differently. People just do their best and hope everyone survives. Now tell me, how did you find out?"

"Danny had come over to the house to borrow a movie the night you babysat, and he witnessed the rape. I know it happened downstairs because he would never come up to our bedroom, especially at night. He got frightened and ran out. He had no idea you were in the house that weekend. He told Dr. Patrick about the attack and naturally took it for granted that it was me. The doctor said there was another event Danny witnessed but he couldn't talk about it now. I'm certain it involves Arnie and that it was pretty major. I figure Danny wouldn't have had to be admitted for something he saw years ago. It must have been a recent event. Dr.

Patrick questioned me about the rape to see if Danny was a reliable witness. On my way home, everything suddenly fell into place. You were the victim that night, not me. May God forgive me for my stupidity. What happened to you afterwards?"

Lara thought for a few moments, searching for the proper words.

"My love, whatever happened, I finally learned to live with it without going completely to pieces. Mind you, it took almost two years on a couple of psychiatrists' couches, but as you can see, I got through it. I went back to university, graduated and found myself a great job. There's really nothing more to tell. As you probably guessed, I threatened Arnie with the evidence on file in Halifax. With his prison record, he wasn't in the mood to go before a judge again, especially for sexual assault with violence. I'm glad the story worked. Naturally it has to stay between us. If my dad found out, there wouldn't be anything left of Arnie to ship off to prison, and Dad would be doing time. In any case, you're the only person who knows about this."

Lara didn't dare mention the trauma, the pregnancy and the abortion. She decided Hilda had already shed enough tears for one day.

"Lara, I swear to God that I'll love you as you love me. Always and forever."

"Look, whatever I did, I would do again. I'll protect you as long as I have the strength. If I told you that your marriage didn't cause me grief, I'd be telling you a lie. It left a large vacuum in my life. I simply couldn't imagine myself with anyone else. Had he not raped me, I probably would have finished university and then left town later anyhow. Now tell me about this business with Arnie. Did he actually tell your mom he's moving out?"

"Yes, yes, she just called me and said that Arnie was planning to leave. I can't handle all of this at one time. I think I'm going to burst. You endured your personal hell just for me, and now you've turned my life around. My God, I'm speechless."

They laughed and they cried and they drank sherry until there was nothing left to toast but the empty bottle. They held each other while reminiscing about the past and daring to plan the future. Eventually, with cautious steps, they managed to reach the upstairs bedroom, and lost themselves in each other's arms.

TWENTY EIGHT

Tony dialed Arnie's cell phone.

"Hello Arnold, it's me. When can we meet? Let's make it a different place this time. There's a little Greek restaurant, Theo's, corner Harbor and First. It's quieter there and I've got more time today. What do you say to one o'clock?"

They arrived at almost the same time and took a table at the rear. Arnie thought, 'Shit, this guy doesn't stop twitching. I'm sure he needs a fix. He never looks me straight in the eye, his head's on a fuckin' swivel like he's worried someone's watching him. The bastard makes me nervous.'

"Arnold, we've made good progress. You've got a large sum in your name at the Shelter Island Trust Co. in George Town, Cayman. The money from the gold should come through in a few weeks. You're a rich man. Things worked out as I promised. By the beginning of July, you should be worth close to four million U.S. You did well."

"Tony, so far we've both kept our ends of the deal, so let's just say we both did well."

Arnie was surprised when Tony actually smiled. He was at a momentary loss for words but managed to avoid displaying any real emotion in spite of the elation he felt.

"Arnold, have you made any plans? Like I mentioned to you, it'll be difficult bringing that kind of money into Canada or especially into the States, unless you do it in small amounts. I can think of other places you can stash it, but it'll still be far from home. Cayman is probably your best bet. I wonder though if you'd be happy there. I see it as a retirement place for seniors."

"Yeah, I know. I was going to launder some of it by buying a property and enlarging the café. I figured I'd take a big loan from the bank and then pay the difference for the expansion with my own money. There's always contractors around who work for cash. Something came up that threw a monkey wrench into everything. My wife and I don't see eye to eye. I hear Cayman's not a bad place to live. I once knew an old guy who owned a restaurant and a bar there. I wonder if he's still around. He had a good life and was doing O.K. I'm seriously thinking of splitting and maybe taking off for down there."

Tony pushed the hair away from his glasses.

"You could live a great life in Cayman. They respect people with lots of assets. You won't have trouble getting residency. My connection there is a solid one. I've done deals with Shelter. The chaps there know all the immigration angles. Yes, it's worth thinking about. Let's have some lunch. I've got all the documents for you here in my briefcase. When you get to the bank, you'll present them to a fellow by the name of Beaton. He'll take it from there. But be careful, these are the originals. I assure you there are no copies. Remember, after today there's no connection at all between you and us. It's a clean, done deal."

Arnie left the restaurant in a euphoric state. He felt re-born into another world where providence was endowing him with a new life. Everything he ever dreamed was now his to choose or reject, the ultimate decision was his alone. For the first time in his life he felt in full control. He climbed into his van, turned on the ignition and leaned back. Hands behind his head, he shouted at the top of his voice,

"Hey world, look at me! I'm Arnie Benson, and I'm fuckin' rich! I made it! . . Shit, I made it. I can go anywhere and do anything I fuckin' well please. Just try and stop me!"

TWENTY NINE

Inspector Bill Gallant gave an exasperated sigh and perched himself on constable Mary Callam's desk.

"I'm frustrated as hell; after listening to Danny Willis repeat the same story over and over again, I'm certain it's factual and not his imagination. But how the hell did Arnie get to Lunenburg that Friday evening? His car was parked all night in the hotel garage and the rest of the cars were owned by registered guests."

Gallant had verified that no cab, bus or rental car had taken Arnie to Lunenburg. He certainly wouldn't have taken a lift with someone on such a mission. He figured that Arnie must have borrowed a car from a close friend.

Mary offered, "Inspector, what about overnight parkers near the hotel?"

"I checked it out; there were no illegals on the streets around the hotel. Only one vehicle received a ticket, and that was on the mall parking lot behind the hotel. The other cars in the mall were all owned by the clean-up staff who work through the night."

Bill had sought out the name of the owner of the ticketed vehicle and found it was registered to a John W. Cullen. He phoned the owner's home and was told by a woman that Mr. Cullen was in the military and currently a peacekeeper in the Middle East. As far as the parking offense was concerned, she claimed she had lost her car keys while shopping and taken a cab home. Gallant had a further thought.

"Mary, contact that traffic cop and get him in here. I'd like to speak with him."

The policeman came in around 3:00 p.m. Mary showed him into Gallant's office. Bill drew out the ticket and lay it on the desk.

"Officer, here's a ticket you issued recently. Can you possibly recall anything unusual about the incident? It was marked a quarter past two a.m. on a Saturday morning at the mall parking lot."

"Yeah, I don't give out many tickets at the mall, but I remember that one. When I drove by at around eight o'clock in the evening, the car was parked all by itself just across from the hotel. I came back at my usual time and it was still there in exactly the same place. It was a cold night, but when I leaned on the car to write the ticket, the hood was warm. It felt real good, but I found it a little strange. The owner must have used it after eight and then re-parked it for the rest of the night. I guess they didn't know that overnight parking was illegal."

Bill Gallant looked at Mary and gave her a wink.

"Officer, you've been a great help. Thanks a million for your time."

"It's a long shot," said Mary, "but do you think there's a connection between the Cullen woman and Arnie? Her husband's overseas. When the cat's away, the mice will play."

Gallant laughed. "It takes a woman to think like a woman. Let's go over and question her a bit. Constable, maybe you've hit on something."

They dropped in without warning. Madge Cullen answered the door and was shaken by the unexpected visit. She denied knowing Arnie Benson and again claimed that she had misplaced her car keys and taken a taxi home. Mary took a seat beside her.

"Mrs. Cullen, here's a photo of a certain gentleman. If you deny knowing him, but it's later revealed he's an acquaintance, you could be in big trouble. Now tell me the truth. I assure you that your husband will not be informed about this."

Madge broke down in tears. She admitted spending the night with Arnie, but when questioned about her car, she swore she never loaned it to him.

Mary asked, "Mrs. Cullen, did you not wake up during the night and notice if he was still there with you?"

"I always wake up a couple of times, but for some reason, I slept right through. All I remember was that next morning, I woke up with a terrible headache and nausea that lasted for a couple of days. I haven't heard from him since then. I called him a few times, and he told me he's too busy to talk. Constable, my husband and I were legally separated for over a year before I even met Arnie Benson. I hesitated to talk to you because I was trying to protect Arnie's marriage, not mine."

"Mrs. Cullen, you seem to be a good person. Take some womanly advice. Stay away from this guy, he's bad news."

Back in their car, Callam asked,

"Do you think he fed her Rohypnol?"

"You've got it, Mary," Gallant exclaimed, "that or a reasonable facsimile. But we're still stonewalled. The Cullen woman swears she didn't give Arnie the car keys, and we can't prove she was drugged at the time. Besides, even though the car engine was still warm when ticketed, we still have to prove that it was Arnie who used it."

Bill was convinced of Arnie's guilt; the evidence was strong but nevertheless, circumstantial. Even if they were able to get an indictment, a good defense attorney could tear it apart in court. His only hope would be Danny. Gallant had interviewed the boy twice in front of Dr. Patrick; Danny never altered the facts. But then again, as a Down Syndrome witness, a jury would waver over his testimony in a high-profile murder trial. Besides, a defense attorney would resort to intimidation and harassment of the boy. The scenario was unappealing to Gallant. He buried his head on the desk and pondered.

'Damn, damn, double damn, everything adds up and yet I can't make it stick.'

A couple of days later, Bill Gallant received a phone call from the Toronto insurance company that covered the loss from the airport robbery. They stated that a private detective agency whom they employed had been following the movements of a certain Charlie Schmidt since his release from Kingston Penitentiary.

Their detective had recently followed him to Lunenburg. He said that Schmidt went directly to the marina, located Drifter's boat, and noticed the 'For Sale' sign attached. The harbor-rmaster probably told him about Drifter's death but wouldn't let him get aboard to inspect. He refused permission saying that Schmidt would have to wait till Arnold Benson, the actual owner, returned. The insurance man then asked Gallant about Benson's whereabouts. Gallant replied that he had no idea where Arnie was nor when he would return. Actually, this wasn't true. The RCMP had followed Arnie's trail to George Town in Cayman. Bill Gallant felt positive about the insurance company's interest in Arnie. It was probably their investigation at Dorchester Prison that brought Arnie into the picture, and it gave further credence to Gallant's theory that Arnie had done away with Drifter to avoid sharing the prize. Gallant was certain that Arnie knew all about the gold and that the trip to Cayman was related to the robbery. Gallant mulled things over and eventually came up with an idea. He suspected that if Schmidt was interested in buying the boat, there had to be something important hidden on board. He figured that if Schmidt and Arnie were going to meet, it would probably be on the boat. Gallant was anxious to know what the two men would talk about. He drove down to the marina and invited the harbor-master to a Subway lunch.

"Sam, I need a favor; it's important, and it's confidential. I must get on board *Easy Time*. Arnie has got to come back eventually and I don't want you to get in trouble with him. I'll get a search warrant for you this afternoon. But Sam, I'd like you to keep silent about this whole thing. If Arnie complains later, then we can show him the warrant and we'll take full responsibility."

Sam scratched his ear.

"Bill, you know I'll help you all I can, but what's this all about anyway?"

"Look, I can't reveal any other details. We're trying to put some pieces together to learn the whole story about Drifter's death."

Sam nodded in agreement. After lunch, Bill obtained the warrant for both a search and a wiretap of *Easy Time*.

THIRTY

Jim shouted through the veranda screen door,

"Greta, your scones get better and better. I'm gonna get fat as a pig."

Greta came out and sat down on the milk stool.

"Mr. Cabot, I must fatten you up. You work too hard on that boat of yours."

"Well, it won't be long now. I'm hoping to launch her in about a week or so."

Lara appeared at the screen door entrance.

"What do I hear? A week? I can't believe it. And you're so calm about it. If it were me, after almost four years of hard labor, I'd be doing cartwheels."

"Lara, after all that time I put in, I doubt if I could manage even one cartwheel. It's taken a toll on my back and my knees. I'm ashamed to say how many times I felt like dropping the whole thing. And by the way, how are you feeling this morning?"

"A bit tired, dad. If I could only teach the baby the difference between day and night, I'd get more sleep."

They leafed through the newspapers, sipped coffee and munched on Greta's scones in the warm morning sun.

"By the way," Jim asked, "whatever happened to Arnie? I hear he hasn't been around for a while. Has Hilda mentioned anything to you since they separated?"

"It's all a big mystery. Mavis hasn't had any news at all. We haven't a clue where he could be and frankly Hilda couldn't care less. Since he moved out she's a different person, and so is Jennie. And by the way, Doctor Patrick seems to think Danny has overcome his demons, and even Mavis is her old self again."

"Yeah, I dropped in to the café yesterday at lunchtime and I must say, she was in full command. She was the centre of attention. You know Lara, Mavis Willis is a bright and attractive woman."

"Well, well, well, don't tell me you finally noticed. Listen dad, I'll let you in on a little secret, but knowing you, you'll blush with embarrassment."

Jim laughed.

"Why not try me out, sweetheart, I've become pretty thick skinned. Nothing surprises me at this point."

"O.K., but I warned you. Mavis is dying for you to ask her out. Dad, you and she have a rare something in common. Hilda swears her mom has never looked at another man since her dad died and I can vouch for you. Why, you guys would be like a couple of teenagers. Now that I've said it, are you in shock?"

"Lara, you amaze me. Come over here and sit on my arthritic knee."

His eyes twinkled.

"I must confess that when I watched her move about the café, listened to the way she spoke to some of those rough clients, firmly yet not intimidating, I can see why Arnie's is a huge success. She disarmed a few very loud fishermen with her warm smile and some well-chosen words in that Newfoundland accent."

"Greta, do you hear what I hear? I can hardly believe my ears. Dad, I'm telling Hilda what you said, but don't expect a phone call. Mavis is too independent and old-fashioned. You're going to have to make the first move."

"O.K, fine, I'll think about it. But first I want to see *Lunenburg Lady* launched."

"Dad, this is really something. I'm getting excited. I want to make a big launching ceremony followed by a noisy party. You really deserve it."

"Well, don't rush it. There's still a bunch of odds and ends to be covered. I must admit though, she's pretty well complete. People are stopping by with compliments."

Lara's cell phone rang. It was Hilda.

"Listen Lara, I just got a long-distance call from Arnie. I don't know where he called from, but he said he's coming home in a couple of days and that I should get the remainder of his things ready. He's coming to pick them up."

"Did he mention where he's been all this time?"

"Not a word. He didn't even ask about Jennie."

"Hilda, if you like I can come over and help you gather the stuff. This is one little job we'll both enjoy."

***

There was no further news from Arnie, but three days later, when Hilda and Lara returned from grocery shopping, all the boxes containing his belongings had been removed. Lara put her arm around Hilda.

"Well, my love, maybe now is a good time to change the door locks."

"I thought about it often, but couldn't bring myself to do it. But now that everything of his is gone, I think I will. Lara, let's talk about something real important. How about moving in with us? We could be an ideal family. Jennie loves you as much as I."

"You know, I'm in a difficult situation. Dad is a changed person since I've come home but I admit that living with you has crossed my mind. I need a little time to think about it. I'm really torn."

Jennie looked up at the women.

"Mommy, was daddy here? Is he coming home?"

Hilda picked the baby up and held her close. The two women stared at each other in silence.

THIRTY ONE

A couple of days later, Arnie made a grand entrance during the lunch-hour rush. He wore a big smile, greeted the crowd, gave Mavis a kiss and grabbed Georgie affectionately around the shoulders. The staff was shocked by his gregarious mood. The clientele knew that he and Hilda had separated, and Mavis surmised his behavior was a ploy to take on the 'good guy' role after news of the breakup had spread all over town. This, then, would be the new Arnie Benson, affable, good humored, secure and an unencumbered bachelor. He was confident that the proceeds from the café would cover his family commitments allowing him to be an independent, liberated man, living a carefree life of luxury in the Cayman Islands and able to come and go as he pleased. He and Georgie conversed at their table. Although they spoke at length, Arnie never revealed where he had been, nor if or when he was leaving again.

Mavis came over from time to time and brought Arnie up to date on minor business items. Arnie got up several times to greet some of his drinking partners at the bar. Once, as he walked by Romeo, he yanked the beer from his hand and took himself a good-natured swig from the bottle. Romeo was startled.

"Hey Romeo, hey guys, did you hear about this little Newfie kid who got separated from his old man at the circus? He bawled his head off and the security guard tried to calm him."

"Hey kid, cool it; quieten down, and let's go find your dad. What's he like? C'mon now, stop your hollerin' and tell me about your dad. What's he like?"

The kid looks up at the guard, and blurts out:

"My ma says he likes Jack Daniel's and girls with big tits!'"

The crowd roared. They had never seen Arnie so animated and loud.

Romeo was not to be outdone.

"Arnie, a Newfie's neighbor knocks on the Newfie's door and tells him that he should keep his drapes closed while he's having sex with his wife. He said that yesterday and the day before, all the school kids and the neighbors were walking by, looking in and laughing."

"Tell them the joke's on them," the Newfie says. "I've been out of town the past two days!"

Georgie and Mavis were shocked at the party atmosphere. Mavis shook her head, rolled her eyes, and walked away. Arnie stood on a soda crate behind the bar and shouted,

"Everyone listen! No Happy Hour today. Drinks are free as of right now. C'mon, let's drink up: Who can come up with a special toast?"

Ned, the Newfoundland fisherman held up his glass and shouted, "Arnie, I got a special one for you!

"Whether it's urination or fornication, may your genitalia never fail ya'"

Four and a half million dollars in a Cayman bank was obviously a good reason for out-of-character generosity. Around 5:00 p.m., Mavis informed Arnie that a client at the bar had been asking for him. She said he had also dropped in several times during the week enquiring about the boat. Arnie was unaware that he was finally going to meet Charlie Schmidt face to face. Schmidt planned to take advantage of the 'For Sale' sign on the boat in order to meet with Arnie in a secluded spot where he could safely reveal his true identity; the boat was an ideal location. Arnie walked over and greeted him.

"Hi, I'm Arnie Benson. They tell me you've been looking for me."

"Yeah, I have. My name is Eddie, and I'm interested in that boat you have for sale. Is it still available?"

Arnie looked him over. The man was thin, almost bald and deeply tanned. His handshake was a surprisingly steel-like grip. His suit seemed too large for his body, and his smile revealed the yellow teeth of a heavy smoker.

"Yup, it's still for sale. Have you seen it?"

"Yeah, I did. I looked over the hull and the deck, but the harbor manager wouldn't let me get inside. Do you have time to go down and show it to me?"

"Sure, why not. Wait for me. I can leave in about ten minutes. Have you got a car?"

"Yeah, I do. I can meet you down there."

Schmidt took the precaution of driving a circuitous route to the marina and then parked away from the boat. He didn't want to flaunt his Ontario plates.

When they got aboard *Easy Time*, Schmidt looked over the deck and hull again and waited until Arnie was inside the cabin. He then went in and seated himself next to the cabin entrance. Arnie was up forward, smoking a long Cuban cigar and leaning back, very relaxed.

"So Eddie, what do think of her? The motor's in good shape and she's never been in an accident."

Schmidt looked at Arnie and, after a long moment, spoke.

"You can call me Charlie. That's my real name. Roger and Drifter always called me Charlie."

Arnie's throat closed, and for a moment he choked on the cigar smoke.

"Don't look so surprised, Arnie. You knew I'd show up someday."

It took Arnie a long moment to regain his composure.

"O.K., Eddie or Charlie or whatever the hell you call yourself, if you're here looking for some dough, you've come to the wrong guy. Drifter chose the hiding place and never told me where it was. He was completely stoned when he fell off the dock. When they dragged him out, he smelled like a brewery. All that alcohol must have kept him afloat."

"Arnie, let's be reasonable. Let me tell you why I think you're lying. Better still, let me tell you why I know you're lying."

"Charlie, I warn you, before you go any further, I did hard time too. Drifter probably told you I used to wipe the floors and walls with guys like you, so watch your fuckin' tongue or I'll toss you in the water wearing that baggy suit of yours."

"Arnie, I'm sorry my wardrobe doesn't meet with your approval, but you're behaving exactly as I expected. That's why I brought my loaded .357 magnum and would love to blow a hole in you bigger than your fuckin' mouth."

He had removed the gun from his pocket and placed it on the table, never taking his finger off the trigger.

"Now Arnie, can we have a reasonable conversation? We guys did the planning, took all the risks, and we all did hard time for it. We've got a standoff here, so let's stop the name-calling and talk a little sense."

Arnie was more than surprised; he was overwhelmed by this guy's cool, calm attitude. His ice-blue eyes were devoid of any emotion. If the guy had been his own size and hadn't had a gun, Arnie would still have thought twice before taking him on. Arnie stared at the revolver.

"You've got me at a disadvantage, so go ahead, let's hear."

"Drifter told me that you and he went to our aunt's cellar and stashed the heist inside that false chimney base he built. When I arrived in town, the first thing I did was try to check the boat. Last Christmas, when he visited me in prison, Drifter told me where he hid the key. When your dock manager or whatever you call him wouldn't let me get aboard, I took matters into my own hands. I came back during the night and broke into the boat. You'll pardon me, but for the kind of money that's due me, I wasn't ready to take no for an answer. I looked under the floorboards and found something very disappointing . . . no key. Then I went over to my aunt's place. Drifter told me the lock on the cellar door was a real monster. I managed to smash it anyway. No surprise. The heist was gone. Drifter told me that you pushed Roger off the roof, and by the way, I gotta thank you for that. I never trusted the bastard and he treated Drifter like crap. Now Arnie, I haven't a clue where the fuckin' dough is but I know for sure that you do. But you know something, I don't really give a shit where it is. I just want you to hand over half of it. A conservative estimate would be at least two million."

Arnie reached out slowly and knocked some ash off his cigar. He thought for a few moments.

"Charlie boy, it's time for you to start talkin' reasonable. Are you forgetting the risk I took? I could be rotting forever in Dorchester. What I did, I did for Drifter and me. Where the hell do you come in? Roger and Drifter planned the whole deal and took all the risk. They could have been killed by the security guards. You sat on your ass behind the wheel like a fancy chauffeur and didn't do a fuckin' thing. You want to talk about twenty-five percent, maybe I'll consider it. In any case, I'll need a little time. But one thing though, next time leave your fuckin' gun at home, O.K.?"

"No way O.K., either I get half or nothin'. And Arnie, if I get nothin', you get nothin'. Understand?"

"You sure talk a big game, Charlie, especially when you pack a gun."

"Hey Arnie, I'm not an unreasonable guy. I didn't bring this gun to kill you, I brought it to prevent you from killing me. You see, I'd bet my life that Drifter's death wasn't an accident. Oh, he drowned alright, but you helped. Let me tell you how I know. Drifter's mother is in a nursing home in Halifax. She has two sisters. One of them owns the house in Halifax where the heist was stashed. The other one is my mother in Kingston. Drifter never held a job for long, but that wasn't where he got his nickname. When we were kids, they sent us to scout camp. Drifter would swim out to the middle of the lake and drift around for hours before coming ashore. No one knew how he did it. Even if he was stinkin' drunk, no way could Drifter drown. Not even the swimming instructors could match him. So you see, Arnie, it's too bad Drifter didn't have a gun like mine when you did him in. Maybe he'd be alive today."

Charlie Schmidt got up to leave but kept the weapon pointed at Arnie. As he climbed onto the dock, he stashed it in his pocket, but Arnie could see the outline of his fingers through the fabric, lingering on the trigger. Arnie stood in the cabin doorway while Schmidt stood on the dock looking at him.

"Remember, I'll meet you at noon here, outside your boat, in a week, and not a fuckin' minute longer. Even if you stashed it in Timbuctoo, a week'll give you plenty of time. And Arnie, if you disappear, I'll find you."

He turned and walked quickly to his car. Arnie stood there, shook his head in disbelief and watched as Schmidt drove away.

THIRTY TWO

While in the midst of supper, Bill Gallant grabbed at the phone for an anxiously awaited call.

"Inspector, sorry to disturb you, but we have the activity on the boat tap. It came in clear and pretty complete."

"Does it sound interesting?"

"Sir, I think you're going to be pleased."

"Thanks, constable, I'll be down right after my meal. Don't let anyone touch the tape before I get there."

An hour later, Bill sat back in his office chair, a satisfied smile on his face. He had listened to the tape several times and couldn't believe his ears. Everything he had suspected was there. Tomorrow morning he would start preparing a brief for the Crown Prosecutor. He was elated. He had gone fishing and caught more than he anticipated.

But Gallant didn't get much sleep that night. Some new and disturbing thoughts entered his mind. Arnie had made self-incriminating statements, but he was doing so under duress, with a gun pointed at him. A good defense lawyer would certainly use that. Another thing came to mind...the prison authorities would probably insist that Roger had really slipped off the roof accidentally in order to protect the integrity of their guard's account of the incident. Arnie could have told Drifter he pushed Roger off the roof in order to justify getting his share of the promised money. It could have been a lie, and perhaps it really was an accident. Again, a good attorney would be expected to use that argument. Gallant could get Danny's statement, but the defense would say it was unreliable because of the boy's affliction. Even though Arnie may have possession of the gold and had said he would negotiate with Schmidt, was that really hard and fast proof he actually had it? With a .357 magnum pointed at him, he could be expected to say anything just to get rid of Schmidt and end the confrontation. The more Bill thought about it, the more he realized that he didn't have ironclad proof, even with the tape. The paradox was that the only charges that would stick from the wiretap were a parole violation and the illegal possession of an unregistered weapon on the part of Charlie Schmidt. It would probably send him back to prison for a while, and Arnie wouldn't have to look at that .357 magnum again.

"Damn," Gallant muttered to himself, "Arnie Benson has a horseshoe up his rear. The bastard has more lives than an alley cat."

Gallant had planned to get a court order in the morning to seize Arnie's passport and keep him in town and away from his money in Cayman. But then again, the court might refuse to seize the passport, since they had no proof that Arnie actually had any illicit funds in Cayman, and Shelter Trust certainly couldn't be expected to offer any information. After much thought, he decided he would try anyhow. Perhaps he could convince the judge that the overwhelming amount of circumstantial evidence warranted some action. Early the next morning, after an almost sleepless night, Bill Gallant met with Judge Elliott in his chambers.

"Good morning, Inspector; I gather you've an interesting story for me."

Sipping coffee, the judge listened attentively to every detail. Gallant explained why Arnie was an important person in a homicide case. He recounted how their RCMP connection in George Town had furnished information about who Arnie had met with, but that they couldn't provide any hard, written proof of financial activity. The judge pondered the story for a while and then, out of respect for Bill Gallant's reputation, granted the request. The insurance detective from Toronto had told Gallant where Schmidt was staying. Gallant called the office and gave the order to take him into custody warning his deputies that the man was armed. He waited to hear that Schmidt was arrested and then went over to Arnie's with the court order. He arrived there at 11:00 a.m., drank more black coffee and waited. Arnie walked in just before noon and greeted Bill like an old friend. After shaking hands and making some small talk, Gallant asked him for a few minutes of his time.

"Sure, no problem. Let's sit at my table at the back."

Arnie sat back, lit up a Havana and smiled at the Inspector.

"C'mon Bill, the RCMP is rarely the bearer of glad tidings. What's the deal?"

Gallant came right to the point.

"Arnie, Charlie Schmidt, a guy who did time for the Halifax airport robbery, is in town looking for Drifter. He was arrested a short time ago for parole violation. He was in possession of a firearm. I have no idea who he intended using it on, but in any case we'll be shipping him back to Kingston to do more time. We got a call from Toronto saying that Schmidt was followed to Lunenberg about a week ago driving his mother's car and without notifying his parole officer. It seems that he's already visited the café a couple of times looking for you. Now Arnie, I must ask if you happen to have your passport with you. We've got a court order to seize it. We'd like you to hang around for a while."

Arnie turned pale, a tight knot churning in his gut. This request was more than enough to kill the good news about Charlie Schmidt's arrest.

"Bill, for Christ's sake, you're not serious. You guys have nothing on me. Why are you hounding me like this? Sam called me from the harbor this morning and asked if I've sold the boat. I also heard that you guys went aboard last week. What the hell were you looking for, anyhow?"

"Arnie, listen, it's all in the RCMP records; your connection with Drifter goes back years. Drifter was living on your boat and now he's dead. Schmidt shows up in Lunenburg looking for Drifter. It's true, you're not charged with anything, but you took off recently for quite a spell and we don't want to have to wait another few weeks in case you decide to travel again. We need you to hang around until we clear up these loose ends. You're an important person in this whole affair."

The Inspector lay the court order on the table. Arnie picked it up, glanced at it and muttered some choice curse words. He reached inside his jacket, unzipped a pocket, withdrew the passport and threw it on the table. Bill Gallant quickly placed it in his briefcase.

"Thanks, Arnie. Look after yourself. We'll be in touch."

Arnie shook his head in disbelief. He leaned back in his chair, closed his eyes and reached for his cell phone. He called Tony's cell, but there was no answer. Arnie was devastated by this sudden turn of events. Against his better judgement, he decided to try Tony's office.

"Hello Tony, it's me."

Tony was shocked.

"Are you out of your mind? This call is a no-no. We're through with each other. You've got no friggin' business calling me here."

"Listen carefully, Tony, I've got a big problem. They've taken away my passport. What the hell am I gonna do? I can't get to my stuff."

"I told you you're on your own. Do you expect me to order them to give it back?"

"Don't smart-ass me or I'll come over there and break your fuckin' head. Now listen. Is there any way to get the stuff back into Canada, to some fuckin' out-of-the-way place, like the Yukon or Labrador? I'll make it worth your while."

Tony cut the conversation short.

"Let me work on it. I'll call you in about ten days. I can't do better. Remember, I'll call you, don't you call me."

Arnie slammed down his cell phone.

"Fuck, I can't believe this! What the hell is gonna happen to my dough?"

THIRTY THREE

"Dad, Hilda has asked me to move in with her. What do you think of the idea?"

"Hey, you're really full of surprises. Lemme absorb this."

"Dad, as close as she and I were years ago, we've become even closer, especially since Arnie has left. We're filling the vacuums in each other's lives. With her Jennie, and then me giving birth soon, we're going to have a lot in common. We could be a great family."

"Lara, just having you back in Lunenburg was something I always hoped for. That alone makes me happy. Asking more would be selfish on my part."

***

Hilda's house was now filled with laughter and love. The women moved furniture, freshened up curtains and rugs and bought a trunk-load of toys for Jennie. If there was a void created around the little girl because of Arnie's absence, Lara's presence more than made up for it. The love and attention showered upon Jennie was a godsend. Her nursery teacher phoned and reported a remarkable change in her behavior and a positive improvement in her interaction with the other children. In short, she was a much happier child.

Hilda arranged for the wood sidings of the house to be repaired and the exterior repainted an even brighter red. She created an artistic rock garden that drew envious looks from the neighbors. Junk was cleared out of the garage and Hilda's car was now parked inside. It was no longer a house, it was a home. At the end of each exhausting day, the women fell asleep in each other's arms. In the mornings, they literally leaped out of bed to undertake another home improvement project.

"It feels like Christmas," Hilda commented, "we're surrounded with love and warmth. I love the sound of Jennie running around the house, laughing and following us from room to room."

"Yeah, I agree, the only things missing are the tree and the Christmas carols."

They gave Jennie little odd jobs and each time she finished one, she was rewarded with a hug, a kiss and a gigantic "thank you". Lara kept the boat-launching party at the top of her agenda. She spent hours on the phone inviting relatives and acquaintances from St. John, Moncton and Charlottetown. She arranged for the celebration to take place at Mario's. Mario, himself a sailor, agreed to close the restaurant on Saturday evening and prepare a private buffet dinner for about fifty guests. Mrs. Mario promised to set up nautical decor and relocate the tables to allow dancing. Mavis's neighbor's son had a small but popular jazz band that was hired for the evening. With Lara and Hilda's input, they arranged a delightful menu.

In the meantime, although back from abroad for over three weeks, Arnie hadn't inquired at all about the baby. Separated from his money and restricted from traveling, he was like a starving, imprisoned animal whose food was there but just out of reach. As time passed and he was denied his wealth and the free and independent life he had envisioned, he became more and more angry and frustrated. Under normal circumstances, he would seek out ways to vent his anger. The easiest prey would be his own family, but his emotions were tempered by the thought of another prison term.

THIRTY FOUR

On Tuesday around noon, Lara, Hilda and baby Jennie drove to the marina to see Jim. He was surprised by their visit and hurried down the ladder.

"Dad, we're taking you to Mario's for lunch."

"No you aren't, sweetheart, not with me dressed like this. Let's go across to that new *SUBWAY*. I'd take you all aboard and show you the cabins but the varnish is still sticky and some of the bilge boards are out."

They found a table in a quiet corner, but with their spirited conversation, their laughter and Jennie's antics, it wasn't quiet for long.

"Dad, we're coming to the marina on Thursday afternoon to decorate the boat with ribbons and flags. We checked the weather, and the chance of rain for the weekend is minimal. We want the boat launch to be a memorable occasion for you. Everyone who should be there has been invited. At around three o'clock on Saturday afternoon we're setting up a table of hors d'oeuvres right on the dock. There'll be lots to eat and drink. Father McCrory has agreed to do the blessing, and Jake promised to smash an expensive bottle of champagne against the bow. We've worked out the details with the Mario's for the evening celebration. We should have around fifty guests. There'll even be some family you haven't seen for a while. I know that aunt Cora is coming in from Moncton with her latest beau. Dad, he's an old salt of a sailor and can't wait to see the boat."

"Lara. this is all too much. You're getting me nervous. You know I'm not very good in a crowd."

"Dad, let's be frank, since mom passed away you haven't been the most socially conscious person."

Jim reflected for a moment.

"Well, on second thought, it could be an occasion to get together with people with whom I've been out of touch. The only time I see a few of my old friends and family seems to be at someone's funeral. O.K., fine, but I think I ought to be getting back to the boat. I've still got a lot of small stuff to do. Oh, I almost forgot . . . come have a look at the stern plaque I installed this morning. That artist friend of yours did a beautiful job with the gold paint. He even refused to take any money. Tell me what you think of it."

The varnished wooden plaque glistened in the sun, and the gold-painted letters *Lunenburg Lady* glowed as if illuminated. The women stared in silence. They knew for whom the boat was named. Lara moved over to Jim, clutched his arm and rested her head on his shoulder. He watched her tears roll down his sleeve. Hilda turned and walked away, her skin invaded by goose bumps. Later, as they drove home, Hilda's cell phone rang.

"It's me. I'm calling about the baby."

Her stomach tightened. She sat there speechless and looked at Lara. By the expression on her face, the caller could only be Arnie. After a long moment, she blurted, "Yes, yes, I hear you."

"Listen, I want you to come over to the bar with Jennie. When can you make it?"

Hilda covered the mouthpiece and asked, "Arnie wants me to bring Jennie over to the café. Will you come with me?"

"Sure, why not, better there than at the house."

"Hello Arnie, I'm in the car and I can drop over in a few minutes."

"O.K., I guess the dyke is with you. I'll see you soon."

"Lara, are we doing the right thing? I'm nervous about this. I'm worried about a scene."

"Look, he won't do anything foolish in public. I'm actually glad you'll see him there and not at home. Besides, until the separation arrangement is finalized, you can't regulate his visiting hours."

When they arrived at Arnie's, Lara suggested that Hilda go in with Jennie and she'd wait outside. Hilda wouldn't hear of it.

"Hilda, you must accept that he's entitled to some time with the baby."

"I know, I know, but I'd feel more comfortable with you around. Why not come in a few minutes later and sit at another table?"

"I don't see the point, but if it makes you feel better, O.K., I will."

Hilda carried Jennie into the café and sat down in the back at Arnie's table. He came over and, without any acknowledgement of his wife, knelt down on one knee and held his little girl's hand.

"Hi Jennie, daddy misses you; did you miss Daddy?"

"Daddy, daddy, when are you coming home?"

Arnie looked at Hilda with a sarcastic smile.

"Why don't you tell her when?"

"Arnie, right now there's no arguing and swearing at home. Jennie's a different child. She's not tense, and she laughs all the time. If you have one bit of feeling for her, you'd appreciate how happy and relaxed she is since we're apart."

"So I guess that means it's all my fault, eh?"

"Do you hear me placing all the blame on you? It takes two people to get into our situation. Please, let's not argue in front of her. Your daughter's here with you in Lunenburg, and you know very well I'll do my best for her."

Hilda understood Arnie like no one else. She did her best to soothe his paranoia without sounding patronizing, while in her mind she visualized him raping her beloved soul mate. She caught sight of a steak knife on the table and shocked herself with a fleeting image of the knife handle protruding from her husband's throat.

Arnie took Jennie's hand and held it to his mouth for a long moment. He got up, shook his head and walked away without uttering a word. Hilda picked Jennie up and left. Lara was waiting in the car.

"Sorry Hilda, but at the last minute I thought it better not to be around."

"I understand. Actually, it went better than I expected. He seemed subdued. He wasn't obnoxious, but I suspect that seeing Jennie again is not the real reason for his civil behavior. I'm certain there's other things on his mind. I wouldn't be surprised if he's in some kind of trouble."

"Hilda, at best he'll never be a Dr. Jekyll. He's a beast. He's always been one, and he'll never change. Meeting you and the baby in the bar instead of at home served his purpose. Here, he's able to put on a display of concerned fatherhood in front of the staff and clients." Lara paused. "Am I being too hard on him, Hilda?"

"No, not really. He's left us both with scars. The physical ones heal, but the mental ones are forever. No matter how he tries to impress, it's pure theatre and very temporary. He's essentially evil. When I was in there with him, I realized I wouldn't feel free unless we're divorced; it'll give me the kind of closure I need for my own peace of mind."

They were stopped at a red light. Lara leaned over, put her arm around Hilda and pressed her lips to her forehead.

"I love you," she whispered.

THIRTY FIVE

News of the impending launch of *Lady Lunenburg* had circulated throughout the marina and even made the local newspaper. There were almost as many party crashers as invited guests. No matter, it added more excitement to the event. Many of the attendees, steeped in seagoing tradition, understood that in this day and age, one seldom hears of a forty-foot seagoing vessel built with exotic woods by the hands of just one dedicated person. It was a rare event that brought old friends and acquaintances back together. Lara was ecstatic.

"Look at them, Hilda, all those hugs, kisses and handshakes. It's like a big family wedding."

Uncle Jake walked around showing off his magnum of champagne trailing fifteen feet of ribbon. Jim Cabot was busy explaining to a group of sailors why he had chosen that particular shape for the keel and rudder. Most everyone carried a glass of something, and the canapés disappeared within the hour. There was laughter, there were screaming kids running here and there and photos of children and grandchildren being passed around. After more than an hour of noisy celebration, Sam the harbor-master climbed aboard the boat holding Jake's bottle of champagne. He tied the ribbons to the jib halyard*, adjusting it until the suspended bottle leaned outboard against the bow. Sam climbed down, mounted a wooden platform and, in a booming voice, announced that the launch was about to begin.

"Folks, before we get started, let's welcome Father James McCrory, who's been kind enough to come down to deliver the benediction. Father McCrory, the podium is yours."

The priest removed his pipe, leaned on his trusty cane and rose slowly from his chair. With some effort, he climbed the three steps to the makeshift platform and turned slowly to the audience.

"Good afternoon, ladies and gentlemen and all you youngsters out there. My, my, what a lovely crowd we have here. It would be nice to see as many people at St. Christopher's Sunday Mass. I hope I don't have to build a boat to bring you all in, because although I'm a Maritimer like you, I know very little about boats. This is indeed a memorable occasion, not just for me but for all of us here today. Jim Cabot and his late wife Celia were committed parishioners in Lunenburg all of their lives. Their loyalty to their religion and to their community was exemplary. This four-year labor of love standing before us today is a fitting tribute to Celia Cabot's memory. Jim Cabot, may the *Lunenburg Lady* watch over you and take you and yours to wherever you venture and bring you safely home. To quote an old Irish expression, "May the wind always be at your back." In the name of the Father, the Son and the Holy Ghost, I pray that the Cabot family, together with this magnificent vessel and all who are here today, be blessed to eternity."

The crowd applauded enthusiastically as the priest returned to his chair; Jim and Lara rose to embrace him. Sam remounted his podium.

"Everyone, please back away from the boat, we're bringing in the marine lift and it needs lots of space."

The huge machine with its four gigantic wheels approached the boat and hovered over it while Sam jumped down, attached two canvas support straps beneath the hull and then started the lifting process; the straps became taut under the weight of over ten tons. The crowd grew quiet as the vessel rose slowly from its steel tripod supports until it was suspended in midair. Sam climbed down, pulled aside the tripods and brought a ladder to the bow of the boat. Jake climbed up, reached out for the champagne bottle and turned to the crowd.

"Folks, this is not your ordinary everyday launching. This is not a boat moulded in plastic and designed by a bunch of high-tech nautical engineers. Neither is this a vessel built on a mass production line, not knowing which week or month its owner will appear, nor even who its owner will be. This sailboat was not built for profit. It was lovingly and carefully crafted and named to honor the memory of Celia Cabot, a person whose dedication to the welfare of the town of Lunenburg was legendary. She was someone to whom all of us here today, man, woman and child, can truly aspire."

Jake could have gone on, but tears were running down his face. The last time he had cried over Celia was over twenty-five years ago, when she told him she would marry Jim Cabot. He turned to face the boat and, holding the champagne in his right hand, exclaimed in a breaking voice,

"I christen thee *Lunenburg Lady*."

The bottle swung down, crashed against the bow and exploded with a loud shattering to the applause and shouts from the onlookers. Sam wheeled the marine lift onto the pier and gently lowered *Lunenburg Lady* into the water. Lara, Jim and Hilda stood at the edge of the crowd and turned their heads away from the ceremony. The tears they shed were private and not to be shared. Later, as the crowd melted away, Jim boarded the boat to check for any leakage; newly launched wooden boats must remain suspended in water for several days to allow the seams to swell and seal themselves. The girls climbed aboard and marveled at the elegant teak and the varnish finish of the interior.

Jim remarked,

"Hilda, I missed your mom today. I was under the impression Mavis was coming."

"She really looked forward to it, Mr. Cabot, but unfortunately, Arnie left town yesterday afternoon without warning. I offered to replace her but she said I was needed here. I promise you we'll figure out some way to get her to Mario's tonight."

Later, as they climbed off the boat, Hilda took Lara's arm.

"I'd really like my mom to be at the party."

166

"I agree. Did you notice how my dad asked about her? I think he's ready."

"Well, I suspect that mom is too. Lara, I think it's only right that I work the bar and let mom come over tonight. I don't really have to be at the party. Between you and the Marios, everything will be under control."

"It's a great idea, and I love you for it. Dad'll appreciate it, but I'm gonna miss you."

Hilda smiled.

"Hang in there, sweetheart, we'll make up for it later."

THIRTY SIX

Mario's Restaurant was popular because of its wholesome food, friendly service and quiet ambience. This particular Saturday night, it had all these things except the quiet. A five-piece musical group played Big-Band-era swing. People were drinking, dancing and laughing. It seemed everyone was talking and no one was listening. The decorations looked more like New Year's Eve than a launch party. Old friends milled about and congratulations, hugs and kisses were the order of the evening. Jim was struck by how much he had allowed these people to slip out of his life since his Celia had passed away. He lived in Lunenburg, so close to most of them, but had unwittingly exiled himself to the fringes of society. He had all but forgotten them but evidently they hadn't forgotten him. Lara's high school friends reminisced about their school days. They sang their school songs, danced and drank toast after toast to Jim and his *Lunenburg Lady*. A few of them commented to Lara about her round, expanded shape but she was ready with a quick reply:

"Girls, I'm putting the finishing touches on an important laboratory experiment."

Uncle Jake and Jim's sister Cora showed off their jitterbug prowess while her new companion, the old salt, hung onto Jim, giving him much unwanted advice about his sailboat. Bill Gallant dropped in and proposed a toast, and then another and another.

Mavis showed up around 9:00 p.m., but Jim hardly recognized her. She wore a stunning green dress that set off her flaming red hair and enhanced her beautiful figure. People turned their heads to look as she strode across the dance floor to Jim's table wearing patent spiked heels. She kissed him on both cheeks and, although embarrassed, he didn't hesitate to return the gesture. He put his hand about her waist and directed her to a chair next to his. For the first time in years he was moved by the touch of a woman.

Lara came over and greeted Mavis with a warm embrace. Mavis looked upon her as another daughter. She understood how important she had become in Hilda's life and how supportive she was through her daughter's stormy relationship with her estranged husband. Mavis and Jim sat and sipped their drinks as they spoke of the events which shaped their lives. Their eyes seldom left each other.

"Jim, your Lara is like the Rock of Gibraltar for Hilda."

"She's become that for me too. As you probably know, we hadn't been close for a long while. It was mostly my fault. I'm just hoping she decides to remain in Lunenburg."

The music mellowed to the slow tunes of the fifties. Mavis convinced a shy and reticent Jim to dance. As they moved with the music, they became absorbed in each other's physical presence. Their bodies moved in closer unison with each dance. Nature was taking its inevitable course as they rediscovered long-lost sensations. The evening closed with "Stardust", but the couple silently hoped the music would never end.

After all the embraces and goodbyes, families and friends disappeared into the night. Lara headed down to Arnie's to pick up Hilda after closing. She was anxious to share the evening's events, especially how their parents seemed to blend together. Although Lara had brought her dad to Mario's, he declined a lift home. Lara caught site of him driving off with Mavis.

***

Mavis parked the car in Jim's driveway. They sat, neither saying a word. When the silence became awkward, Jim offered,

"Mavis, I must tell you how much I appreciate you coming tonight after your long day at work. You insulated me from the crowds, the noise, the handshakes and the back-slapping. This is my first evening in years in the company of a woman. I gather this is kinda' new for you too, but strangely enough, it doesn't really feel new."

She reached out for Jim's hand and held it fast.

"Jim, I feel comfortable with you. I feel relaxed. You have a quiet strength that calms me. I'm usually kind of tense and hyper, but I don't feel that way around you."

He passed the back of his hand slowly over her cheek in a gentle caress. He pulled her closer, leaned over and kissed her lightly on the lips.

"Let me taste you, Jim."

She pressed her mouth to his. She caressed his thigh with her fingertips as he pulled her even closer and held her tightly.

"I feel like a renewed person," he said, "like a new beginning is happening right here in the car. You arouse me in areas that I forgot existed."

She understood very well. On this night, a platonic friendship had transformed into a reawakening of feelings that descended down to her thighs.

"Mavis, I'd love to spend all night here with you, but it would be selfish of me. You've had a busy day. Let's save it for next time, and hope it's very soon." "Jim, you're a caring and thoughtful person, and I appreciate it. Passion may come and go, but respect is something more reliable and permanent. You're easy to like, Jim, because I've always respected you."

"Well, if all goes according to plan, I'll be making a sea trial with the boat in a few days. I'd like to eventually take a three or four day trip to Halifax. Perhaps you'll join me. You're a Newfoundlander, you must know something about boats."

"I was brought up in boats, but it's been years since I've sailed. Meanwhile, I'm going straight to bed, but I doubt if I'll sleep very much."

He leaned over, placed his mouth over hers and, after a long moment, turned and let himself out of the car.

THIRTY SEVEN

Two months earlier, around the middle of April, the phone rang around 6:00 a.m. in Phyllis Dunham Maitland's Charlottetown home in Prince Edward Island*. She awoke with a start, reached out for the receiver, but hesitated to lift it. This could be the call she had dreaded for years. She slowly placed the receiver to her ear.

"Hello," she heard herself say, but was it really her, Phyllis Maitland, speaking?

"Hello, Phyllis, are you there?"

She looked at the receiver and placed it again to her ear.

"Hello, yes, yes, this is Phyllis. Is that you, Millie? There's a problem, isn't there."

"I'm afraid so. Harvey stopped breathing around 3:00 a.m. We tried to bring him back, but nothing worked. We thought he had lapsed into a deeper coma, but he just slipped away. I assure you he didn't suffer at the end. I'm terribly sorry. Would you like me to send someone over to be with you?"

"No, Millie, no, it's O.K. I'm coming right over. I want to see him again. I want to touch him. I want to talk to him. I have things to say to him."

Phyllis felt a sudden pounding in her head. She got out of bed but had to support herself on the night table. The room seemed to be moving and she fell back on the bed. She closed her eyes, waiting for the dizzy spell to pass.

Phyllis Dunham Maitland, the beautiful, black-haired, green-eyed Miss Canada finalist: Phyllis, happily married to Harvey Maitland, a vice president at Campbell's Brewery. They had been teenage sweethearts, deeply in love and expectant parents. They were celebrating Harvey's promotion with several friends.

'Wait, what was that? Harvey's on the floor! Was that me screaming? God, where am I?'

Phyllis bolted upright and reached over for the bed lamp. She stood up slowly and managed to dress. Realizing her own mental state, she wisely opted for a taxi.

Her hands and arms shook, and as she descended from the cab, she felt a tightness in her chest. Phyllis had made this trip hundreds of times, but this occasion was different. Idle conversation was out of the question so she avoided the elevator and climbed the stairs to the second floor. There it was, Room 221, Harvey Maitland printed on the door. This would be the last time she would read that sign.

'How can I go in? God give me strength.'

She moved around the screen to the head of the bed. Harvey was pale and gaunt but the lines on his forehead had lost some of their depth. There was a placid expression on his face as if a burden had finally been lifted. Phyllis kneeled on the footstool and took his hand in hers, then leaned over and pressed her cheek to his face.

"Harvey, my love. I'll be with you forever. Oh God, my heart is full of sadness. Dear Lord, I hold no forgiveness for the one who did this to us. I'm overwrought with feelings of revulsion and hate. A monster has taken my husband and my child. Years have passed, and there is no quelling the bitterness within me. It's taken hold of my soul and haunts me day and night. My dear, dear husband, I swear to you that I'll exact retribution for the pain and suffering that we've endured all these years."

Millie, the night nurse, had stood quietly by, waiting for her presence to be noticed. Phyllis rose, walked over and embraced her. Not a word was spoken. Millie's teardrops trickled down her cheek and fell onto Phyllis's hair. But Phyllis's eyes were dry; they were wide open, clear, sharp and determined.

THIRTY EIGHT

And now, a couple of months later on a Thursday evening, dusk in Halifax was a blend of red and orange pouring over the roofs of the buildings. Phyllis arrived by car and pulled into the driveway of the home of her friend Janice. The woman had left town for the weekend and Phyllis had often looked after the house while her friend was away traveling. This time, Phyllis purposely opted to leave her Mustang in the driveway rather than park it in the garage. She wanted the P.E.I. plates to be conspicuous the whole weekend. She fished the house key from her leather bag and went inside. She felt a gnaw of nervous tension in the pit of her stomach and knew she wouldn't sleep well, if at all. Phyllis had avoided food on the ferry from Charlottetown, hoping to prepare a light meal on arrival, but a wave of nausea spoiled her appetite. She eased herself onto the sofa and flicked the TV remote from channel to channel but soon dozed off until around 11:00 p.m.; she undressed in the guest room and tried to get more sleep.

After grieving for almost seven years, it was now time to settle accounts. She had slept very little in the weeks following Harvey's passing, mainly preoccupied with her immediate future rather than the recent past. She had meticulously prepared for an encounter with Arnie Benson. She had gone over her plans in detail, writing and rewriting each possible scenario, drawing maps, itineraries and time-tables. She had considered Arnold Benson's violent nature and admitted to having no illusions about the possible risks, especially if he was in a drunken state. She could be the victim of a vicious sexual assault or even worse. Her plan was to confront him in a quiet, private place, not too far from a bustling, crowded area, enabling her to quickly leave and blend into the surroundings. She chose her wardrobe carefully. Arnie must never suspect her identity. In order to further stimulate his curiosity, she would look as attractive as possible and present the image of a sophisticated, worldly woman. Phyllis understood that she must earn a modicum of respect from him if she were to succeed in making him believe their encounter could evolve into a prolonged relationship. She needed to create a relaxed, confident Arnold Benson, a man who would conduct himself in a manner that could convince Phyllis he was a person of character, someone who matched her expectations of a gentleman. Tomorrow, if all went as planned, her life would take a new direction. She awoke several times during the night, drank some warm milk and walked about the house. She leafed through a novel until finally, at around 7:00 a.m., she showered and rinsed off with a stimulating splash of cold water. Around 9:00

a.m., after a light breakfast and a longer than usual stint in front of the mirror, she donned a red beret and a colorful print dress that concealed a white blouse, and slipped into a pair of patent leather black pumps. She carefully folded a black linen suit, a black beret and a long blonde wig into her large leather handbag, together with an old blue frock. She then added a folded shopping bag and a large, plastic zipperlock bag to her handbag.

Phyllis locked the door and strode down to the intersection where she hailed a taxi to within a block of the bus station, disembarked, and walked the rest of the way. She went to a phone booth and made a person-to-person call to Arnie Benson using a prepared amount of change. Georgie, the chef, answered the phone. He asked the operator to hold the line, saying that Arnie would take the call in a moment. Phyllis immediately hung up. She now felt quite certain that Arnie would be at the café and that there was no need to postpone. She went to the ladies' room and changed into the dark blue frock. She folded her print dress and put it in the handbag. Phyllis donned her sunglasses, took several deep breaths and walked around the bus terminal in an effort to calm herself.

The bus ride to Lunenburg was irritating. The stopping and starting in the heavy traffic wore on her nerves, and she arrived in an agitated state. She proceeded to the terminal's ladies' room where she removed the blue frock and put on the black suit, black beret and blonde wig which she had bought with cash at a flea market. She rolled up the frock and the red beret and placed them in her handbag. She donned a pair of black gloves and put on her sunglasses. Phyllis stood in front of the mirror and hardly recognized herself.

"Phyllis, today you are Ellen Davidson."

She had brought a street map to guide her quickly to Arnie's location. Her plan was to arrive as soon as possible after lunch and enter when few clients remained, in order to be certain of Arnie's undivided attention. On nearing the café, she threw the map into a trash can. It was about 1:30 p.m. and so far, her timing was good. When she walked into the café, Arnie was alone at the bar, while Mavis was evidently on her lunch break. Phyllis recognized him immediately and felt her body tense up. She sought out a table near the rear and sat back to read the menu. Arnie usually gave his male clients a cursory greeting, but when it was a woman, he always managed a smile. If she was not a familiar face and happened to be attractive, she could count on his full and prompt attention. He noticed that this particular client was unusually beautiful, with long blonde hair, very smartly dressed. Her body language and determined walk implied she was a sophisticated, self-assured big-city dweller. Arnie followed her to her table and offered a warm greeting.

"Good afternoon to you," she replied, "it's nice being received by the maître d' himself."

"Well, you're not far from wrong, miss. Actually, I'm the owner, I'm Arnold Benson."

He turned on more charm.

"I know most of the people in Lunenburg, but unfortunately, you're not one of them. What's your pleasure today?"

She looked stunning in her black tailored suit and white blouse, together with the black beret that accentuated her blonde hair. Never removing her sunglasses nor gloves, she looked up at Arnie with a disarming smile.

"I think I'll start with a very dry martini; I know it's kind of early, but I've had an aggravating morning and I'm going to treat myself. I'll have a BLT on toasted whole wheat after my drink."

Arnie was so carried away by her appearance and her elegant manner that he felt physically aroused. He wondered if she was married; that could present a challenge but, in any case, it was one he intended to take up. He brought over the martini.

"This should do the trick," he remarked. "When things don't go my way, I do the same, only I rarely stop after one."

"Well, you're a big man, and you can probably hold your liquor better than most."

"Miss, you seem to be alone, and my work is almost done . . . do you mind if I sit here a bit?"

"Not at all. But please make sure I get the check. I always pay my own way."

Arnie thought, 'Who is this dame? This is something really different.'

"Feel like telling me about your morning? It helps to talk."

She laughed. "It's kind of depressing; on my way in from Yarmouth, I hit a bad pothole and got a flat. The garage changed my tire and then announced that something connected to the front wheel was bent and I'd have to wait till Monday for the repair. I'm a medical rep for a pharmaceutical company. I have five doctor appointments in Halifax on Monday, and I need my car. Renting one is no problem, but then I've got the hassle of coming back here to retrieve mine on Monday night. It's a real bummer. Right after this sandwich, I'm going back to Halifax. Do you think a local cab would take me there?"

It was the opening Arnie needed.

"Don't worry your head about a cab. I'm going into Halifax this afternoon for the weekend, and I'll be glad to take you in. Besides, a cab will cost a fortune."

She had fed him the bait, and he had grabbed it exactly as she hoped.

"By the way, you now know I'm Arnie, what's your name?"

"I'm Ellen Davidson. My friends call me Ellie."

Arnie smiled disarmingly. "I'm gonna call you Ellie unless you stop me."

"Fine, then I'll call you Arnie as long as you're a gentleman, and if you're not, I'll call you something worse."

They laughed. He leaned over as if whispering a secret. Concealing his car keys under his hands, he moved them slowly across the table, slipping them under her menu.

"Look Ellie, take my keys. I've got a white Cadillac van in the lot across the street. When you're through with lunch, pay your bill at the bar and cross over to the parking lot. Wait for me in the van. I won't be long. I've got a few things to straighten out here."

"Mr. Benson, or rather Arnie, I really don't mind taking a cab. My company is good like that. They'll pick up the tab."

"No way, don't even think about it, I'll be more than happy to get you there."

"I tell you what, hold onto your car keys. When I'm through eating, I'll walk down to the end of the block and you can pick me up there. I'd rather be discreet about this."

He brought her food to the table, gave her a sly wink and went into the kitchen to speak with Mavis. Phyllis bit into her sandwich but with little appetite to finish it. She took a sip of her martini, picked up her bag and left the check and the cash on the counter. She walked casually to the intersection, glancing occasionally into the store windows.

In the meantime, Arnie was in the kitchen telling Mavis that an urgent matter had come up and he had to take off for Halifax for a couple of days.

"Arnie, how could you do this to me? You knew I was going to Jim Cabot's launching tomorrow. You promised to replace me. You're a real S.O.B."

"This is important. Get Alma to replace you."

"Alma's invited to the party too. You're not human, you're a selfish beast!"

He ignored her and went to the back storeroom to freshen up. Twenty minutes later, he was driving to Halifax with blonde and beautiful Ellen Davidson by his side. They traded small talk, mostly impersonal. As they approached the city, Arnie commenced act two of his performance.

"It's a bloody hot day, Ellie, do you always wear gloves?"

"Yeah, it's an old habit. It keeps my hands from drying out."

"Tell me more about yourself. You look like a well-educated gal. Do you have a profession?"

"Well, I graduated university and got a job in pharmaceuticals. I visit doctors and hospitals, sharing information about our products. It's interesting, but there's a lot of travel. I'm due for a promotion and may soon be tied to a desk job."

"Ellie, I'm trying to guess the color of your eyes behind those sunglasses."

"My husband is an optometrist and he just fitted me with my first set of contact lenses. I'm still getting used to them. Just about any kind of light really bothers me."

"I never forget a face. You look vaguely familiar. We must have bumped into each other years ago at a party. Where do you live in Halifax?"

She felt a little uneasy.

"We have a condo downtown. My husband would have picked me up in Lunenburg this afternoon after work, but he's at a convention in Toronto until next week. Where do you stay in Halifax?"

"Do you know the Ritz Hotel? I've been staying there for years. It's really de-luxe. Hey, I've got an idea; you're all alone this weekend and you've had a bad day. Why not have an early dinner with me at the Ritz Hotel Grill. They've got a great menu. I don't feel like eating alone, and you shouldn't either."

She smiled. "Arnie, you're such a charming man. I'll wager you're never short of female companionship. I must admit you've been pretty decent today. I'll take advantage of your hospitality and accept your offer."

They took a table by the window. The dinner was quiet and relaxed. Arnie was on his best behavior and neither one drank to excess. The music was soft and moody, and the setting sun rendered an orange glow through the restaurant curtains. The atmosphere grew mellow, and so did Arnie. He felt self-assured and confident enough to make his next move. He placed his hand gently over hers, and she didn't move. He squeezed it a little and she returned the gesture. He was so physically aroused that he'd be embarrassed if he tried to get up from the table.

"Ellie, would you consider coming up for a drink? My place is really nice. They tell me the Prime Minister occupies it when he's in town. I'd like to show it to you. We'll have a couple of drinks and perhaps watch some TV. You'll call all the shots. Whatever you say goes."

Ellen remained silent. She sat there with a half smile and just stared at him. He held his breath awaiting an answer. Finally, she said,

"Alright Arnie, but I can't stay too long. It's almost seven now, I've got to be home by ten. I'm expecting a phone call from my husband."

"Ellie, can I pay you a compliment?"

He didn't wait for a reply.

"You're the most beautiful woman I've met in years. I don't give a damn whether or not that's your real hair color or if your eyes are green, blue or orange, but whatever they are, they sure go well with your face."

"Thanks again," she laughed, "but don't go overboard. I've already agreed to come up to the room.

Seriously, Arnie, I'd feel better if you went up alone and I'll join you in a few minutes. I don't want us to be seen together." She smiled, "my mother-in-law wouldn't approve. I'll knock, and I hope you'll let me in."

THIRTY NINE

When the allies landed in Normandy in June of 1944, Canadian forces became involved in a month of heavy fighting around Caen, near the French coast. A Canadian army officer, Captain James Dunham, was on an inspection patrol after the Germans abandoned the town. He came upon a partially destroyed three-story building whose roof had served as a sniper's nest. He gained entrance through a broken window and found himself in a large room where the staircase to the upper levels had collapsed and the floor was littered with debris. He caught sight of a shoe protruding from beneath the fallen staircase. It took every bit of muscle to move it, but he eventually succeeded. Half-hidden beneath some loose boards was the body of a German soldier, a telescopic sniper's rifle by his side. As Dunham pulled the body away from the wreckage, he noticed a gun holster attached to the German's belt, together with a leather ammunition pouch. The items were embossed with swastikas, and the holster held a .25 calibre Walther PPK pistol, a beautifully crafted weapon loaded with a full clip of seven cartridges. The pouch contained an extra full clip along with more ammunition. Dunham brought the items back from overseas. Like most veterans who returned with souvenir weapons, he never bothered registering the gun, but kept it well hidden in a trunk in the attic of his home in Charlottetown. Years later, when he became aware that his grandson and granddaughter had discovered it, he decided to explain to them in detail how it was acquired and impressed upon them how lethal it could be if mishandled. Every few years, he would polish and oil the pistol, and he allowed the children to watch as he loaded the weapon and fired it into a sandpit in their cellar. He then returned it carefully to the bottom of an old trunk next to the leather ammunition pouch. The granddaughter grew up to be the beautiful Phyllis Dunham, the widow of Harvey Maitland. Now, but only for tonight, over twenty years later, she was alias Ellen Davidson.

***

The hotel room was the Prime Minister's Suite. Arnie was rarely alone when he stayed at the Ritz, and this room always impressed his female guests.

"Arnie, I must compliment your good taste. This looks like the Homes & Gardens Revue."

"Well, I only stay here a couple nights a week, so I might as well be comfortable."

"My gosh, a grand piano! Maybe I'll serenade you a little later."

"Ellie, you are something. What'll you have? Lemme order up some drinks."

"Arnie, thanks, but I already had one at supper. You know, I'm really not much of a drinker. Perhaps we'll see each other again after tonight. I'd like us to be clear-headed if and when things between us go somewhere."

"Like I said, Ellie, you call the shots."

Her plan was to avoid being physically close to him while they were in the confines of a private place. She had to act quickly.

"Arnie, after this really humid day, I'll bet we're both a little sweaty and can probably use a shower. You go first and give me a chance to get my makeup off." She winked. "Perhaps I'll even join you. We can order room service later."

Arnie was certain his heart skipped a beat as he disappeared into the bathroom. 'Hell', he thought, 'this is going even better than I expected.'

The bath was a large semicircular affair with several protruding shower heads. He threw off his clothes, climbed in and turned on the taps. As soon as Phyllis heard the shower, she turned on the TV and raised the volume to its highest level. She moved quickly into the second bathroom, removed her blonde wig and her sunglasses and brought out a small towel. Without removing her gloves, she went into her purse, opened the ziplock bag and removed the Walther pistol. She wrapped the towel around it and ran back into the main bathroom, closing the door behind her. She stood back at a safe distance, using both hands to steady the weapon.

"Arnie, would you like me to join you?"

"Ellie, are you kidding?"

"Then open the curtain, I'm coming in."

He pulled back the shower curtain, revealing his enormous body, his private parts erect in anticipation.

Arnie looked at her, and the color drained from his face. He gasped.

"It's you! I fuckin' knew you looked familiar. What the hell are you doing here? What's inside that towel? What do you have there? Is that a gun? Are you fuckin' crazy?"

Before he could finish the sentence, she pointed the weapon at his lower abdomen and pulled the trigger. She aimed at his crotch and fired again.

"Yes Arnie, it's me, Phyllis Maitland. Look, my hair is still black. I'm a black widow, and I'm going to bite you, just like you bit Harvey and my baby."

He reached for the wall for support. His jaw hung open and his eyes bulged as he stared at the blood running down his legs. He moved toward her, but she had kept her distance. She fired twice again, the bullets penetrating his shoulder and neck. He grabbed wildly at the shower curtain for support, bringing it down with him as he collapsed. He looked up and mumbled,

"Stop, stop, please stop!"

"Why should I stop, Arnie, why? I begged you to stop that night and you wouldn't."

He lay back in the bath, one leg bent under his body, his head against the wall, eyes blinking at the ceiling. She extended her arm to within a foot of him and emptied the gun into his heaving chest. She ran back into the room, turned down the TV volume and returned the gun to the ziplock bag. She quickly changed back into the red print dress and red beret. She unfolded the large shopping bag from her purse and placed the discarded clothing and her purse inside. She returned to the bathroom and turned off the shower; Arnie's lifeless body lay there, eyes open and staring at nothing. She closed the bathroom door and looked around, assuring herself everything in the room appeared normal. She cracked open the door to check the hallway and then hung the "Do Not Disturb" sign on the doorknob. She donned her sunglasses and walked casually down the two flights of stairs. No one took special notice of a woman with black hair, wearing a red dress and sunglasses and carrying a large shopping bag, strolling nonchalantly across the lobby. Phyllis walked to the corner, hailed a cab and rode it to a few blocks from her girlfriend's home. She walked the rest of the way, went into the guest room and collapsed onto the bed. Her head throbbed as she felt a migraine coming on. After resting awhile she prepared some chamomile tea to steady her nerves, but the headache was now full-blown and she was overcome with nausea. She turned on the TV and settled into a soft chair.

She awoke with a start around 3:00 a.m. Her stomach felt better. She got into a hot shower and scrubbed her body repeatedly as if to wash away the night's events. She put on a bathrobe and lay down, hugging the pillow tightly. She slept better than the night before.

The next morning, Phyllis went over each detail again and suddenly remembered that the bus ticket stub was still in her purse. She tore it into small pieces and flushed them down the toilet. Satisfied that no traces of her Lunenburg visit remained in Halifax, she carefully rolled up her frock, black suit and white blouse together with her black beret, blonde wig and gloves. She placed everything into a sturdy plastic garbage bag, along with a stone she had gleaned from the landscaped lawn. She put the heavy package into a large shopping bag and carried it to the trunk of the Mustang. Phyllis sat in the car for a few minutes going over every detail. The neighbors may have seen her wearing a print dress, the bus driver a blue frock and the café and hotel staff in her black suit. She was confident there would be little chance of connecting the three outfits. She turned out of the driveway and headed for the Charlottetown ferry.

***

Phyllis sat for a time in the ferry garage below decks, reliving the previous day's events. She eventually got out of her car, reached into the trunk for a shiny metal box and placed it into the large shopping bag. She moved to the upper deck using the nearest stairway. Assuring herself that she was unobserved, she moved casually to the stern of the vessel and removed the garbage bag containing the stone and the rolled-up clothing. She dropped it overboard and watched it disappear in the churning wake. She then reached for the small metal box containing the ashes of her late husband, removed the cover and sprinkled the contents into the sea. She stood silently at the rail for a few moments and then whispered, just loud enough to hear her own voice,

"Goodbye, Harvey my love. It's all over . . . finished. The beast is dead. Please beg forgiveness from God for what I've done. It will stay with me forever, but it's a small burden compared to the one that Arnold Benson placed on our lives the past seven years. Our suffering and anguish are all in the past. We're left with the legacy of a beautiful, undying love. Harvey, may you rest in peace together with our child. My love, I'm going to try to get on with my life, but I'll always love you and never forget what we were to each other."

FORTY

The rays of the rising sun washed over the rooftops on Montague Street and heralded another beautiful day. The blue of the morning sky was a perfect background for the fluffy white clouds, their shapes changing as they moved slowly out to sea. Jim stood in the doorway and sampled the brisk morning air with a half-dozen deep breaths. He opened the Sunday paper and settled into the verandah couch. It had been a restless night, but he wasn't complaining. He had walked about the house recalling the feeling of Mavis's small, lithe shape pressing against him as they moved to the music. The color and texture of her hair, her green eyes, her moist mouth against his, vivid images that appeared in his mind's eye. He slept very little but felt filled with life. The boat project and its aura of urgency which had hung over him like a cloud were fading away. This unexpected relationship with a beautiful and intelligent woman provided a new resurgence of energy, an opportunity to experience and enjoy the fruits of his labor with someone he loved and who loved him.

Loud voices and the odor of coffee interrupted his thoughts. It had slipped his mind that his sister Cora and the old salt were house guests. Cora and her beau appeared with coffee and muffins and a cheery "good morning". Jim didn't particularly care for Cora's most recent choice. The man simply wouldn't stop talking. He characterized himself as an authority on all things nautical. Jim wasn't easily fooled. Clues from their conversation suggested his knowledge was confined to small power boats and that he had probably never been out of sight of land. Cora was Jim's only sibling and he loved her dearly. She was a sensitive woman, so Jim avoided commenting on some of her life choices, a number of which merited criticism. They had lost their mother at a young age, and Cora stepped in and took over. She was childless and now widowed, so Jim was pleased that she had a companion. His real concern was that someday, in the not-too-distant future, his sister could become a round-the-clock caregiver to a chronically sick old man.

Cora ran back into the house to answer the phone.

"Good morning, Lara. My, it was good to see you last night. Jim and I talked about the soon-to-be addition to the family. I'm so happy for you. I hope it's a boy and that it looks like your dad. Jim was such a gorgeous baby."

"Aunt Cora, I wish for the same thing. Your new friend seems to be nice. I hope he makes you happy."

"Let's be honest, dear, it's better than being alone. Actually, it's quite restful when he's around. I don't get tired talking,.....he does it all."

Jim took the phone.

"Hi Lara, how are you? How can I ever thank you for that party? I'm still flying high."

"You deserved it. I hope the party wasn't the only thing you enjoyed."

"Alright, I know what you're driving at. Yes, she's a wonderful woman. I must confess I lost a little sleep over her. Maybe I'll drop in to Arnie's for lunch today."

"Wow, that's great. Give Mavis my best. I was actually calling to invite you to lunch at the house, but never mind. We'll drop by your place later this afternoon and say goodbye to Cora."

Jim walked into Arnie's around noon. The weekends were always slow before the tourist season. As usual, Baby Face Romeo was there, attached to a Moosehead and expounding on the IQ of Newfoundlanders.

"Mavis, d'ya hear why the Newfie father walked his son to public school every day? They were in the same class!"

Mavis snapped back,

"Romeo, someone told me you missed a flight recently 'cause the moving sidewalk in the airport stalled for an hour. Now go home, Baby Face, you've had enough."

Mavis greeted Jim with a smile and a kiss on both cheeks.

"What a pleasant surprise. Take a table at the back. It's not busy. I'll sit with you."

She hovered over him while he looked over the menu.

"The soup today is green split pea. It's Georgie's secret recipe."

"Sounds good, ...I'll have a turkey sandwich with it on toasted whole wheat."

When he was almost through lunch, Mavis came over and sat with him.

"That was quite a party last night. A couple of people who were there dropped in this morning. They're still talking about it."

Jim reached over and squeezed her hand.

"It was special for me for several reasons. By the way, you owe me a night's sleep."

"Well, you owe me one too, so we're even."

"Mavis, you put in a lot of time here. Have you made any long-term plans?"

"jim, it's difficult to think ahead these days. Right now my job is our sole source of income."

"Jake mentioned he'd give you a management training position any time. As a bank manager, you could do well and not have to put up with this rowdy crowd every day."

"Yes, but what if they send me to work in another city? I've got too many commitments in Lunenburg. Danny needs me here. I want to be near Hilda and the baby. And besides," she whispered with a mischievous smile, "I really don't want to be far from you."

"That's fine with me, but I'm warning you, I'll nag you every day to come sailing."

He sipped his coffee and after a few moments of idle conversation asked,

"Tell me about St. John's.* Jake mentioned how you ended up in Lunenburg. What was your life like before?"

"Jim, does the name Hugh Kennedy mean anything to you?"

"Yeah, it sounds familiar, but I can't quite place it."

"Hugh Kennedy was a professor of medicine at Memorial and chief of cardiovascular surgery."

"O.K., now that you mention it, I do recall him. As a matter of fact, I believe he operated on a couple of people in our engineering firm."

"Well, any surgeon will tell you he was among the best in the country."

"The way you talk about him, is there some connection?"

"Jim, he was my father; he died years ago. He had become a recluse. He not only retired from medicine, he retired from the world. My mother predeceased him by about three years. When she passed away, he went into a nursing home. Let me tell you the whole story."

"I was a medical student at Memorial. I had done well in high school and university and was the youngest in the class. I'd always been 'Mavis Kennedy', but in medicine, I became 'Hugh Kennedy's daughter'. It was constantly thrown in my face, as if my name came with special privileges. They didn't realize that all it brought was discomfort."

"Heck, that's understandable, but was that enough to make you change your career?"

"You're right, it wasn't. When I was in my second year, an event in dad's life turned my world around. There was an international cardiology meeting in St. John's, and my father was the keynote speaker. During the closing dinner there was one toast after another, mostly honoring dad. When he and mom were driving home, he approached an intersection with the green light in his favor. According to several witnesses, a woman driving a van carrying two young children without safety harnesses ran the red light. My father couldn't stop in time and slammed into them. A little girl sustained a fractured skull and died in the ambulance. The mother had a concussion and was semi-comatose for about a month. The other child miraculously escaped injury. The police smelled alcohol on my father's breath and subjected him to a Breathalyzer test. The result was a virtually undetectable amount above .08, but he still got the DUI citation. With three witnesses, the police agreed that the other driver was in the wrong and absolved my dad of any responsibility. But the DUI charge stuck. He was so depressed about the death of the child, he could hardly speak. A police reporter found out who he was and needless to say, the newspapers had a field day. Jim, they crucified him. Within a week, he resigned his positions both at the university and the hospital. He came home one day and went into his room; he would stay there for weeks at a time. I continued my education for a couple of months, but the whispers and the finger pointing were starting to get to me. One day I passed a group of students in the corridor and I could hear the words, "Kennedy, alcoholic, a little girl". Something snapped inside my head. I walked straight to the front office and resigned from the faculty. I hated to do this to my parents. I was an only child and they had such great expectations. I simply couldn't take it anymore and just gave up. I registered in the MBA program and did quite well. But then I met Bert Willis, a handsome, bright engineering student who swept me off my feet. I guess the emotional aftermath of the events in the family affected my judgement and I was an easy mark. A year before graduating, I found myself pregnant. I quit school, got married and went to work for Jake at the bank."

They sat in silence for several long moments. Jim reached out and held her hands tightly. His eyes never left her as he watched a faint smile envelope her face.

"Jim, it's a strange world, isn't it? My father had encouraged me to eventually specialize in pediatric and adolescent psychiatry. We spoke often of helping unusual and special children, kids who needed extra care and understanding, youngsters who could eventually blend into this crazy, complex world. I guess God answered our prayers, eh Jim? He bestowed upon me a son with Down Syndrome and a daughter who marches to a different drum."

Jim bit his lip and remained silent. Her words were hitting home.

"Mavis, God Himself will attest to the magnificent job you've done. He threw you a heavy burden and you ran with it. The more I hear you speak, the more my respect for you grows and overwhelms me."

He paused to choose his words.

"This is only our second day together, and perhaps I shouldn't be saying this, but I'll say it anyhow. It may sound like an old-fashioned proposal, but if I were to spend the rest of my days with someone like you, I'd consider myself a very lucky man.

FORTY ONE

Bill Gallant propped himself up in bed and clicked on the 10 p.m. news. In fewer than ten minutes he was fast asleep. He maintained that he couldn't sleep unless the TV was on, but this time his rest was short-lived. The ringing phone startled him.

"Hello, who's this?"

"Hello Bill, it's Les Howland, did I disturb you? Hope it's not too late."

"No problem Chief, what's happening in Halifax?"

"Probably stuff that would interest you. We got a call from the Ritz Hotel, and when we went up to look, we found a body in the bathtub. Looks like he may have been dead for a couple of days."

"Was there any ID? Was it a homicide?"

"The hotel desk tells us it's Arnold Benson, a regular guest who lives in Lunenburg. He had seven neat bullet holes in him, more than enough to send him on his way."

It took Gallant a few moments to absorb what he had just heard. He was disappointed but not surprised.

A number of people would be pleased to see Arnie Benson on a slab in the morgue. The women he seduced and abandoned after making grandiose promises, jealous boyfriends and husbands and certainly a few of the shady characters with whom he had dealings.

"Hello Bill, are you there? I can call again in the morning. This thing can keep."

"Yes, I'm here. Well, it so happens I know the family. No sense telling them at this hour. I'll take a female constable with me in the morning and visit Benson's wife. You know Les, we had a full investigation going on this guy. He was someone of special interest in both a robbery and a murder. This news kinda complicates things."

"Maybe it really simplifies things. It depends from which end you look."

"Is there an autopsy planned?"

"Not yet, it appears that the cause of death is pretty straightforward. I'll know more in the morning. By the way, something interesting,...the bullets were from a .25 calibre pistol, certainly not a choice murder weapon. Two of the shots were low down in the groin." He laughed,..."I guess somebody tried to blow his balls off."

Bill stared up into the darkness. Sleep was out of the question.

***

"Mr. Gallant, Mr. Gallant, are you alright?"

The housekeeper shook him gently after wakeup calls by the alarm clock failed. Bill woke with a start and stumbled quickly into a cool shower, berating himself for oversleeping. The cold water left him breathless, but he needed that kick start. He passed up breakfast and pulled into the RCMP parking lot an hour later than usual. Constable Mary Callam gave him a cheery greeting.

"Good Monday morning to you, Inspector! Can I bring my late boss a cup of coffee?"

"Do that, please, and then get me Arnie Benson's home on the line. The number's in his file."

He gulped down the coffee and picked up the phone.

"Hello, good morning, is this Hilda Benson?"

"No," answered Lara, "it's her house guest. Just a moment, I'll get her. Shall I tell her who's calling?"

"I'm Inspector Gallant. It's a personal call."

"Oh hello sir, it's me, Lara Cabot. I'll get Hilda for you right away."

"Hi, this is Hilda."

"Good morning, Mrs. Benson, it's Inspector Gallant. I wonder if I may drop over to your house and speak with you."

"Oh, there's something wrong, isn't there. Is it about my husband? He's out of town now."

"Yes, I'm aware. May I drop by? It's a personal matter, but it's quite important."

"Yes, certainly. I'm in all morning."

Twenty minutes later, Gallant arrived with Mary Callam. Lara answered the door.

"Good morning, Miss Cabot, we meet again after Saturday night's party. I'm here on official business.

May I ask you to please stay close to Mrs. Benson while we speak with her."

Hilda walked into the room.

"Good morning, Mrs. Benson, this is our Constable Mary Callam. May we all sit down?"

They settled into comfortable chairs. Lara offered drinks but they refused.

"No thanks, this is just fine. Mrs. Benson, we have some disturbing news about your husband. Our Halifax detachment informed us late last night that he met with an unfortunate accident."

"My God, was he driving drunk again? Did he hurt anyone?"

"Nothing like that, Mrs. Benson."

He paused for a moment and said,

"I'm afraid he was the victim in a fatal shooting."

Lara leapt from her seat and wrapped her arms around Hilda. The woman just sat there, frozen. Lara turned to Gallant.

"When did this happen—where? Who did this?"

"It happened over the weekend. It was at the Ritz Hotel in downtown Halifax. There was a 'Do Not Disturb' sign on the hotel room door for at least thirty-six hours before they actually found him. He was in the bath and had suffered several bullet wounds. We have no indication who may be responsible. The hotel staff was under the impression he was alone. No one else was seen entering the room."

Constable Callam returned from the kitchen with water and handed it to Hilda. She took a sip and turned to Lara.

"I'm O.K. I'll be O.K. Inspector, where is he now? Will they be sending him back here?"

"You'll get a call from Halifax giving you some further details."

The room was silent for a while.

"Inspector, I often told him something bad would happen to him someday, and he laughed at me. I guess his past finally caught up with him. How am I going to tell my little girl?"

She took another long sip of water, sat back in her chair and gazed at the glass with unseeing eyes.

"Mrs. Benson, we would like to know who did this because there's several loose ends that need tying up. In any case, we'll leave you now, but I'll have to meet with you after the final services. We're hoping you'll enlighten us about some of Mr. Benson's associates."

The Inspector and the constable left shortly after.

Lara and Hilda sat and held each other. Not a word was spoken. There was a death in the family; there was shock and surprise, there were questions to be answered, decisions to be made. There were so many issues. But there were no tears.

FORTY TWO

Hilda asked Lara to break the news to Mavis in person.

"Hilda, I don't want to leave you alone."

"I'm fine. I'm really O.K. I'm going to make myself a hot cup of tea and lie down for a while. Please do me a favor and run over to the café. I want mom to hear it from us and not from a client. I want to give her the news before someone else does."

Lara walked into Arnie's just before the noon rush. Mavis was surprised to see her so early in the day.

"What brings you here at this hour?"

"Mavis, can we talk in the kitchen for a few minutes? I think Georgie should be in on this. You can tell Danny later. Can your help take over a bit?"

"No problem, Alma's here. Is something wrong at Hilda's?"

"She and Jennie are fine, but I do have some news."

They gathered in the kitchen.

"I'm glad you're all seated. I don't want to sound flippant, but fasten your seat-belts. Hilda had a visit from the RCMP about ten this morning. The news was as follows. Arnie Benson passed away over the weekend in Halifax. They found him in the bathtub in his hotel room at the downtown Ritz. Someone sent him on his way with several well-aimed bullets. The cops haven't any clues as yet. And that's it. I don't know about you, but frankly I'm not too surprised."

Mavis was speechless. Georgie was the first to react. "Well for Christ's sake, someone finally got to him. I do not believe this. Sweet Jesus! Is this for real?"

Lara moved over to Mavis's chair, knelt down beside her and grasped her hands tightly.

"Mavis, it's an unexpected shock, but it could be a new beginning for you and your family."

Georgie brought her a glass of water. She sat there silently, staring straight ahead. She rubbed her face with her hands.

"My cheeks feel all tingly. I'm cold. Georgie, there's a woolen blanket in the storeroom."

He brought it over and covered her shoulders. She looked up, her glistening tears intensifying the brightness of her eyes. A tiny smile curled on her lips; she looked around as she said to no one in particular,

"Isn't this strange? This is Arnie's blanket. I covered him whenever he came in cold, wet and drunk."

She paused, then, in a voice that shook with emotion, uttered a prayer.

"Oh Lord, may Your love and compassion be bestowed upon him and finally bring him peace."

Lara held her close.

"Let me stay awhile and help. I did some bartending in Toronto."

"Lara, you're an angel. I really feel a bit shaky. I'd like to go home and rest a bit."

"Knowing my dad, I think he'd like to be with you today. You shouldn't be alone, and it'll be good to have someone to talk to."

"Lara, you're not only beautiful and smart but you're a mind reader."

"Great, I'll call him now and tell him to come and pick you up."

Georgie walked over to Mavis, squeezed her hand and whispered,

"You can count on us. Just you watch; you made this place into a little gold mine, but now we're all gonna turn it into a great big diamond mine!"

Lara put on an apron and walked out front. After a couple of minutes of instruction, she took over the bar from Alma. Her first client was Jake Allen.

"Lara, I just heard from Bill Gallant. I can't believe the news. What a hell of a shocker. We're supposed to meet here for lunch."

"Uncle Jake, I don't believe in capital punishment, but between you and me, in Arnie's case I think I would have made an exception. People may say 'rest in peace'. I say 'may he rot in hell'."

"Wow, I never expected such strong words from my sweet little 'niece'."

"Jake, someday, because I'm a 'niece' and not a 'nephew', I'll explain why I feel that way about him. I only knew Arnie's bad side, but I knew him well enough to know it was the only side he had. O.K., now can I at least buy you a beer for getting me that mortgage renewal?"

"Lara, are you trying to bribe your bank manager? By the way, the mortgage papers are ready for your signature. I'll pay for a coffee, though."

Bill Gallant walked in and took a seat beside Jake.

"Mr. Gallant, we meet for the second time today. What can I get you?"

"Thanks, Lara, I'll have what Jake is having. How is Mrs. Benson doing?"

"She's going to be O.K. Things will work out just fine. I'm anxious for the final services to be over so she can have closure on a very unpleasant part of her life."

Jake raised his coffee mug.

"I'll drink to that."

FORTY THREE

Tony Manolo drove out of his office garage and turned on the 5:00 p.m. news. The report of Arnie's murder hit him like a hammer. He pulled over to the side of the road and tried several stations for more details, but without success. He rushed home and waited impatiently for the 6:00 o'clock TV news. There was little new information, but enough to make him sit back in his chair and mull over the possible opportunities. Tony prided himself on being meticulous in all of his dealings, especially the illicit ones outside his law practice. The late-night TV news didn't elaborate any further.. He went to bed soon after but slept very little. So many thoughts and possibilities whirled about in his head. By the time he fell asleep, around 3:00 a.m., he had concocted a plan whereby he could benefit from Arnie's sudden death and from his Cayman assets. The following morning, he called his bank in George Town.

"Hello Beaton, it's me, Tony. How are you doing?"

"Fine Tony, good to hear from you. What's happening in Canada?"

"Beaton, I need some information. The chap whom I sent to your office about a month ago passed away suddenly and violently over the weekend. I had lost touch with him recently. Can you shed any light on his sudden demise?"

"This is news to me. I assure you there was nothing unusual at this end. Is it possible that the 'child' he left here is now without a 'father'. Are there any other 'relatives'?

"No, I'm virtually certain there's no 'family'."

"In that case, this could bear looking into."

"We agree, Beaton. I can't get away right now, but I'll fly in early next week. Don't bother sending a car, I'll take a cab from the airport."

Tony sat back and thought.

'Yes, yes. This rainbow could be worth following right to the end. Let's see if I can move in and take over where the late 'daddy' left off.'

***

Arnold Benson was laid to rest the following Saturday. A standing-room-only crowd attended services at St. Christopher's. It was more out of curiosity than the payment of respects. Gruesome murders provoke the imagination; they're a rare occurrence, even for a city the size of Halifax, and especially in a luxury hotel. The late Arnold Benson had placed the town of Lunenburg in the media limelight. Since no one offered to speak on his behalf, Georgie agreed to recite the eulogy.

"Folks, Arnold Benson was a loyal Canadian. At the age of twenty-one, he volunteered and served in the

Canadian Special Forces. As owner of Arnie's Café, he could always be counted upon to lend financial and moral support to our local sports teams. Any client of Arnie's will agree that he was friendly and charming and never failed to greet his fellow Lunenburgers, either on the street or in his café. Left to mourn him is a wonderful wife, Hilda, and a beautiful baby daughter, Jennifer. Lunenburg won't be the same without him. God rest his soul."

Lara thought, 'It's a pretty short and lame eulogy, but a hell of a lot more than he deserves. But then again, Georgie's right. Lunenburg won't be the same without him. As a matter of fact, it'll be a much better place.'

The RCMP was especially attracted to Arnie's interment. A police photographer moved discreetly about the cemetery, his telephoto lens recording every visible face. Bill Gallant knew that if the underworld was involved in Arnie's murder it was a tradition to have one of their lesser-known members attend the burial just to make certain the victim was expedited.

There was little negative publicity about Arnie Benson in the news media, although they did allude to his possible connections to some unsavory people. Instead, there were discussions regarding the future of Arnie's Café. Hilda decided that in spite of the circumstances surrounding Arnie's death, the name "Arnie's" should be retained. Human nature, being what it is, people find it exciting to identify with the mystique of a place where rules are broken, police and the law defied, and rumor and controversy rampant. The café was now busier than ever and extra help was needed.

Evidently its newly acquired notoriety attracted many new and curious clients.

FORTY FOUR

Jim Cabot arrived at Arnie's just after the lunch rush and Mavis joined him at a table at the rear.

"Hey, you're spoiling me, Jim. This is your fourth visit this week."

"I can't believe you're counting them. Hope that tells you something. I've hardly had any quality time with you in almost a week. Are you planning to take some evenings off? Since Arnie passed on, you're working day and night."

"Arnie never put in very much time here. I'm working extra because I want to change a lot of things. This place will be Hilda's future. By the way, are you still putting the finishing touches on the boat?"

"Well, it's just about done. I'd like to talk to you about our maiden voyage."

"Our maiden voyage? When and where are you taking me?"

"I thought we'd leave Thursday morning and stay over in Chester. Maybe go on to Halifax from there and be back next Tuesday or Wednesday."

"Jim Cabot, it sounds more like a honeymoon cruise. If that's what you're planning, I'll really have to think about it." He laughed.

"I don't want to rush you. Let's call it a 'getting to know you' cruise."

"I confess I have been looking forward to the two of us getting away. I could rearrange the work schedule here. This'll be my first holiday in several years. I don't know how I'm gonna finish up today just thinking about it. By the way, can I sleep in the V-berth*? It's cozier. If you promise to behave yourself, maybe I'll let you join me."

"If you let me join you, how can I behave myself?"

"Jim, I used to crew for my dad on his sailboat. We were members of the yacht club in St. John's, and I did a fair amount of sailing when I was a kid."

"Wonderful, if we get into trouble out there, I'm depending on you to save us. I'm going to do a sea trial on Tuesday. I'm pretty confident everything will be O.K. How about if we get aboard on Wednesday night and take off the following morning. Can you arrange it?"

"Yup, I've got extra help and Hilda will keep an eye on the place. I'm not worried. It'll be alright."

***

Mavis worked late that night, going over details with Alma and Hilda. Georgie now had a young assistant in the kitchen, which allowed him to keep an eye out front.

When Jim got home he started a checklist of the things they would need. Next morning he provisioned the boat with food, drink and fuel. Lara and Hilda had outfited the galley and installed nautical-design linens and bedclothes. On Tuesday afternoon, he motored out of his slip for the sea trial. He set the autopilot, tested the electronics and bent on the sails. He was alone and in his glory. The boat heeled gently and cut silently through the water. The afternoon breeze was a steady eight knots, and the wheel was light and responsive. The new sails could use some minor alterations, but for cruising, they were more than adequate. Jim was exhilarated.

'Damn, it doesn't get much better than this.'

Jim didn't get home from the marina until well after dark. Greta had left supper in the fridge, but his stomach was in knots and he ignored the food. He laid out new nautical charts on the kitchen table and reviewed them repeatedly. He had sailed this course before, but for this special trip he wanted every detail to be perfect. He paced the floor, turned on the TV and tried to concentrate on the news. He dozed off but awoke with a start about 3:00 a.m. He went to the fridge for a glass of milk, set the alarm and went to bed

***

Hilda hung up the phone and grabbed Lara's arm.

"Wow, they're getting on the boat tomorrow night and taking off for Halifax on Thursday morning."

"Hey, it's finally gonna happen, and on board a sailboat. How romantic."

"I agree. I hope it goes well."

"Oh, it'll go well alright. They're both lonely and in good health. They may even forget about the trip and just rock the boat all weekend."

Hilda mockingly scolded her.

"You're impossible, you're talking about my mother! Let's change the subject. Mom gave me some new information. Arnie sat with an attractive blonde woman on that Friday at the café. As soon as she left, Arnie changed his plans and said he was going to Halifax. I bumped into Bill Gallant yesterday, and he told me the restaurant at the hotel served dinner to Arnie and a blonde woman. However, the hotel claims he was alone when he registered, and no one was seen entering his room. That was the last time they saw him alive. Bill Gallant suspects someone may have been using the blonde as bait to lure Arnie to Halifax, where a homicide would be easier and less conspicuous than in Lunenburg."

"It sounds to me that they're making progress," said Lara, "you'll forgive me, but as far as I'm concerned, I don't really care who did it."

"Well, you know me, Lara, even when I see an animal in pain I go to pieces. I just hope he didn't suffer when he died."

But Lara was unrelenting.

"Let's be frank, he was more than an animal. Calling him a beast would be more appropriate."

She was tempted to continue the tirade, but Hilda again changed the subject.

"I'm having a problem with Jennie. She keeps asking about her father."

"What are you telling her?"

"I tell her he's in heaven with the angels."

Lara had to control herself from laughing.

"Hilda, I can't say that I blame you. There are occasions when telling lies is a necessary evil, especially when kids are involved."

"Lara, I'm not kidding myself; sometime in the future, Jennie is bound to learn all about him. I wonder and worry how she's going to react."

"Fine, but until then, don't bother your head about it."

FORTY FIVE

Mavis and Jim arrived at the marina around 5:00 p.m. It was drizzling but the forecast called for clear skies by morning. The boat was cold and damp but warmed quickly with the portable heaters. Mavis immediately took over the cooking. She prepared a salad and microwaved a salmon manicotti meal. Jim opened a bottle of wine and proposed a toast. They sat facing each other, both at a loss for words.

"Mavis, so many wonderful things have happened the last couple of weeks. I can't express how good it feels."

They ate slowly and spoke very little, each sip of wine preceded by a toast to themselves and to their future. They stood at the galley sink doing dishes and embracing at every opportunity. They settled in front of the TV, oblivious to the images on the screen. They held each other close, each embrace a deep and new experience, exploring and caressing each other. Mavis eventually pulled away.

"Jim, I've got to get into something more comfortable. How about you?"

"Fine. I'll wait for you in the V-berth."

He slid beneath the covers. The new bedclothes were smooth and cool against his naked body.

"Everything is new," he thought, "a new boat and a new life."

Mavis soon joined him. Jim was overwhelmed by her beauty. She wore a short, pale-green nightie that accentuated her beautiful lithe legs and radiant red hair. She moved closer and wrapped her arms around him, her head snuggled under his chin. He slipped the nightie from her shoulder, lowered his head and enveloped her breasts with his mouth. He caressed her gently and his body responded to the feel of her velvet-like skin.

"Jim, I'm very warm, but please . . . slowly. It's been a long time."

She reached down and placed his rigid member between her thighs. Ever so gently, he penetrated her; the heat and passion he felt was more intense than he could ever remember. Together they moved slowly in unison, their ardor building to an intensity beyond their control. The urgent sounds of their climax were muffled as their mouths locked together.

They fell asleep in each other's arms and awoke around 3:00 a.m. They spoke about all sorts of things and made love again.

***

At around 8:00 a.m. the view through the portholes was of dense, white fog. Jim looked down at Mavis sleeping peacefully, her head against his shoulder, her hair spread over the pillow. He lifted her nightie and gently caressed her breasts. He drew light circles with his fingertips on her stomach, moving slowly to the silky red triangle and firm thighs. Her body seemed years younger than her age. He felt a momentary uneasiness, wondering that perhaps people would mistake him for her father.

Later, they squeezed into the boat's shower stall. It was designed for one occupant, but two was certainly more exciting. They were pleased that there was virtually no one in the marina this early in the season, their laughter would likely have disturbed the neighbors. Breakfast was bacon, eggs and scones, served on the blue-and-white nautical plates that Lara had purchased.

Jim moved about the deck checking the lifelines and anchor rode. The fog lifted around 10:00 a.m. and they could now make out the details of the harbor. They cast off and motored slowly toward the open water.

"Mavis, please take the wheel. I'll put up the sails."

She maneuvered in and out of anchored boats of all sizes and colors and then headed out into a light morning breeze. Offshore, they bore off to the east and eased the main and jib sheets, setting a course for Mahone Bay. *Lunenburg Lady* glided silently through the water. The sun had burned through the fog and reflected off the bow waves like dancing diamonds. Jim was impressed at how adeptly Mavis managed the wheel. She steered a proper course while he stood behind, his arms wrapped around her, his cheek snuggled in her hair. The wind gradually increased and became gusty; the boat leapt forward, cutting easily through the building swells.

"Looks like we'll arrive sooner than I thought," Jim exclaimed, "we should be there between three and four."

They sailed into the bay and steered an irregular course past numerous picturesque islands.

"I reserved an overnight berth and a table at the Maritime Den, a lovely little marina restaurant for big appetites," said Jim.

Mavis's cell phone rang. It was Hilda. A lengthy conversation ensued, and Jim was concerned by the expression on Mavis's face.

"Anything wrong?"

"Not really, Jim. Hilda got a call from Inspector Gallant. He wants to see her again and talk more about Arnie's past. He said something had just come up that could be important but he didn't want to talk about it on the phone."

"I'm not surprised. I believe the more they dig, the more they'll find."

They tied up in Chester just after 4:00 p.m. Although it was still early in the season, numerous boats were already docked in this beautiful, picturesque harbor. Jim signed in, topped off the water tanks and connected the electric cables. They relaxed on the restaurant deck under an unseasonably warm sun.

"Jim, just look at your boat; she's such a beauty. The more I admire every detail, the more I wonder how you were able to do all this singlehandedly. You're really a special human being."

"Mavis, every time I look at you I discover something new and overwhelming."

"Seriously, Jim, it has such salty lines. You have great talent in those hands of yours".....she smiled..."but of course I know that from personal experience."

"You're a she-devil. I may have talented hands for boat building, but I'm not too well versed in other, more important things."

"Never mind," she laughed, "let me be the judge."

They chose to dine on the restaurant deck with its magnificent view overlooking the marina. The sun was setting and its soft, reddish hues reflected off Mavis's face and hair. Jim reached across the table and caressed the smooth skin of her arm. They gazed at one another with a smile which meant much more than any words could express. They were sharing a mutual affection they never dreamt could be theirs again.

"Mavis, I never want to lose this feeling. I doubt if I could ever go back to the loneliness I've lived with after spending the past couple of weeks with you. I guess we should consider ourselves lucky that life offered us a second chance."

"I feel the same, but keep in mind that I bring along some special baggage. Danny is bright and well-behaved, but he's growing up pretty quickly and could be a much bigger problem as an adult. So far, and perhaps into the near future, I can be a positive influence on him, but what happens when he's grown and manifests strong opinions of his own with the physical and intellectual strength to make his own

decisions, some of which may not be totally rational .
. ."

"Mavis, I'm not sweeping your arguments under
the carpet. We all have uncertainties about our kids.
It comes with parenthood. I think you'll agree though
that the only way is to take things one day at a time.
Danny is a kind and compassionate boy. I'm confident
he'll make his way in the world and find his own place
in society. Keep in mind he's very bright and cognizant
of things going on about him. I'm not worried. Look, it's
been a long day and you must be hungry. Let's order.
How about starting out with a nice bottle of white wine.
Aha, I've already spotted my mussels and shrimp on
the menu."

"I'll have the grilled salmon with a little pasta.
It's a difficult dish to ruin, even in the hands of an
amateur chef."

"Tell me, how are things going at the café? Are you
pleased with the results of your efforts?"

"Well, we're up about fifteen percent over the same
month last year; if things keep up, there'll be more than
enough for Hilda and myself to give Jennie and Danny
a good education. We'll be financially secure. It was a
constant battle keeping Arnie's hands out of the till."

She paused while they drank another toast to
each other.

"Jim, making a living is not as important as making a
life. Perhaps now we'll have an opportunity to put some
normalcy back into our lives. The will is being probated
next week, and our attorney has assured us that Hilda
will be declared sole proprietor of both the business
and the building."

They enjoyed a delightful meal to the sounds of a live trio playing soft jazz.

"Well what do you know, Jim, the guitarist is my next-door neighbor's kid, the same one who played at your launch party. His mother is the town gossip. As of tomorrow morning, my darling, our love affair's no longer a secret."

FORTY SIX

Early next morning, *Lunenburg Lady* dropped her lines and eased her way out of the marina. Visibility was poor but by the time they reached open water the sky had cleared. They unfurled the sails and bore off to the northeast in a ten knot breeze. Jim made a few calls on his cell phone.

"I booked a reservation for this evening at a great restaurant on the Halifax waterfront with dockage nearby. Tomorrow we'll tour and shop Halifax like a couple of foreigners and misbehave in our floating hotel."

"Jim, I've been to Halifax a hundred times but never arrived by water. I feel like a cruise tourist."

It was an easy forty-mile sail, but a long day. Again, the boat behaved beautifully, and the autopilot took over most of the steering. They docked before sunset, showered and relaxed in the cockpit. Mavis called Lunenburg and spoke to Georgie. There had been no issues that the chef or Alma couldn't handle. Danny took the line, sounding excited.

"Hi mommy, are you having a good time?"

"Danny, I'm really enjoying myself, but I miss you. Are you O.K.? How is Hilda managing?"

"Hilda's O.K. She was here this afternoon with Auntie Lara. Jennie was eating an ice cream cone for the first time. She's really funny. When are you coming home? I miss you."

"Mommy will be back on Wednesday. I'm getting a real good rest, and it was fun coming to Halifax by water. Mr. Cabot's new boat is beautiful."

"O.K. mommy, have a good time. I love you. Bye."

***

"Good evening, Mr. Cabot. Your table is ready. It's by the window as you requested. Your server this evening will be Marcel. He'll be over shortly with the wine list and menu."

"Mavis, this a great place for seafood; a two pound lobster is no problem for them. Think you can handle it? There's no shortage of restaurants in Halifax, but this one is really special. Let's order the lobster. If we can't finish it, we'll have the rest in the morning."

"God, lobster for breakfast, now that's living! You're spoiling me, Jim."

"Spoiling you gives me pleasure. I just look at your face and I lose track of time. Whenever I hold you, it feels like the first time."

"Let's hope it stays that way. You make me feel so relaxed, so comfortable. I don't think I was ever as happy as I am today. You've turned my world around. You overwhelm me, Jim."

After a splendid meal they retired to the boat, took in the evening news and fell asleep in each other's arms. It had been a long but beautiful day.

The next morning, Mavis woke early and went ashore for eggs and fresh croissants. She surprised Jim with a delicious lobster omelet.

"Mavis, now you're spoiling me. What can I do for you today?"

"Jim, when I was a kid, my dad used to take me to the Halifax museum whenever he had a medical meeting here. According to the morning paper, there's a Bouguereau exhibition in town. Lara told me you used to do a lot of photography. Well, this artist paints in oils, but so delicately detailed you'd swear his works were photographs."

The next few days were idyllic. They toured the city, ate and drank and visited the sights that most Haligonians* rarely see.

On Wednesday, they awoke at 6:00 a.m to a cold, damp fog. Mavis put up coffee while Jim prepared the boat for the return voyage. They weaved their way out of the harbor into open water. The weather had cleared but remained cool. The wind was a steady nor'wester, which suited Jim fine. It would allow them to sail a more direct course, at least to the approaches to Lunenburg. Mavis brought the croissants and coffee up on deck. They ate and drank, absorbing every minute of an adventure that was drawing to a close. The boat heeled to port in a chilly breeze blowing out over St. Margaret's Bay. Jim turned on the autopilot, maintaining a course to the Lunenburg headland. They moved at a steady six knots, and by 3:00 in the afternoon, they were only twelve miles from home. They furled the sails in an unfavorable wind and motored the rest of the way. At about 5:00 p.m., *Lunenburg Lady* ended her maiden voyage.

But an unexpected welcome awaited them on shore. Jim had already spotted the girls through the binoculars. Lara, Hilda and Jennie stood on the main dock waving frantically.

"This is embarrassing," he said, "we're being greeted by our children on our return from a kind of unofficial honeymoon."

Jim threw Lara a dock line while Mavis jumped ashore and scooped up Jennie, smothering her with kisses. She caught Hilda's eye and gave her a knowing smile. Lara greeted her dad, staring and smiling until he turned away in embarrassment.

"Ladies," he exclaimed, "we just arrived from Halifax, not China. Why all the fuss?"

Hilda and Lara rolled their eyes and burst out laughing. Mavis blushed and tried to change the subject.

"O.K. folks, enough said. We had an enjoyable trip and we're both very happy. The details shall remain private."

FORTY SEVEN

Bill Gallant was haunted by the slow progress of a near fruitless investigation. Then, in the midst of it all, he received a disturbing call from the Charlottetown precinct. A couple of RCMP constables recalled a prominent obituary that had appeared in their local paper about two months earlier. It was placed by Campbell Breweries and was entitled "In Memory of Harvey Maitland", a popular vice president of a local brewing firm. It displayed a photo of the deceased, announcing his death due to an unfortunate incident which had taken place in Halifax years ago. The constables then referred to the recent news reporting Arnold Benson's murder. Both names were familiar, so they checked the police records. The order of the deaths and the proximity to each other was a coincidence that provoked their curiosity.

"Very interesting," Bill offered. "I've got to hand it to you guys. It's the kind of stuff worth looking into. See if you can find out where Maitland was a patient when he died. Let's interview the staff and see if we can get more information. Have you any idea where his widow could be?"

"No, Inspector, but if she's in Canada, we'll find her."

"O.K. I want to thank you chaps again. This may be important. I'll be over there on Monday."

Gallant was more surprised than happy. The phone call threw a monkey wrench into his line of reasoning. He had felt certain that the murder was tied to the airport robbery money. Now a new scenario presented itself. Could it have been a revenge killing, or just a coincidence that Maitland's and Arnie's deaths happened so close together? Yet maybe there was some substance to it. Bill thought again about the bullets extracted from Arnie's body. They were .25 calibre, certainly not from a professional murder weapon. It was a great pistol for target practice, but then again, it was adequately lethal at close range. Who knows, perhaps it was the only weapon available.

The police managed to identify both the nursing home in question and the location of Phyllis Maitland. The following Monday, Gallant visited the nursing home in Charlottetown and questioned the late Maitland's nurse, Millie, about the circumstances of his death. He was interested in the widow's reaction when she visited the hospital for the last time. During the interview, Millie recalled some of the words that Phyllis had uttered while she spoke to the lifeless body of her husband. She was certain she had heard "retribution" and "monster". Gallant then contacted Phyllis Maitland herself and set up a meeting at RCMP headquarters. She denied having visited Lunenburg in recent years but admitted visiting Halifax occasionally and staying at her girlfriend Janice's home. She stated that she never owned a gun and couldn't recall anyone in her family who did. Gallant thanked her for her cooperation and said that he may call upon her again.

Gallant decided to stop over in Halifax on his way home and meet with Phyllis's girlfriend, Janice. The woman confirmed Phyllis's presence in her home the weekend of the murder, and her next-door neighbor corroborated that a Mustang bearing a Prince Edward Island license plate never left the driveway until Sunday around noon. Gallant didn't get much sleep that night, but it wasn't because of the Maitland case. He had turned on the 11:00 p.m. TV news and was greeted by a headline story.

> *"An attorney from the office of Grierson & Hamel, a prominent Halifax law firm, drowned while on a fishing vacation in the Cayman Islands. Anthony Manolo had left his hotel room in George Town about a week ago. His body was retrieved yesterday morning about two miles offshore. When police were asked if the death is being treated as an accident, they offered no comment."*

Gallant was familiar with the law firm but had never heard of Anthony Manolo. He went directly to his office early the following morning.

"Hello Inspector, how was P.E.I?"

"Mary, I haven't had much luck there. I guess you heard about this guy Manolo from Grierson's office."

"Yes Inspector, it's on the front page."

"Mary, look up the phone tracings on Arnie Benson and tell me if he ever made a call to the Grierson office."

"The file is close by . . .O.K, here it is. Yes, there were a couple of calls to Grierson's office number from Arnold Benson's cell phone."

"Bless you. Let me have Alex Grierson's personal number? It's in my private file."

Gallant called the attorney.

"Alex, it's Bill Gallant, sorry to hear about your man. Saw it on TV last night."

"Hi Bill, yeah, we're all in a state of shock. We're waiting for more details from the police down there."

"Alex, what I'm asking you now is a police matter. Was the late Arnold Benson a client of yours?"

"The name is familiar. Wasn't he the guy who made a violent exit recently in some hotel room?"

"You've got it, that's him."

"I can tell you without checking he never set foot in this office, nor did he ever use our services. To my knowledge, I have no clients who ever had any dealings with him. Has our name come up in your investigation?"

"Don't worry your head. You've been a great help."

'Well, well, well,' Gallant thought. 'Arnie and Manolo were obviously involved in an out-of-the-office business deal in Cayman.'

Gallant phoned his police connection in George Town. It seemed that a bank official named Beaton had also disappeared at about the same time Tony went missing. He said the police now considered Beaton an important person in the case.

"Confidentially," the informant added, "I found out that Manolo was dead before he hit the water."

Gallant pondered, 'Arnie spent time in Cayman to store his acquired wealth, but was possibly set up by Manolo and Beaton, the bank associate. Beaton was probably affiliated with an international money-laundering syndicate. They eliminated Arnie, and when greedy Tony goes to Cayman for an extra share of Arnie's dough, they turned on him and got rid of him too. How bloody neat. So Tony Manolo, acting outside of his Halifax practice, set up the whole deal and ended up dead for his trouble. Admittedly it's all conjecture, but it makes for a credible plot.'

Gallant was relieved in a way. The pressure to come up with a suspect's name or at least a lead had diminished. If an international crime syndicate was involved in Arnie's murder, there wasn't much an RCMP constable in Nova Scotia could accomplish. He doubted if even the Cayman police could make any headway.

FORTY EIGHT

Hilda was working the café when Lara called.

"Sweetheart, I forgot to mention that I'm going for my monthly check-up this afternoon. My appointment is at 2:30. Can I drop Jennie off at the bar for a couple of hours? I'll pick her up afterwards. If not, no problem, I'll take her with me."

"Lara, take Jennie with you by cab, and I'll meet you at the doctor's office. We'll all come home together."

Lara made the beds and did some washing. It wasn't difficult keeping an eye on Jennie; the child followed her from room to room, chatting endlessly.

The medical exam went well. Dr. Ellis predicted a September birth. Back in the car, Hilda commented, "Why so glum? The doc found you in great shape."

"Listen, after I spoke to you this morning I phoned Jake at the bank. His secretary told me he wasn't feeling too well and would be in at noon. I called again later, and she said he wouldn't be in today. I phoned his home and spoke to the housekeeper. She knows me and said Jake was at the emergency room. I have to pop in and see what's going on."

"You seem unusually concerned. Is he that close to the family?"

"Hilda, It's a long story."

The women walked into the ER visiting area. Jake was surprised and delighted to see them.

"Uncle Jake, what happened? I hope you feel as good as you look. Is there a problem?"

"Bless you, Lara, how did you find out?"

"Never mind, just tell me what's going on."

"Well, I woke up this morning short of breath. I had a couple of aches and pains in my arm and my jaw. The doctor says I've had a lucky warning. It's my heart, but he said there was no damage. They did all sorts of tests, put me on this IV you see here and I really feel fine. I'm scheduled for an angiogram tomorrow and I may end up with a bypass."

In a commanding voice that was almost a shout, Lara burst out,

"Well, you've got to give up those damned cigarettes!"

'People don't usually speak to their bank managers in that tone of voice,' thought Hilda. She noticed tears in Lara's eyes and curiosity haunted her. She looked forward to an explanation.

Back in the car, Lara spoke first.

"I have to share a situation with you with which I've been living with for years. I really need to talk about it, more-so now than ever. If Jennie's not too tired, I want to stop at the bank."

"You seem upset. Maybe we ought to go straight home and relax."

"'No, no, I'm fine. This is something you should know. We're close enough to share everything, but in any case it'll be a hell of a surprise. Heaven knows, it was for me."

They parked at the bank and proceeded to the vault room in the rear. Lara removed a business envelope from her safety deposit box and handed it to Hilda.

"Let's go into the private room. I'll hold Jennie while you read."

Hilda stared at her apprehensively as she removed the document and unfolded it.

My Dearest Lara:

I hope this letter finds you and dad in good health and that your differences have been ironed out. I am writing this a few weeks before your twentieth birthday. Lara, I have no idea how long I shall live. You are well aware I suffer from acute hypertension, the same condition that carried my mother away at an early age. I am sealing this message and handing it to Rogers & Gordon, our attorneys. They have been instructed to give it to you on the occasion of my passing.

My darling, there is a part of my life I have shared only with Dr. Ellis and my priest, but which I must now share with you. It's a burden that I have carried with me since almost the day you were conceived. Before I met your dad, I had a teenage infatuation with Jake which developed into a relationship during our sophomore year at Dalhousie. Jake subsequently transferred to McGill, and time and distance took their toll on our love affair. We still spoke occasionally, but then I met your dad. I confessed to him that I had had a prior relationship. He never asked with whom, nor did we ever speak of it again. Dad was a much quieter man than Jake, and he was the kindest, most gentle person I had ever known. He gave me an engagement ring about a year after I graduated and we married the following September. After about a year, we planned a family, but I was unable to conceive. Tests indicated the fault was mine. In the meantime, Jake moved back to Lunenburg, and we would often meet and speak at the bank. Almost another year went by and Dr. Ellis decided to place me on hormone therapy. A couple of months after the therapy started, Dad was on an overnight trip to Halifax, and I attended the St. Christopher's Church Bazaar, which I had organized and which was a great success. Jake was there and I was in a celebratory mood. Perhaps I had too much champagne, but I certainly had my wits about me. Nevertheless, when Jake gave me a lift home, our being together again for a few hours was like déjà vu. We ended up in each other's arms. I'll leave the rest to your imagination. I rationalized that it could have happened to anyone, but then again, it shouldn't have happened to me. Your dad deserved better. A couple of months later, my doctor confirmed that I was pregnant. Dr. Ellis said that DNA testing would be the only sure way of determining the father, but that would have meant confessing to dad and informing Jake. It would have destroyed your father and would have been a reason for Jake to continually intrude upon your life. Needless to say, I was in shock. I seriously considered terminating the pregnancy, but how could I explain that to my husband? After meeting several times with Father McCrory, he convinced me it was best to leave things as they were.

Jake once swore that I was the only woman he'd marry. It seems he plans to keep his promise. Lara . .this is the reason I have written you this letter. Jake has very few relatives. Thirty or so years from now, he may be a lonely old man with no one to look after his interests. I ask you to use your judgement and intelligence to make his final years comfortable. No one but God Himself knows if I deprived Jake of the joy of knowing his daughter; show some interest in his welfare and allow him the occasional pleasure of your company. I love you, my sweet angel, with all my heart and soul. May the Lord bless you and keep you and dad in good health. Tell dad over and over again how much you need his love . . . as much as he needs yours.

Your loving mom.

Hilda felt the blood drain from her face. She looked up at Lara and reached for her arm.

"I'm glad I'm sitting. You would have had to pick me up off the floor."

"Hilda, just think about it for a moment; I lost my mother, and five days later, when I read this letter, I may have lost my dad too."

"Has Father McCrory or Doc Ellis ever spoken to you about this?"

"Nope, they wouldn't betray a confidence. We've never spoken to each other on the subject, and they're unaware that I know. Hilda, my mom wanted to know the truth, but she wasn't able. Even if I were able, I doubt if I'd have the courage to seek it out."

"Lara, I've just read something awesome. Trust my silence. I promise to carry this to my grave."

"I believe you, sweetheart, but there may come a time when I'll need your support on all of this. It's the kind of thing I've got to face sooner or later. It's too deeply implanted in my mind to simply sweep under the carpet. Please put the letter through the paper shredder over there under the table. It was stupid of me to keep it this long. I should have destroyed it years ago. Can you imagine if something had happened to me and my dad was given the contents of my safety deposit box?"

FORTY NINE

That evening, after a light supper and with Jennie fast asleep, Lara said, "Let's talk in the living room. I want to tell you of a decision I've made about Toronto."

She settled in her favorite chair and watched Hilda pour the wine. Once again she thoughtfully observed her lover:

'Beautiful Hilda, so much suffering and heartache, and yet look at her, a person full of empathy and compassion. A carbon copy of Mavis. I love her now more than ever. She fills me with the same warmth and excitement I felt when we were teenagers.'

"Hilda, I've decided to put the condo up for sale. I took a long-range view of my life, and I can't see myself living without you and Jennie."

"My God, stop! I want to hug you and kiss you. How many times have I told you the same since you came back? Come September, we'll be a happy family of four."

"Well, the fourth member is certainly anxious to get out. It doesn't seem to want to wait that long."

"Lara, caressing your stomach and feeling the baby moving about is a spiritual experience for me."

"Is that what it's doing, just moving about? Feels more like football practice in the dark. I'm not getting much sleep. Now, about the condo,…Jake has already renewed my mortgage, so I'm not under any pressure. I'm going to give it to an agent in Toronto and hope for an acceptable offer."

"Hey, I'm in ecstasy!" They raised their glasses. "Here's to us and to everyone we love. But seriously, this is a major career decision. I know you and I'm sure you've spoken with your company in Toronto."

"I talked with them on several occasions. Officially I'm on maternity leave. In any case, they told me there'll always be a place for me if I should ever come back."

"Aha, I guess I'm not the only one who thinks you're special."

"Actually, I was more than a little surprised when they made that offer. The way things are now, though, I can't ever see myself going back. To change the subject, what's happening with our parents? Dad complained to me he doesn't see enough of your mom. He's got it real bad. I think he's rushing her a little."

"That's right. She told me he is and she loves it. They're like a couple of young lovers. But there's an interesting situation going on. Your dad thinks that it would be inappropriate for them to be together at his home out of deference to past family memories. Mom feels the same way about her house."

"Hilda, whatever they decide about where they're gonna live, I can tell you that my dad's too straight and conservative to have an extended relationship outside of marriage. I'm certain he has that in mind."

"Look, mom is crazy about him and I'm sure she'd like to make it permanent. But there's one big obstacle, and that's Danny. Did it occur to you she doesn't want your dad to feel that he may be taking on more than a wife?"

"What you say may be true. I wonder though if they haven't already discussed it."

"I hope you're right."

"Well, dad's always been a careful planner. He's also highly principled. I think he's addressing the situation with Danny as a challenge and as further proof of his feelings about Mavis."

"It wouldn't surprise me. Mom thinks he's a very unusual man. In the meantime, they spend their intimate moments on the boat."

Lara laughed. "How exciting, but what happens when winter comes? The boat's heated, but if there's a snowstorm, they could be trapped for days."

They burst into laughter. More wine was consumed, a few more toasts to their parents were made, and they eventually fell asleep harmonizing their old songs.

FIFTY

Beautiful Maritime weather persisted, at times as long as a week without a threat of rain. Arnie's Café was more popular than ever. Mavis brought in a four-piece band on weekends, and it became the 'in place' for the college crowd from as far away as Prince Edward Island and New Brunswick. The menu was upgraded and Georgie showed off some of his exotic dishes to the Canadian and American tourists. Good summer help was abundant, and the servers were bright and eager college students.

Hilda and Lara couldn't recall a happier time. They watched Jennie progress and planned for the new baby. It was a full-time, happy adventure for both women. Hilda pampered her expanding lover and forbade her to do any heavy work around the house. Back at Arnie's, Mavis worked longer hours but enjoyed it more than ever. Jim made himself useful when visiting the café by offering Georgie kitchen help when it was unusually busy. Alma and Danny were the mainstays out front. The anxiety the boy had suffered in Arnie's presence disappeared. Danny was happy in his job and often volunteered a double shift on exceptionally busy weekends. Uncle Jake underwent the angiogram but managed to avoid a bypass, settling instead for an arterial stent.

***

On a hot, humid evening, Lara stopped over at her dad's home to say hello. No one was in, but as she returned to the car, a voice from across the street called her name.

"Lara, I'm over here. C'mon over and join us."

Uncle Jake, Bill Gallant and her dad were seated on the Inspector's front porch lifting beer mugs in the sweltering heat. She crossed over, pulled up a chair and commented,

"Such a small town; all this talent gathered in one place and all they're doing is quaffing beer. Tsk, tsk, what a waste of brain power."

Jake laughed.

"We'll take that as a compliment; I'm referring to the brain power."

Gallant countered,

"Don't be fooled by our apparent inactivity, we're sitting here solving the world's problems."

Jim asked,

"Lara, how you're doing and how are Hilda and the baby?"

"Fine, Dad, all is well. I feel like a horse ready to foal. This heat doesn't help. Speaking of solving problems, rumor has it our Inspector here is making great progress with his investigation. Is that true, Bill? Am I allowed to ask?"

"Well, you might as well hear it from me. After sewing the pieces together, we're of the opinion that an international cartel of criminals got Arnie's number and did him in, together with at least one other individual. I can't talk any more about it at this time."

Lara exclaimed, "Bill, if I were in your place, I'd send them a thank-you note. I must admit though, I thought for sure it would be a jealous husband or an abandoned girlfriend."

The Inspector laughed.

"You ladies are all romanticists. In my professional experience, money is a far greater cause of crime then love."

"Maybe so, but a lot of women were probably happy about Arnie's sudden demise. As a matter of fact, I believe I bumped into one of them at the cemetery right after Arnie's funeral."

Bill Gallant was surprised.

"Are you serious, Lara? Who was she? Did she talk to you?

"I was getting into my car to leave. I was the last one on the parking lot. If you recall, it was very foggy and damp that morning. I happened to glance back in the direction of the burial and noticed this woman coming out the mist and walking over to the plot. She stooped over and starting talking to the grave. She spoke loud enough for me to hear, but I couldn't make out what she was saying. I can tell you though, her words were angry and her tone was abusive. It had started to drizzle so I walked over to offer her a lift back to town.

She must have thought she was alone because I think I startled her. She thanked me anyway and said that today was a special one and she didn't mind the rain at all. I mentioned this to Mavis and Hilda, and we all agreed she sounded strange."

Gallant put his mug down abruptly.

"Do you know who she was? Can you describe her to me?"

"I never saw her before, but I can tell you that she was beautiful. She had shining black hair, unusual green eyes and skin like ivory. She was really gorgeous and without a stitch of makeup."

Jake was impressed.

"How could you notice all these things in such a brief encounter?"

Lara laughed.

"Uncle Jake, let's just say it's my nature."

"Gentlemen and lady," Gallant announced, "I'm certain you'll survive five or ten minutes without my enthralling company. I've got to make a few phone calls."

Gallant reappeared a short while later.

"Jake, I've got to cancel tomorrow's lunch. I'm going out of town in the morning," He turned to Lara,

"Look, I want to thank you for being so observant. You've been a great help. I'm glad you dropped around."

"You see, gentlemen," Lara observed, "very few problems can be solved without a woman being involved."

Jake intervened, "Yep, and we'd have very few problems if it weren't for them."

She shot him the dirty look he expected and then turned to Gallant.

"Inspector, I've got to call Hilda. Will you show me to your phone?"

She followed him into the house but startled him when she suddenly grabbed his arm.

"Bill, I don't need the phone. I just want to speak with you in private for a minute. I know it's none of my business but since my remarks were obviously the reason for your sudden change of plans for tomorrow, can I try to read your mind and share a hunch with you?"

"Go ahead. I've learned that nothing you say will surprise me."

"If you're going out of town on account of that woman I described, I'd like you to tell me just how important she is."

"Lara, how can any of this concern you? I'll only say it involves Arnie."

"That's precisely why. I have a feeling that I may know who that woman is and why she behaved the way she did at the cemetery."

"This is most unusual, . . . Lara, off the record, her name is Phyllis Maitland. Her husband died a short while ago after being in a coma for years. He was a victim of Arnie Benson's violent nature. You met her at the cemetery. I just called her and arranged to see her again tomorrow. I want to know why she attended the funeral and why she lied to me about never being in Lunenburg."

"Bill, Hilda told me the whole story of that incident in Halifax at that hotel bar. I want to ask a favor of you. I have no idea what you're going to come back with, but before you act upon it, please talk to me. I have my own victim's impact story about Arnie that I've never fully revealed to anyone. If you allow me to share it with you, I'm certain you'll agree it was worth hearing."

"I don't understand what you have in mind, but O.K., I'll talk to you when I get back."

The group joked and drank for another while, eventually parting company. Lara walked her father across the street. They sat on the porch and held hands.

"Sweetheart, what do you think of me selling this house? You realize, of course, that if you want it for yourself, then it's yours."

"Dad, let's speak first about marriage. I presume that's why you want to sell. Hilda and I talked about it, and I've mentioned this before. You and Mavis complement each other. Whenever we see you folks together, you're both radiating warmth. Is it true, or is it our imagination?"

"You're probably right. At times, I think I was as happy as this with your mother, but it's so long ago, I can't remember. All I can say is that we enjoy each other's company. We can sit and talk for hours."

"Then don't wait. Do something about it. These mutual feelings are kinda' rare. Hold onto them and don't let them slip away. And if you're thinking about mom, I know she'd agree."

"But Lara, what about the houses? Mavis would like to sell hers and buy one together. That makes sense to me, but I want you to have final say on this one. It's a big house, and it could be quite comfortable for you, Hilda and the children."

"Dad, go ahead and sell. Hilda's put a lot of work and a fair amount of money into her place. It's real cosy."

"Lara, I could talk to you for hours, but you look bushed. It's past your baby's bedtime. He'll be complaining soon."

"Did you say 'he'? That was a Freudian slip. I'll do my best for a grandson, but I'm afraid it's out of my hands. But don't fret, I'm young and I can have another one or two."

"Listen, I'll settle for a healthy baby girl on one condition: she's gotta look exactly like you."

"Dad, you're prejudiced. I love you. Have a good night. I'm taking off."

FIFTY ONE

Around 7:00 the following morning, Bill Gallant boarded the ferry to Charlottetown and drove directly to RCMP headquarters for a short meeting with the detachment chief, Hal Ross.

"Hal, thanks for allowing me to horn in on you. As I mentioned on the phone, this case involves a lot of acquaintances in my home town."

"No problem, Bill. Here, I've prepared the search warrant. Are you sure you don't want another constable with you?"

"No thanks. I must tell you, though, if this Maitland woman were as dangerous as she is beautiful, I'd take the whole detachment along, fully armed."

Phyllis's home reminded Gallant of the Maritime architecture of yesteryear. A narrow curved walk led to her front door, and a well-tended vegetable garden extended back from the sidewalk. She greeted him wearing a plain black dress. Once again, Gallant was overwhelmed by her beauty, his attention drawn to her green eyes and the elegant black hair that reflected highlights from the midday sun. He greeted her politely and presented the search warrant.

"Come in, Inspector, I've nothing to hide."

"Mrs. Maitland, may we sit for a while and talk a little over coffee? I'd like to get an idea of the impact these events had upon your family."

Gallant was looking for signs of intense emotion, hate, vengeance, anything which, nurtured for an extended period, could evoke a lethal response from a relative or friend of a murder victim.

"Mrs. Maitland, would you please recount again what happened that evening, and then elaborate how these unfortunate events impinged on your life in the subsequent years?"

Phyllis looked at him strangely. This was the last question she expected from someone seeking to pin a murder on her.

"You surprise me, Inspector. I was always under the impression that the Canadian justice system was more concerned with rehabilitating violent criminals than showing any interest or compassion for their victims."

"Mrs. Maitland, it would seem that way when you read the newspapers, and it's true to a certain extent. We feed, clothe and house our criminals in comfortable quarters with civilized amenities. We educate them and oversee their health. The sad part is that we do little to alleviate the suffering of their victims. Please tell me about your life before and after the incident."

"Inspector, Harvey and I were married for just over three years. We were both from middle-income Maritime stock. I worked while I was in high school and actually met him while employed at McDonald's. We were good students and managed to graduate university using our savings and scholarships. We married soon after and were broke following our honeymoon. We got jobs in industry, and Harvey rose quickly up the corporate ladder at Campbell's Brewery. He was a very innovative salesperson and had a wonderful personality. In less than three years, he was promoted to vice president of marketing and elected a member of the board. I started out as a medical representative for a pharmaceutical company and eventually worked my way up to supervisor of marketing. Inspector, we had a great future. We were celebrating Harvey's promotion in Halifax with two couples from our college days and I had just become pregnant. One evening, we were all seated at a hotel sports bar in Halifax. Harvey was in the men's room when Arnie Benson walked up quietly behind me, slipped his hands under my sweater and grabbed at my breasts. At the same time, he put his mouth to my neck and bit me. I screamed. I can still smell his filthy breath. Just then, Harvey returned and shouted,

"Get your hands off my wife!"

"Benson shouted back, fuck off, she's too pretty for a wife, she's a whore working the bar!"

"Harvey lashed out and punched him hard on the nose. Benson started bleeding heavily. When he saw his blood, he went crazy. This monster knocked my husband to the floor and started kicking him in the head. Benson was lame and wore a heavy orthopedic boot; he kept pounding Harvey's head with it, screaming hysterically. Our friends jumped on him and tried to pull him away, but he was like a wild animal. It took four or five men to overpower him. Harvey was lying unconscious on the floor, covered with blood. But Benson broke away and started kicking him again. It was surreal, worse than anything you'd see in a violent movie. His facial features were unrecognizable. The doctors were amazed he survived. I passed out and when I awoke in the hospital three or four hours later, I couldn't recall a thing. The next morning, they came into the room and broke the news. Harvey was in a coma, and I had lost the baby."

She arose abruptly from the table, opened the fridge and poured herself a glass of water. Her face was expressionless. She dabbed her lips with a tissue, sat down and continued.

"I had a nervous breakdown and went to live with my parents. My mother quit her teaching job in order to look after me. She lost many of her retirement benefits because of it. My dad continued working, but he was never the same. He suffered a fatal heart attack the following year. Harvey's parents were devastated. He was an only son. His mother was chronically ill, and his dad was a reformed alcoholic with a good-paying job as an administrator with the city of Halifax. Needless to say, he went back to drinking and lost his job. I eventually returned to the labor force and brought my husband home for a couple of years. I had been visiting him at the long-term nursing facility, but it was very far and going there every day after work became too much of a burden. I brought him back and my mother took care of him. My mother passed away a year ago, and Harvey went back to the nursing home."

She paused and took another sip of water.

"I feel like I'm only partially alive. I see, I hear, I carry out my basic bodily functions, and that's it. I don't live, I exist. Inspector, it's hard to believe one individual could inflict so much death and misery on so many people."

She paused and wiped her eyes.

"So, Inspector, you now have my recent history. I keep up-to-date with things going on in our country. Forgive me, but my feelings are that Canada, in many respects, is a criminal's paradise. Three teenagers break into a home on the outskirts of Montreal, bludgeon a pastor and his wife to death with baseball bats, and three years later a couple of them are free and committing crimes on the streets of Toronto. If a crime reporter mentions their names in the papers, even though they're now adults, the reporter may go to jail. Surely you recall that nightclub fire in 1972 in Montreal that killed thirty-seven young people. The perpetrators were sentenced to life imprisonment, but just eleven years later they were all walking around free on the streets of Montreal. Think of it, eleven years for murdering thirty-seven young people in the prime of their lives. Repeat sexual predators are released time and again after serving light sentences. Drunk drivers who kill innocent pedestrians are convicted of manslaughter and freed in a couple years for good behavior. I once read of a woman whose daughter was strangled by a live-in boyfriend. Just four years later, she came face-to-face with him on a Montreal subway train. She passed out in a state of shock. It's incredible. We even try to force our policies upon other countries. American criminals fleeing charges of murder try to make their way to Canada because they know that if they're captured, Canada will not extradite them without written assurance from the U.S. that they will not be executed. Inspector, our system is a joke, a sad, sad joke."

"Mrs. Maitland, listening to you and with what you've personally experienced, I have nothing but sympathy. It's utterly frustrating for law officers like myself to have to protect the public from the same criminals over and over again."

Gallant wanted to ask her what she thought about the death penalty, if it were legal, could she imagine herself being the executioner after all she had suffered? It was now obvious to him where she stood on punishment and perhaps even revenge.

"Mrs. Maitland, I must carry out this search warrant. I won't be long. I'll make the rounds of the house, and I'll be careful not to leave anything in disorder. You don't have to accompany me, I'll do it alone and reasonably quick."

"Take your time, I usually occupy myself in my garden at this time of the afternoon."

He took out his pad and looked for the items he had noted, a black beret, gloves, sunglasses, and possibly a blonde wig. He went through the closets and the drawers and examined numerous documents and papers in her office filing cabinet. They were virtually all medically related. He was about to end the search when he noticed a heavy red velvet curtain. He presumed it covered the entrance to another closet, but when he pulled it aside, he could make out a darkened, narrow staircase which led to a second floor attic. He hesitated, trying to decide whether to go up.

He could imagine the accumulated dust and debris in such an old house. He climbed the stairs, pushed on the door and was surprised at how easily it opened. He turned on his flashlight and looked around. Antique items were everywhere; they held the history of four or five generations of an old Maritime family. Tucked away in the corner beneath some blankets was an ancient looking trunk. Gallant lifted the blankets and opened the lid. It was a revelation, an adventure into the past. There were several well-preserved wedding gowns, meticulously wrapped, together with bundles of old letters dating back to World Wars I and II. There were albums of cracked and faded photos. Gallant was always fascinated by old gravestones and ancient history; he now found himself digging deeper, more out of curiosity than for his real purpose. As he neared the bottom, he lifted two old photo albums and came upon a high school graduation yearbook dating back to 1930. Beneath the book was a large Havana cigar box tucked neatly into a corner. He lifted it out, opened the lid and shone his light on the contents. Gallant was startled. The light beam fell upon a swastika embossed on a leather gun holster. He unsnapped it to reveal the Walther .25 calibre pistol. Beside the gun lay a leather pouch, similarly embossed, containing about thirty cartridges in addition to a spare clip holding seven more. To avoid smudging any fingerprints, he carefully handled the items with a handkerchief. He lifted the gun to his nose and sniffed the barrel. He knew immediately it had been fired recently. The cartridge clip in the gun was empty, but the number and calibre of the bullets found in Arnie's body was an exact match. He dusted off a stool with an old newspaper and sat down. Gallant fondled the holster, opening and snapping it closed several times. It had dried out and cracked over the years. He examined the cartridges and noted they were well lubricated. He shook his head in disbelief. He carefully placed all the items into his briefcase, closed the cigar box and replaced it in its former position. He closed the trunk and covered it carefully with the wrapped blankets. Gallant remained seated on the stool, pondering both the discovery and the situation when suddenly the attic lit up.

"Inspector, you missed the light switch on the wall. There's no point sitting in the dark."

Phyllis stood there, hands folded, a trace of a smile on her face. Gallant was surprised by her sudden appearance and her casual manner.

"Attics are interesting places, aren't they?" she continued. "I come up here every once in a while and recall the pleasant memories of my childhood. I escape for an hour or so into a former and better world."

"Mrs. Maitland, we have an attic at home, and I do the same. You're right, it brings back childhood memories. In the meantime, can we go back to your kitchen and talk a bit more?"

Bill Gallant was unaware that Phyllis had stood quietly in the dark attic for about ten minutes before turning on the lights. She had observed Gallant's discovery of the incriminating evidence and had watched him place everything into his briefcase.

Gallant sat down at the table facing her.

"Coffee or tea?" she asked.

"Thank you. I'll have coffee."

He marveled at her composure. Yet it shouldn't have surprised him. He thought of what her life had been since the incident. She had become impervious to shock and the unexpected. She was drained of all emotion. It was as she had described, she wasn't living, she was existing.

"Mrs. Maitland, although you denied it, I now know you did attend Arnold Benson's burial. What were your reasons? Your presence at the cemetery was what prompted my visit today."

Taken by surprise, she hesitated for a moment.

"I'm sorry, Inspector, but I couldn't help myself. I wanted to watch him being buried. I wanted to see this personification of evil placed in a hole in the ground with a ton of earth entrapping him. I wanted to be certain Arnold Benson will never hurt anyone again, as he hurt so many before me and probably after. Inspector, during the past few years and through various sources I acquired information which should have been given to the prosecution at the trial. I don't know if the military try to keep these things under wraps but Benson was a problem in the army. We had acquaintances in Special Forces and the rumors about him were mind-boggling. He raped a couple of soldier's wives; he claimed it was consensual sex. There were no witnesses and no DNA proof. Another woman on the base whom he was seeing swore that Arnie asked her to tamper with a rival's parachute. She refused, but the army dropped any further investigation. It was her word against his, and Benson had already been given a general discharge."

Bill exhaled a long sigh.

"It's been quite a day. Mrs. Maitland, your victim story is impressive. Do you have any plans to leave the country in the near future? Until we can clear this matter up, I'd like you to be available for further questioning if necessary."

She nodded in agreement. They sat in silence for a few long moments, maintaining eye contact, neither flinching. Gallant finally offered a smile and said,

"I'll be leaving now, but let me offer you some advice. Do not discuss this affair with anyone until you hear further on the matter."

It was a beautiful day for a leisurely drive. Gallant decided to return home via the Confederation Bridge.

**

The drive back to Lunenburg allowed time to ponder the situation. He wondered whether Phyllis Maitland had been alone with Arnie when he died. Did she have an accomplice? Did she have a friend or relative or perhaps a lover whom she convinced to commit the act? After speaking with her, all the evidence seemed to point to her and no one else. Her behavior today, cold and almost detached, convinced him she was capable of masterminding the whole event, singlehandedly. All the discreet enquiries indicated she had no close male friends. She was alone at Arnie's Café and in the hotel restaurant, and knowing Arnie, she was almost certainly alone in the hotel room with him. No, it must have been her and her alone.

Gallant thought, 'there's no doubt in my mind the markings on the bullets that killed Benson and those on the gun barrel will be a match.'

Meanwhile, Phyllis settled into her favorite chair and stared out the living room window. The RCMP now had ample evidence for an indictment. She knew enough about ballistics to conclude that Bill Gallant had what he needed to close the case. She had already lied to Gallant in a previous interview when she said that no one in her family owned a weapon. Even though Gallant had removed the evidence illegally, how could she question him about it?

She whispered to her late husband,

"Harvey, my love, I have no intention of ever spending time in prison. My darling, we may soon be together again."

FIFTY TWO

Bill Gallant arrived back in Lunenburg around 9:00 p.m. He had travelled for more than eight hours and it had been a tiring day. He decided to stop at Mario's for a light supper instead of bothering his housekeeper. He sat down at a quiet table and dialed Hilda's home.

"Hello, this is Inspector Gallant. Is Lara Cabot home this evening?"

"This is Lara. Hi, Inspector, I didn't expect your call so soon."

"Good evening Lara, I'm over at Mario's. I just got in from out of town. Would it be possible for me to hear what you have to say this evening? The rest of my week is taken up with a giant backlog. Can we do this thing tonight?"

"Inspector, you're a gentleman for keeping me in mind. I can be there in about fifteen minutes."

A short while later, Lara walked in and sought out Gallant at the back of the restaurant.

"Hello, Inspector. Thanks again for seeing me. You look as if you've had a tiring day, so I won't keep you for long. Can I speak while you're eating?"

"Certainly, pull up a chair."

"Bill, about four years ago I was a student at St. Mary's. I was doing well and was looking forward to a career in economics. As it happens, I had arranged to spend two days with Hilda. I never visited her or stayed over if Arnie was in town. I always felt uncomfortable in his presence. On this particular Friday night, Hilda unexpectedly had to replace Mavis's assistant who was off sick. Arnie was supposed to be in Halifax all weekend, but around nine o'clock he stumbled into the house, extremely drunk. He was cursing the weather, the traffic and everything else he could think of. He was surprised to see me and asked about Hilda. I told him she got called in unexpectedly and had to work until closing. I bade him goodnight and turned to get my things. He reached out, grabbed me and forcibly kissed me on the mouth. His odor nauseated me. I pushed his face away with all my strength but accidentally stuck my fingernail into his eye and it started to bleed. When he saw his blood, he went crazy. He screamed and cursed and smashed me in the face with his fist. I fell down, hit my head and must have been unconscious for a while because when I came to, I saw that he had taken off his coat and pants and was standing over me in his underwear. I thought I was having a nightmare. Then I saw the hunting knife in his hand. He held the point of the knife to my face and pressed his erection against my cheek. He screamed that if I didn't put it in my mouth he'd stick the knife in my eye. Through

clenched teeth, I yelled, "Kill me, kill me, you bastard."
He threw down the knife and hit me again with his fist.
I passed out, and when I awoke, I had adhesive tape
over my mouth and my hands were tied behind my
back. When I saw that my blouse and bra had been
ripped apart and I was naked from the waist down, I
passed out again. I woke in incredible pain. He had
forced himself into me. Bill, I was a virgin, and he tore
me apart."

Gallant had put down his knife and fork. Lara
was pale and trembling. Tears streamed down her
cheeks. She leaned her head forward, supporting it
on clenched fists, her body shaking convulsively. Bill
sat there frozen, enveloped by a feeling of disgust and
frustration. He made a valiant but unsuccessful effort to
hold back his own tears. He moved his glass of water
over to her and watched her sip it slowly, then took her
free hand and squeezed it gently.

"Perhaps you've told me enough, Lara. Let's leave it
for now."

"No, no, Bill. I can't go all through this thing again."
She poured water on a napkin and freshened her face.

"I watched him as he rested for a while, and then
he raped me again. He cursed and called me every
name you can imagine. I was a fucking dyke and a
filthy whore. Bill, I swear I begged Jesus to take me. I
pleaded with Him."

"Lara, Lara, Lara," he whispered and held her
hand tightly.

"Then, just like that, he untied my hands and simply
went upstairs without another word. He walked away
calmly, like he was going for a stroll. I tore off the tape,

dragged myself to the bathroom and splashed water all over me. When I saw myself in the mirror, I had to grab onto the sink to avoid collapsing. My cheek and lip were bright red and swollen, and one eye was almost closed. I had scratches all over my neck and chest, and my breasts had teeth marks where he had bitten me. I left the house, got into my car and drove to the Rape Center in Halifax. I was in terrible pain; I can't even recall the trip to the hospital."

Lara took another sip of water. Before Bill could comment, she continued.

"That was the end of the physical violence. The mental anguish was much more prolonged. I called my dad and told him I'd gone back to Halifax because I wasn't feeling well, but I forbade him to visit me. I was released the next afternoon and took a flight to Toronto. I checked into a hotel, called my dad again and told him I was transferring to another school and I'd call him again in a few days. We weren't close at the time, so he accepted everything without demanding an explanation. I guess he was just glad that I was in touch. It took me about ten days to recuperate sufficiently from the trauma and injuries. A little later on, I realized I must be pregnant. Coming from a Catholic family, entertaining the thought of an abortion was mind-wrenching. The local hospital referred me to a psychiatrist who put me on medication to treat a nervous breakdown. Bill, I couldn't possibly have lived for nine months with part of Arnie Benson in my body. I went ahead with the abortion."

"The following month, I went up to York University and signed into the MBA program. I passed my year at school and remained in therapy for almost two years. I managed to obtain copies of all the medical reports from Halifax and Toronto, including some DNA results. I have them all in a safe place. You're probably wondering why I didn't report the rape to the authorities. Well, my dad is a quiet guy, but I've seen him lose his temper. He would have killed Arnie and then spent years in jail. Hilda was my best friend, and she was two months pregnant. This would have destroyed both her and my dad. Lunenburg suddenly became too small for me to live a normal life. Although relocating to Toronto was a quick decision, I think it was the right thing to do at the time."

Lara had regained her composure a little and managed a smile.

"Now look at you, Inspector, you've hardly eaten anything, and your food is cold. I owe you a deluxe meal."

Gallant dabbed his forehead and eyes with his napkin, put it down and gripped Lara's wrists with both hands. He looked into her eyes and shook his head without uttering a word.

"Bill, it's hard to believe, but some good actually came from all of this. I'm a different person. I'm stronger now than I ever was, and this transformation has allowed me to make some recent decisions that would have been impossible for the old Lara. I guess every event in life is a learning experience, whether it's good or bad."

Gallant walked Lara to her car. As he held open the door, he leaned over and kissed her on the forehead.

"Lara, stories like yours make people in my business feel grossly inadequate and frustrated. For a few moments, we forget who we are and how we're expected to respect due process of law. Our immediate thought is to lash out and exact revenge. Fortunately, we soon come to our senses and realize the purpose of the law is, or at least should be, separating the criminal from the general population. Watching you relive those events, I couldn't help but regret calling you tonight. One thing I can assure you though is that it's provided much food for thought, and as tired as I am, I doubt if sleep will come easily tonight."

FIFTY THREE

When the doors of Maritime Bank opened at precisely 10:00 on Monday morning, the first client was Mavis Willis. She strode in and took a seat near Jake's office. He arrived about ten minutes later and greeted her with his usual kiss on both cheeks, a cultural carry-over from two years of living in Montreal.

"Mavis, this reminds me of the good old days. You always arrived at work before me."

"I loved my work then, but even more so, I enjoyed working for you. You were the best boss I ever had."

"Well, you were an unusual employee. You were so devoted to your job, some clients thought you were the bank Inspector."

"You exaggerate, but it makes me feel good. Jake, to change the subject, I'm going to need a temporary mortgage on a new home."

"That's a major decision, congratulations."

"Let me explain. Perhaps you noticed at the launch party that Jim Cabot and I were quite friendly. I know you well enough to tell you it's blossomed into a real romance. We've been seeing each other on a regular basis and we want to make it permanent. Jake, living together with Jim in my home or in his is out of the question for obvious reasons. You were my kids' godfather, you were my late husband's friend, you understand."

Jake was both surprised and a little perturbed. He had looked upon Mavis as a younger sister, and now it was suddenly brought home to him that perhaps she could have been more had he done something about it. It was déjà vu, Jim Cabot again marrying a woman that Jake admired.

"Yes Mavis, I certainly do understand. I kinda noticed you and Jim had become friendly. I didn't realize it had come this far."

"Jim's family and ours have been close for years. Neither of us ever considered another partner until about a month ago. It just happened. I think Hilda and Lara were working on this behind the scenes."

Jake forced a smile.

"You said 'temporary mortgage", I presume you'll need some bridge financing until your current home is sold?"

"Here's what happened, Jake. Jim is a real gentleman. He offered to buy another home and wouldn't hear of me contributing any of my money. He's very old-fashioned. I, on the other hand, felt that at this stage in our lives we should share the responsibilities. Besides, I've got Danny with me; he's my son, and feeding and housing him is my responsibility, not Jim's."

"Mavis, from what you tell me it sounds better than a partnership. You don't have a mortgage on your present home, so let's just make it a temporary loan. Go ahead, make a decision, and don't worry, the money will be available."

Mavis hurried over to Arnie's for the noon rush. She was greeted by Baby Face Romeo.

"Mavis, I've got a great story for you. You gotta listen to this."

"Do I have a choice? Go ahead and get it over with."

"This Newfie gal is sitting at a bar, and a guy offers her a drink. She thanks him but turns him down and says she doesn't drink 'cause alcohol affects her legs. The guy asks, "Does it make them swell?" She smiles sweetly and says, "No, it makes them spread.'"

"Romeo, one more of those and I'll drag you to the kitchen and have Georgie wash your mouth with soap. Now finish your beer and go home."

Mavis went to the rear to change. Georgie greeted her.

"Mavis, I got the Halifax paper here. Take a look at this headline story on page one."

CAYMAN CORONER RULES HOMICIDE IN LOCAL ATTORNEY'S DEATH

An autopsy performed on the late Anthony Manolo, a Halifax attorney, determined that the victim was dead before entering the water off George Town in Grand Cayman. The police in both Halifax and Lunenburg are interested in this latest development.

"Mavis, this is international stuff. They mentioned Lunenburg. I wonder if it has something to do with Arnie's death. Do you think he knew that lawyer?"

Mavis sat there, shaking her head.

"Georgie, do you think Arnie's associations could have placed Hilda and the baby at risk? You know, like threats or blackmail or something?"

"Relax, Mavis, you've read too many murder mysteries. These are sophisticated people. They're not messy. They don't go after innocent women and children. Everything's done with surgical precision."

Around lunchtime, the kitchen phone rang; it was Jim Cabot.

"Hi Mavis, it's me. How are you, sweetheart?"

"Hi there, I was just going to call you. Jake gave his blessings for a new home. I told the agent we're ready to sign the listings. She told me there was an unusual opportunity that just came up on a property on your street."

"Sounds exciting, we'll see it together tomorrow. I'll come over tonight for supper around six or seven. I love you."

The next evening, Mavis and Jim rang the girls' doorbell. Hilda greeted them.

"You're too late for the main course, folks, how about dessert?"

Mavis exclaimed, "never mind, we're too excited to eat. We just came from this property on Montague Street not far from Jim's house. It's a gem. It belongs to a retired diplomat who's in a nursing home in Toronto. It hasn't been lived in for months, but there's a resident housekeeper who keeps the place spotless and in move-in condition. Believe it or not, even the beds are made and covered with plastic sheeting. They're leaving most of the furniture. Real elegant stuff. We'd really like you and Lara to see it before it gets dark."

"Forget the dirty dishes, Lara," Hilda shouted. "We're going over to see a house."

They parked their cars in the driveway of an old and beautiful looking home. From outside, it looked more like a big-city stately residence than the standard wooden Maritime design. The stone and brick construction had an air of permanence. The interior walls were a rich wooden finish with handsome carvings and trim. There was an ornate staircase which led to two upstairs bedrooms. A small library held leather-bound editions on dark oak shelving. The kitchen was yesteryear but evidently in good working order. The dining and living areas were spacious and the furniture had been well maintained. There was even a beautiful Steinway grand piano; it wasn't included but nevertheless negotiable.

"Dad, this place has character. How do you like it, Mavis?"

"It reminds me of our old house in St. John's. It must be at least seventy-five years old, but I'd say it could outlast most homes in Lunenburg."

Jim offered,

"Hell, it's like a fort. They certainly don't build this way anymore. I looked into the cellar earlier today. I was surprised; no damp odor, lovely clean walls and no cracks in the foundation. There's a modern furnace and the darn house is air conditioned. It's a one car garage, but the floor is clean and smooth, and the door has a remote control."

"Everyone seems to agree. Jim, shall we make an offer?"

Jim looked at the girls.

"Well, what do you think? It hasn't been on the market very long."

"Dad, if you don't take it, someone else surely will. Hilda, what's your opinion?"

"I would grab it. It looks like a one-of-a-kind to me. It seems out of place in Lunenburg."

"Great," Jim exclaimed.

"Mavis, let's call the agent tonight and make an appointment."

They walked back to the cars. Lara pulled Jim aside and whispered,

"Hey Dad, the living room is a very nice size. It's ideal for a small private wedding."

Mavis overheard the remark.

"Hilda just told me the same thing. You girls are a couple of scheming witches."

"Lara, I'm reminding you again about the Labor Day Race this Saturday. We'll have a real picnic on board, courtesy of Georgie. Jake is joining us too. Hilda, you kept turning me down each time we sailed this summer; will you reconsider?"

"Thanks, Mr. Cabot, but you wouldn't want me on board. I'd spoil it for everyone. I'd be hanging over the rail, sick as a dog and hoping to die. I didn't inherit my mom's cast-iron stomach."

Lara chimed in,

"Never mind, you inherited her brains and her looks . . . that's more important."

The following afternoon, Mavis and Jim signed three agreements with their real estate agent, two offers to sell and one to purchase. The market was spotty but both homes were in good condition and the agent was confident she could move them fairly soon. Because the newly listed house's owner was now in Toronto, in poor health and with no family in the Maritimes to look after his interests, the agents told the couple that their modest offer on the house stood a good chance for acceptance.

FIFTY FOUR

Jim awoke early on Saturday and was greeted by a troublesome looking bright red sky. He grabbed a cup of coffee and drove down to the marina where he inspected the boat in detail, checking the engine, the rigging and the anchor lines. Concerned about the possibility of heavy winds, he rechecked the furling lines.The rest of the crew showed up around 11.00 a.m. with Mavis bringing the food` and Jake the liquid refreshments. Lara's burden was the most unwieldy—a large belly holding a very active baby. Jim was a bit concerned.

"Lara, I'm a bit worried about you going out today. It could get a little rough."

"Dad, I love watching the Labor Day Race. I wish we could participate like we used to."

Mavis called out from below decks,

"Don't worry, Jim, I'll keep an eye on her. She's going to sit quiet and behave herself."

They dropped anchor near the race committee boat and settled back for a light lunch. Jake peered through his binoculars, scanning each boat that sailed into the starting area.

"Who do you see out there?" asked Jim. "Any of our old gang?"

"Skipper, I'm making a mental note of all the boats I financed. It's more than half the fleet. It's better than even money that one of my team will win."

Lara remarked,

"Uncle Jake, you're a banker even when the bank is closed. Mavis, these shrimps are delicious. Is this dip one of Georgie's secrets?"

"Georgie's full of surprises. He can turn out a mean burger or an elegant coq au vin with trimmings that are actually photogenic."

"What else do you see that's interesting?" Jim asked, "bathing beauties?"

"It's really unbelievable, folks. I recognize a few skippers out there who struggle to meet the mortgage payments on their homes, and they're sailing gorgeous looking boats."

Everyone laughed. Jim commented,

"It's a matter of priorities. What's more important to a sailor, his house or his boat? You should give up financing homes and just do boats. Maybe it's not as risky."

It was a beautiful sight, the large white sails shifting from side to side, the boats gracefully turning and zigzagging to avoid each other, the shouting of orders and the sounds of the ratcheting winches that hauled in or released the lines controlling the sails.

The race committee boat was anchored at one end of the starting line. Ten minutes before the start, their crew sounded a warning call from a shotgun and raised a small white flag. Five minutes before the start, the white flag was replaced by a blue, again with a shotgun blast. The boats moved closer and closer to the start line as each sought out a strategic position. Five minutes later, the gun sounded again and a red flag replaced the blue. The race was on! Virtually all the boats had lined up, pointing in the same general direction, about forty-five degrees away from the wind. They commenced their journey, turning from side to side as they edged forward to reach the first anchored race buoy.

Lunenburg Lady pulled up anchor and followed the progress of the fleet from the outer perimeter of the course. Jim recognized several of his old competitors.

"Hey, I see guys we used to race against. Hell, some are way older than me and they're still at it."

"Dad, doesn't that tell you something? We used to beat most of them in our old boat. I'll bet we still can."

Mavis joined in.

"I sailed almost every weekend with my dad. I'd like to compete again next summer. Jim, you'd better be in shape or I'll take over as skipper."

"You're already skipper in more ways than one. Doesn't bother me at all."

The last leg of the race was exciting. Giant spinnaker sails of various colors and designs flew from the bow of each boat and paraded down the final leg in a blaze of color. Another blast from the gun announced the first boat over the finish line. One by one the fleet crossed, just as the wind started to pick up.

The humidity had noticeably increased. Jim watched as dark clouds began moving in from the southwest.

"Jake, look over there, it looks like a rain squall on the horizon. Better bring the foul weather gear up on deck. Mavis, let's move all the dishes and food below decks."

Lara had gone below more than half an hour earlier, and Mavis wondered why she hadn't returned. She stuck her head into the cabin.

"Lara, are you O.K.?"

"Mavis, can you come down here, please?"

Mavis went below and found her lying stretched out in the V-berth.

"Lara, are you O.K.? What's happening?"

"Mavis, please tell Dad we should get back as quickly as possible. I think I'm about to become a mother. I'm soaking wet. God, what a mess. I've even had a couple of contractions."

Mavis dashed up on deck and grabbed Jim's arm.

"Better get back to shore real quick, you're going to be a grandfather sooner than you expected. Give me your cell phone. I'm calling 911. Let's hope we make it in time."

Jim and Jake looked at each other, wide-eyed and startled.

"Jake, tell me this is not happening! Shit, let's get the anchor up."

Jim started the engine and turned the boat into the wind. He set the autopilot while Jake moved quickly about the deck and closed all the hatches. He released the main halyard, dropped the mainsail to the deck. Jim grabbed the furling line and wound up the jib. He turned the boat toward shore, reset the autopilot and went to the mast to help Jake. They folded the mainsail, tied it, and dropped down into the cockpit. They donned their foul weather gear as Jake grabbed the binoculars and looked out in the direction of the incoming weather.

"This squall's a biggie, Jim. It's already hit some of the boats. Jesus, I've lost sight of most of them in the rain."

"Put on your life jacket and hand me mine. Tell them down below that everything is fine and that we'll be kicked around a bit. I figure we're about four miles offshore. We should be able to make it back in about an hour."

"The weather came in pretty fast . . . Jim, some of the guys were caught with their sails up when it hit."

The noise of the wind and the rain pounding the deck was deafening.

"Jake, I'll be O.K. up here; go below and see how they're managing."

Jake eased himself down the companionway as *Lunenburg Lady* rolled gently in the surf.

He put on a reassuring smile.

"Ladies, the skipper wants to know if you're O.K."

"We're doing fine," said Mavis. "I got through to 911 and they should be waiting at the marina. Are things rough on deck? How's Jim doing?"

"He's O.K. Lara, what about you?"

"So far I'm O.K., I think. It's a new experience for me."

"Well, it's more exciting than a hospital bed."

Mavis had taken two bath towels and spread them beneath Lara. She had stuffed pillows between Lara and the bulkheads of the V-berth to prevent her from rolling from side to side.

"It's getting cool down here. Lara, you gotta keep warm. Lemme throw this blanket over you."

The pounding of the rain on the cabin roof was nerve-wracking, and the boat was hit by rolling waves on her port quarter. It made for an uncomfortable ride, but the vessel wasn't too difficult to control. Jim had taken over the steering from the autopilot and was zigzagging his course to keep the boat as steady as possible. Mavis was tense. The frequency of Lara's contractions had increased, and she wondered if they'd make it on time. She shouted out,

"Jake, ask Jim how much longer to shore."

Lara squeezed Mavis's hand.

"I must be dilating, the pain is really bad. Hilda told me you delivered babies in med school, I hope you haven't forgotten how."

"Lara, just squeeze those overhead handgrips as tight as you can. Let's get your jeans off. It's time I had a look."

Jake shouted down the companionway,

"The marina's in sight and we'll tie up in about twenty minutes. I can make out the ambulance parked near the dock."

Lara clenched her fists in excruciating pain.

"Geez, Mavis, I'm being ripped apart."

"Hang in, even if the head starts showing and we're still on the boat, don't worry: I know what to do. Just be calm. With the ambulance crew close by, you and the baby will be fine. Try to breathe slowly and deeply."

Lara's face was contorted with pain. Mavis applied a cold cloth to her forehead. The next twenty minutes seemed like hours. Lara whispered a prayer of thanks when she heard her father's voice shouting landing instructions and felt the boat bump up against the wharf. Jake and Jim threw the mooring lines to the dock boys and grabbed the stretcher from the waiting ambulance crew. Fortunately, the rain had abated somewhat. The medics leaped aboard and went below decks. They placed Lara on a stretcher and threw a waterproof cover over her. In fewer than ten minutes, they were on their way to the hospital.

Lara grabbed Mavis's arm.

"Gawd, I think I'm going to have it right here in the ambulance."

Mavis looked at the medic and whispered,

"I think I can see the head."

"There's no real problem," he replied, "we're only about seven minutes from the hospital. At this point, she won't have it in the ambulance. Let things take their course. There won't be anything we can't handle before getting her to the case room."

Jim and Jake followed in Jake's car.

"This is all like déjà vu," said Jim. "It's seems like yesterday that I followed the ambulance to the hospital when Celia was giving birth."

"Lucky she didn't start having it on your boat," he laughed. "If I remember, in those days you were sailing a fifteen-foot dinghy."

At the hospital, Jim got up every few minutes and paced back and forth in the corridor. Mavis was in the case room but came out about half an hour later.

"Well, Lara made a quick start, but things have slowed down a bit. The baby's taking a recess. They expect her to give birth within the hour. Dr. Ellis is out of town, but the chief resident says everything's under control. I'm going to call Hilda, I think she'd like to be here."

Twenty minutes later, Hilda rushed in.

"I can't believe it. Mr. Cabot, you've got to be excited. I'm beside myself. Is my mom with her?"

Just then, Mavis and the resident strolled into the waiting room, grinning.

"Where's the proud father?" he asked.

Mavis turned to him.

"Doctor, I forgot to mention, actually there is no father."

"Well, well," he exclaimed, "haven't had that happen for a couple thousand years. Sounds like another biblical event."

Jim burst out,

"Doctor, you mean it's a boy?"

"It sure is. Congratulations. He's just under six pounds, but he's a feisty little guy."

Jim felt shaky and moved over to a chair. Mavis congratulated him and kissed him. He got to his feet again and shook hands with the doctor.

"Thank you, Doctor. Thanks again. By the way, I just want to clarify a point. I'm the grandfather; the father is an intelligent and handsome laboratory specimen."

The waiting room erupted in laughter.

Two days later, Lara and the baby were at home. He was a sturdy, active little fellow with an insatiable appetite. His shock of brown hair and his blue eyes were more Jim's coloring than Lara's. There was general disagreement whom he resembled, but that didn't bother Jim at all. His prayers had been answered;

he was blessed with a beautiful, healthy grandson, and nothing else mattered.

Jim thought, 'I intend to unpack those trophies, shine them up and place them over the fireplace. And I plan to be around to share the mantelpiece with my grandson.'

FIFTY FIVE

Bill Gallant was undergoing a new experience. Sleep usually came easily to him, but the images of Lara's encounter with Arnold Benson followed him day and night. He had personally performed and confirmed the ballistic tests and yet, almost a week later, he had still not reported the results, nor the details of the search of Phyllis Maitland's home. For the first time in his career, he was defying both the law and RCMP regulations.

'Why am I doing this?' he demanded of himself. 'With the evidence I've got, I can go ahead and procure an indictment. Why am I stalling? What's holding me back?'

On the following Friday afternoon, upon leaving the office, his secretary called him on the intercom.

"Inspector, I have a long-distance call from your daughter in Boston. Can you pick it up now?"

"Yes, by all means, thanks..... Hello Hazel, how are you? How are the girls doing?

"Dad, you promised to come to Boston this summer. You're now a couple of months late, and the girls keep asking for you. I wonder if they'll still remember their Gramps."

The remark was a jolt. Bill suddenly realized how current events in his job had pushed the important things in his life aside.

"Hazel, you know something, I've just made a decision. I've got to get away from lots of things. To heck with it. The girls don't miss me as much as I miss them. I'll be down in a few days. Just let me clear up some stuff here."

Gallant spent most of the weekend writing his final report on the Arnold Benson case. He would submit it to the head office on Monday. After studying the conclusion and acting upon the evidence, HQ would censor out any confidential or sensitive information and then issue a statement to the news media.

On Monday morning, Bill Gallant handed the document to his secretary to send on to Halifax. He knew that this was the last report he would file in his career. He closed the office door, sat down at his desk and wrote a letter of resignation to Les Howland in Halifax. Gallant leaned back in his chair, closed his eyes and allowed his mind to wander back over the years. Professionally, it had been a rewarding and glorious time. He had accomplished great things, solved numerous cold and complicated cases and garnered much respect from his peers. Nature had robbed him of sharing his remaining years with a spouse who couldn't recognize him. But he would reap the rewards of retirement, share his life with his daughter and grandchildren and nurse a wife whose love and loyalty had always been a source of wonderment.

After supper, Bill turned to his housekeeper and announced,

"I'll be taking off for Boston in a couple of days. Please get my things together for a one-week trip. I'm going in to work tomorrow for the last time. I should be home by 2:00 p.m."

The caregiver was stunned and shook her head in disbelief.

Bill walked into the office at 8:00 a.m. the following morning. When word got around that he was cleaning out his desk, the precinct descended into a state of turmoil. Gallant was like the Rock of Gibraltar in the Lunenburg detachment. Lunch was a series of toasts to his health. A couple of handshaking men and teary women moved in and out of his office. By the time things had calmed down, it was 3:00 in the afternoon and Bill had yet to clean out his desk. However, by 5:00 p.m. everything was packed into two cardboard boxes. Finally, his throat tight with emotion, he carefully removed his shoulder holster with its weapon and placed them in the security vault.

Gallant arrived home to a meticulously prepared meal.

"Rack of lamb, my favorite dish! Daisy, you must have been in the kitchen all afternoon. It wasn't really necessary, but I thank you. By the way, I'm taking the ferry to Bar Harbor tomorrow. I'll stay there overnight and I'll call you from Boston on Thursday."

The next morning, Bill went into his wife's room. She lay there, glassy-eyed and staring at the ceiling. He bent over and held her.

"Darling, you may or may not hear me. I'm off to Boston. I'll kiss the family for you. I love you, my sweet."

The road trip to the Yarmouth ferry was hampered by heavy traffic, but it didn't bother Gallant. He had anticipated this and sat back and relaxed. He thought about the retirement letter he had written and kept staring down at it, lying on the seat beside him. Upon arrival at the terminal, he parked the car and stood awhile beside a mailbox, the letter in his hand. He finally reached out and dropped it into the slot.

It was a beautiful day in spite of a dismal forecast. The ocean was calm, and Gallant relaxed by the stern rail, filling his lungs with the cool sea air. When the ferry was about an hour out of Bar Harbor, he reached down for his briefcase and carefully removed Phyllis Maitland's holstered pistol, the leather ammunition pouch holding thirty or so cartridges, and the ammunition clip. He held them in his hands for a few moments and then flung everything overboard into the foaming wake. He knew very well that at the instant the items disappeared from view, his career as Inspector William Gallant of the Royal Canadian Mounted Police, had come to an end.

***

On Thursday morning, Gallant sat at the breakfast table in Boston with his daughter, son-in-law and two granddaughters. The little ones competed for his attention, and he soon found himself eating breakfast with both girls on his lap. His son-in-law commented,

"Inspector, now that you're retired, will we see more of you? I've got a great little fishing boat you'd enjoy."

"Son, don't call me 'Inspector' anymore, I'm just plain old Bill Gallant. I no longer merit the title."

Hazel interjected,

"C'mon Dad, once a Mountie, always a Mountie; you often told me that."

"Hazel, there was once an old Hebrew philosopher by the name of Maimonides. He maintained that the deadliest of all sins was the one where a person 'does the right thing, but for the wrong reason.' I've never committed that sin, Hazel, but I wonder what Maimonides would have said if I told him I did the opposite . . . I did the wrong thing, but for the right reason."

The phone rang, and Hazel passed the receiver to her dad. The retirement letter that Bill had written had a profound effect on Les Howland, his boss and close friend. Howland's reaction was expected.

"Bill, I finally tracked you down. Your housekeeper gave me your number and I hope I'm not intruding. I got your letter yesterday afternoon. You shocked me. After tying up a complicated case, you go ahead and retire. Why, Bill, why? Is there a health problem?"

"Not at all, Les, but thanks for your concern. I should have handed in my weapon a few years ago, but at the time, if you recall, I just couldn't accept the diagnosis of my wife's condition, and I guess I was in a state of denial. I felt that retiring and caring for her meant I was acknowledging her illness. And you know me, I'm a stubborn old goat."

FIFTY SIX

The following Tuesday morning, Phyllis Maitland sat at the breakfast table in her girlfriend Janice's home in Halifax. The uncertainty of what to expect from the RCMP investigation made for long, sleepless nights. She was mentally exhausted and decided to visit her friend, hoping a change of scenery would ease her mind. Janice brought in the morning paper, took out the obituaries and handed the first section to Phyllis. Phyllis stared down at the headline story.

POLICE MAKE PROGRESS: RCMP AND INTERPOL INVESTIGATE DOUBLE HOMICIDE; BANKER MISSING

"RCMP officials today confirmed that a Halifax attorney, Anthony Manolo, and a Lunenburg businessman, Arnold Benson, were the victims in a double homicide carried out by what they believe is an international money-

laundering crime syndicate. Cayman Islands police are currently investigating the disappearance of a third person, said to be an officer of a Cayman Bank. At present they are withholding details, but unofficial sources suggest that an armored car robbery at Halifax airport a number of years ago was an important issue in the case."

"Janice, excuse me, I've got a sudden cramp."

She got up and rushed into the bathroom with the newspaper. She sat down and burst into tears, reading and rereading the news story. She turned on the water tap to drown out the sounds of her sobbing.

"Thank you, thank you. Oh my God, thank you," she cried.

She sat there, reading and rereading. She splashed cold water on her face and, making a supreme effort to act casual, returned to the kitchen. She showed the report to Janice. Her friend remarked sarcastically,

"Well, what do you know? Whoever that Mountie was who came poking around, I hope he realizes what a damned fool he made of himself questioning me and my neighbor about you."

***

Lara and Hilda watched the same news story on the evening TV news. Lara sighed.

"I guess we'll never know for sure who did Arnie in, but I for one am glad that woman I met at the cemetery was not involved. I'll probably never meet her again, but I can't help thinking that you, me and her are tied together with some invisible bond."

"Arnie probably got in trouble over money. He was always complaining to me how rich everyone seemed compared to him. It was a toss-up whether he would come to a bad end because of money or because of a woman."

"Hilda, listen, I've got an idea. I must go to Toronto and discuss an offer on the condo. I have to close up the place and bring back my personal stuff. My Chevy has been sitting in my garage for months and my dog has probably forgotten my scent. Why don't we all fly out there and come back by car? The trip back would only take about four or five days. The baby is a good sleeper, and thankfully there's no need for bottles. It could be a fun time. On the way back we could stop over in Montreal for a day or two. What do you think?"

"Do you want to travel so soon with the baby?"

"I'm not worried. I checked with the doctor. He's healthy, and he's got his food supply close by."

"Well, I'm sure Jennie would love a plane ride; the last one I took was on my honeymoon. It was very forgettable. With all the attention Arnie paid the stewardesses, I could have stayed home."

"Great, now there's something else I want to mention. Did you know that Toronto is a great place for same-sex marriages?"

Hilda sat there and stared.

"What did you say? Lara, what did you say?"

"I was just mentioning a fact. Don't get me wrong. It's not a proposal."

"C'mon, I know you better than that. Why isn't it a proposal?"

"Hey, it can be anything you want it to be. I feel so close to you, I can't imagine not being with you forever."

"Lara, that sounds like me talking. If it is a proposal, it's an unusual one. So I'll give you an unusual answer."

She got up, walked over and pressed her lips to Lara's. A long moment later, she pulled away, looked her lover in the eyes and said,

"Let's go to Toronto. We lost each other once before. I don't want it to happen again."

FIFTY SEVEN

Mavis was busy chasing Romeo out when Jim walked in. Romeo complained.

"Mr. Cabot, Mavis doesn't appreciate my humor. She's kicking me out again."

"Romeo, did you ever think of becoming a professional comedian? I once had a friend who did well as a stand-up comic. Of course you'd have to improve your material. You can't go on forever telling Newfie jokes. Some Newfoundlanders may take offense. They're arguably the nicest people in the country. It's a shame the way we disparage them."

"Mr. Cabot, I like kidding around with Mavis 'cause she's a Newfie. But I got lots of other material. Listen to this . . . there's these two rednecks sitting at a bar in Kentucky; after killing a dozen beers, one says to the other,

"Bubba, if I went to your house now, made love to your wife and she had a baby, would you and me be related?'

"Bubba rubs his chin, thinks a bit and then says,

'No, but we'd be even.'"

Quiet, conservative Jim burst out laughing.

"Romeo, you should take my advice. Somewhere out there, an opportunity is beckoning."

"Yeah, Romeo," Mavis chimed in, "I often meet your mom in the supermarket and she's wondering when and if you're ever going to move out."

Jim took his usual table at the rear. Mavis eventually came over.

"Any news from Toronto? I haven't heard a thing from Hilda. I wonder how they're managing with the kids."

"I wouldn't worry, sweetheart." Jim slipped his arm around her waist. She leaned over and gave him a long kiss on the mouth.

"I shouldn't have done that, now I won't be able to work."

"It's fine with me, I'd love to have you all to myself."

She squeezed his hand, leaned over and whispered in his ear,

"It's been almost a week, I'm getting lonely."

"Tell you what, it's going to be warm tonight, so let's sleep on the boat. What do you say?"

"Fine with me. I'll be through about six. Do we eat here?"

"No way. I'm taking you over to Mario's for a quiet dinner. I'm in the mood for lobster and you know something, why don't we bring Danny with us? He rarely has a restaurant outing, and I know he loves lobster. I think he'll enjoy it."

"Jim, you're a special man. Here we were, under each other's noses for years, and nothing came of it. We have our kids to thank for all this. Hilda's choice of a partner for me was a hell of a lot better than the one I made for her."

"You're not alone. When I think back over the years, I could have been a more sympathetic and understanding father to my daughter. I was always trying to give her advice. Thank God they love us in spite of our errors of judgement. That old cliché "The road to hell is paved with good intentions" certainly applies to us."

"Not at all, Jim, not at all," she countered. "Clichés can be disputed, and I'd certainly dispute that one. I believe the road to hell is paved with bad intentions. Jim, every act of kindness or compassion is preceded by a good intention. True, good judgement and timing may be lacking on occasion, but that's irrelevant. Human beings behaving in a sincere and civilized manner toward each other do so because of good intentions."

Jim stared at her for a long moment and smiled.

"Mavis, you'll forgive me, but a raunchy old college professor of mine who often used off-color language once described his own aging process as follows:

"I've reached a point in life where my interest in the opposite sex is mainly what a woman has between her ears rather than what she has between her thighs." Mavis, maybe it's happening to me. I'm in love with your mind. The more you speak and the more I listen, the more your intelligence impresses."

"God forbid," she laughed. "I hope that is *not* happening to you!"

***

Mrs. Mario always welcomed them as friends rather than clients. She was especially delighted to see Danny.

"Goodness, Mavis, Danny's taller than you. He's a fine-looking young man."

Danny bowed his head in embarrassment.

"Yep, the customers are crazy about him."

"We do have the lobster special this evening. They're nice big ones too."

"For sure," Jim interjected. "Lobster all around, but it must be up to your usual standards, because Danny here is our lobster connoisseur."

It was an excellent meal and a delightful evening. Danny participated in virtually every aspect of the conversation. Down syndrome may have robbed him of a certain sophistication but he more than compensated with his inner warmth and sharp observations. On the way home, he surprised them with a remark.

"I know you sleep together on the boat."

Mavis was taken aback, but Jim responded immediately.

"Yes Danny, your mom and I love each other very much and we enjoy being together."

"Mr. Cabot, when two people really love each other, I think it's O.K. if they sleep together."

Mavis offered,

"Danny, Mr. Cabot and I are soon going to be married. I was going to save it as a surprise, but I might as well tell you now."

"Mommy, that makes me happy. Mr. Cabot, I like you, and I love Lara."

They pulled into the driveway. Danny kissed his mom goodnight, shook Jim's hand and thanked him for supper. As he crossed the porch and opened the door, he was bowled over by Boxer,....ending up in a wrestling match with the little dog.

"Goodnight, Danny," Jim and Mavis shouted as they turned and headed for the marina.

FIFTY EIGHT

Mavis awoke in Jim's arms. The heat was oppressive and they had kicked off the blanket during the night. Her fingers glided slowly over Jim's naked body. Sunbeams shone through the port holes and danced on his bare chest. The boat rocked gently to the sound of tiny wavelets caressing the hull. Chirping birds, searching for food scraps, walked about on the cabin roof, their tiny feet making clicking sounds. Mavis released herself slowly from Jim's embrace, reached for her cell phone and dialed Toronto.

"Hilda, it's me. What's going on there? We've had no news."

"I'm sorry, mom, we've been busy for four days straight. First of all, the kids are well. Jennie is having a ball. We took her to the Science Centre and she had a great time at the kiddies' displays. The baby is fine. He gets a little cranky at times, but Lara gives him the breast and he's O.K. Gawd that kid has an appetite! He's going to be at least six feet two."

"How's Lara doing, what's happening with the condo?"

"We've been packing non-stop, but we're getting help from the concierge in the building. Lara's discarding lots of stuff, but the rest will have to be shipped. As far as the condo is concerned, it's not sold yet, but the agent has several serious prospects. Lara's leaving all the furniture, so that'll make things go smoother."

"You're not staying till it's sold, are you?"

"No, mom, the agent will look after it. She's a close friend of Lara's. Both she and her husband are agents. Lara's known them for years and gave them power of attorney. We're starting our trip back in three or four days. And by the way, I've got a big surprise for you. I'll save it till we get back."

"Really? Don't tell me you've had an in-vitro too."

"No, but I must admit it's crossed my mind."

"I'm calling from the boat. We slept out last night. Jim is still asleep. Maybe he'll call Lara later."

"Great. Hey mom, you really sound perky; hope you didn't get seasick from all that rockin'."

"Hilda, you're disgusting. Goodbye."

***

"Lara, I just spoke to my mom, they're on the boat, still rehearsing for their honeymoon."

"Stop your speculating, they're old enough to do anything they like. Marriage is going to be great for them. Now, can I change the subject and talk about us?"

"Sure, go ahead; is our big event still on for this week?"

"I confirmed with the pastor. He'll meet us at his chapel on Thursday at 2:00 p.m. My agent friend and her husband will be witnesses. Jennie'll be our flower girl. We'll get her a giant bouquet of roses."

She approached Hilda and held her close.

"Sweetheart, any second thoughts about what we're about to do?"

"Lara, I've never been so certain about anything. I love you forever."

***

Mavis called a cab and headed downtown to the café. A while later, Jim awoke and was surprised at how late he had slept. He dressed quickly and drove over to Arnie's for breakfast.

"You walked out on me this morning," he complained to Mavis.

She came over to him and whispered,

"You really slept in, Jim. Looks like I tired you out last night. Anyhow, I gave you a warm good-morning kiss, but it didn't even move you. I hope you were dreaming about me."

"To be honest, I never dream. But if I ever start, I promise it'll be about you. How about joining me for breakfast?"

"Sure, if you don't mind the usual interruptions."

Jim relaxed with the morning paper. Mavis joined him a few minutes later. No sooner had she sat down, his cell phone rang. It was their real estate agent.

"Jim, some good news; the offer is officially accepted. The house is yours. Their agent is in a hurry to close the deal. He can arrange the signing for the day after tomorrow at around two p.m. We're going to meet at the agent's office. His name is Grant, and he's in that two-story office building directly across from Maritime Bank."

Jim was elated.

"Great! Everything will be taken care of, and we'll be there on time."

He grabbed Mavis's hands.

"The house is ours! We get the keys in a couple of days."

***

Lara was breastfeeding the baby when a call came in. Hilda picked up the phone.

"It's for you, it's your dad. Sounds like the news you were waiting for."

"Hi Dad, I'm going crazy waiting to hear. Did the offer go through?"

"Lara, first of all, tell me, is everything O.K.? I haven't heard from you for days."

"Everything is fine, I'll fill you in later. Tell us about the house."

"Well, it looks like Mavis and I will soon own three homes. A minor disagreement was resolved at our last meeting with their agent. He just called and we're scheduled to take possession in a couple of days""

"Dad, I'm so happy for you both. That house is a real jewel. You're going to love it. When do we start moving you in?"

"Hold on . . . Mavis and I have made a decision, a rather old-fashioned one."

"Let's hear."

"Well, she wants me to carry her over the threshold of the new place. Now, you know as well as I that an honorable man can't do that unless he's married to the woman."

"Geez, I shouldn't be surprised. You're really special."

"Well anyhow, we figured we'd furnish the place with mostly family heirlooms and let you girls help yourself to everything else. Then we'd have a small nuptial ceremony in Father McCrory's study. We want it quiet and low-key. We're doing it out of respect for two other people, and you know very well who they are."

"I understand. By the way, while we're on the subject of Father McCrory, I've already registered at the parish for a proper baptism in a couple of weeks. I'll give you the details when I get back. I gotta go now and help with the kids. What great news! Congratulate Mavis for us. Tell her to call Hilda again when she has a chance. Love you, dad."

***

"Mavis, what do you think?"

"I can't think. This is too much. Everything is happening so quickly. It would be nice if we were wed and all the excitement was behind us."

"I have some thoughts I want to share with you. The launching party that the girls threw was greatly appreciated, but frankly, all the hoopla and attention were sort of overwhelming. I'm just not that kind of person. Don't misunderstand, I was happy, but a bit uncomfortable. If we're going to have a marriage service, I know the girls will want to take over, just as they did with the boat party. I'd like to know what you think about another celebration like that."

"You know, we're not a couple of starry-eyed youngsters. I'd prefer something quiet, dignified and brief. Between my Hilda and your Lara, I don't know if that's possible."

"I agree. They won't be back from Toronto for almost a week. Do you know what I'm thinking? That smile tells me you know what I have in mind. Let's go ahead and do it on our own. We can even arrange it to take place in Father McCrory's study, exactly as you described, quiet, dignified and brief."

Mavis thought for a moment.

"Jim, I'm wondering how the girls will handle it. It's an important event in their lives too. Would they feel left out? Would they be resentful? Perhaps we should discuss it with them beforehand."

The next day, just before noon, Jim made a cell phone call to Lara.

"Hi Dad, how are you? How's Mavis?"

"Everything's O.K., what's happening?"

"I've got some interesting news for you. I was going to wait till we got back, but I might as well tell you. I can't go into details 'cause we don't want to be late, but we're on our way to a wedding."

"Who's getting married, anyone I know?"

Yes, Dad. You sure do. Your daughter! I'm getting married." There was silence.

"Dad, are you there?"

"Yeah, I'm here. At least I think I'm here. What's going on?"

"Dad, same-sex marriages are legal in Canada, and Ontario is very accommodating. I know you're crazy about Hilda, and this afternoon she's going to become your daughter-in-law. Dad, can we talk later? I'm really late."

"Yeah, yeah, we'll speak later. Good luck."

Jim closed the cell phone and sat there, dumbstruck. He was seated behind the wheel of the jeep, parked near a busy intersection but completely oblivious to the traffic noise.

'Why God? Why? What's happening? What does this all mean? I want so badly to fit into my daughter's world, but I seem to be out of synch with everything and everyone. The world has passed me by and left me way behind. I can't keep up with the changes. People are different, and so are their ideas. Events take place so rapidly that when I reach out and try to make sense of them, they slip away.'

Jim was unaware how long he was parked. He eventually picked up his cell and called Mavis.

"Hi, it's me. I just spoke to Lara. We have to talk tonight. I'll go into details later, but you should know this . . . I want you to be my wife before the girls return."

FIFTY NINE

It was closing time, and Mavis sat with Jim at their table at the rear of the café.

"Mavis, I know I should be happy because Lara is happy, it's just that I can't wrap my brain around the situation. You may think I'm upset because we weren't in Toronto for the event, but it's not so. I'm just trying to sort out the logic of it all. When you're an engineer, you deal with finite things. You deal with numbers and make scientific conclusions that are mathematically correct. Everything makes sense, everything fits."

"Jim, logic is not a science of numbers, it really depends on character and individual values. Things which seem logical to the girls may not be to us. What makes it even more complicated is that the limits of logic keep expanding in unpredictable directions."

"Fine, then I would really like to go ahead with the original plan. A quiet ceremony in Father McCrory's study. Georgie and Alma could be witnesses. The girls have their hands full with the two children. It would be a blessing to relieve them of a bunch of little nonessential tasks like a reception, guests, food. What do you say?"

"At this point, I'm inclined to agree. If you really feel that way, then let's just go ahead."

Mavis got up, moved over to Jim's chair and sat down in his lap. She put her arms around him and pressed her face against his.

"You make me so happy. You have no idea how much I love you. I know now why I never looked at another man while I was alone. I was waiting for you. I think it was ordained."

"Well, I never believed marriages were made in heaven, but whatever or whoever brought us together is fine with me."

Mavis called out to the chef.

"Georgie, can we talk for a moment before you leave?"

Georgie came in and sat down.

"Is everything O.K.?, any problems?"

"How would you like to cater a wedding?"

"Who's getting married?"

"Jim and me, and probably within the next two or three days. We'd like you and Alma to be witnesses. It'll probably take place over at St. Christopher's."

"Well, I can't say that I'm surprised. Wow, congratulations. You mean I'll have an opportunity to show off my cuisinier talents for a marriage reception?"

"No reception, just marriage vows, a little champagne and perhaps some of your world-famous hors d'oeuvres. We want to keep it simple."

***

"Mavis, close up and leave your car here. I'll drive you home and pick you up in the morning."

They parked in her driveway and held each other close.

"Tomorrow we have a new home, and the day after, a new life. I'm looking forward to carrying you across the threshold."

She gave him a warm kiss and whispered,

"Never mind the threshold. I won't let you stop until you carry me upstairs to our bridal suite."

"That's what makes you so exciting. I never know what's going to come out of your beautiful mouth. Let me give you a goodnight kiss and send you off to bed. We've both had a long day."

The next afternoon, Mavis and Jim became the new owners of 609 Montague Street. Jim, the old-fashioned traditionalist, wouldn't allow Mavis to visit the new house until after the wedding ceremony. The following day, a notice was placed in Arnie's window.

Closed Tomorrow
Mavis and Jim are Getting Married!

A small, intimate ceremony took place in Father McCrory's rectory. Alma served Georgie's hors-d'oeuvres, and Jake opened a few bottles of his inexhaustible supply of champagne. Mavis looked stunning in a floor-length dark green gown. Alma wore a royal blue pant outfit that matched her dark blue eyes. The big surprise was Danny. He arrived wearing a beige worsted suit and a stylish neck tie.

"Danny, where and when did you get that outfit? You look like Gentleman's Quarterly. Gosh, the last time you looked so elegant was at your First Communion."

"Mommy, Mr. Cabot took me shopping and we wanted to surprise you."

She walked over to Jim, and embraced him.

"Thank you, Jim....thank you for you. I'm the luckiest woman in the world."

The couple were united in an inspiring ceremony. Georgie's football ring was Jim's wedding band, and Alma's graduation ring graced Mavis's left hand. The priest was at his best. As usual, he concluded with a blessing of his own creation.

"Dear Lord, we implore you to bestow your blessings upon the bodies and souls of this loving couple standing before us. Make their path through life an easy one, and may they enjoy good health and the eternal friendship of all who love them. May the Lord Jesus Christ cast His light upon them and bring them eternal peace."

Later, after several glasses of champagne, Father McCrory commented,

"People, this is indeed a pleasant change from the regular routine. My study is usually a meeting place for condolences and family arbitration."

The wedding party dispersed around 5:00 in the afternoon. The newly married couple drove to their home and parked in the driveway.

"Jim, let's just sit for a while. Let me absorb what's happened to us. I feel I've been on a roller coaster ride, a magic carpet where reality has taken a holiday, and I'm afraid it may all be just a dream."

"My dear Mrs. Cabot, it's not a dream, and if you're suffering from an overdose of happiness, just relax and enjoy it. It's not toxic, and the side effects are beneficial. You deserve every bit of it."

"O.K., Jim Cabot, let's go in. After all that champagne, I hope you can carry me without falling."

Jim unlocked the door and picked up his bride in his arms. She held him firmly around the neck while he climbed the stairs to the master bedroom. She gave him a lengthy kiss on the mouth and slowly released her arms as he bent over and placed her gently on their marriage bed.

SIXTY

Georgie handed the phone to Mavis.

"Mom, how are you? We just got in from Toronto. What a trip! We're all coming down to the café to visit after lunch. Is Jim going to be there?"

"He'll be back around 3:00. We're anxious to see you. How was the wedding?"

"I'll reveal all this afternoon. Love you mom, see you later."

Jim arrived before the girls. Mavis held him close.

"My loving husband, how do we announce our marriage to our daughters?"

"Same way they announced theirs to us, in a matter-of-fact, off-hand manner."

"They're going to be shocked, Jim."

"Yup, but sure as hell not as shocked as we were."

"Well, let's play it by ear. If you're still upset, please try not to show it. Let's all get off to a good start."

The girls and the children made a noisy entrance around 4:00 p.m. Alma kept Jennie occupied out front while Mavis ushered everyone else into the kitchen. She embraced Lara.

"You're now my daughter-in-law. I couldn't love you more even if you were my daughter."

Jim embraced his daughter, then turned and reached over and held Hilda.

"The same goes for me, Hilda; God bless you."

Mavis pleaded, "Tell us about the service!"

Hilda took Lara's hand and held it in her lap.

"Mom, it was beautiful. The pastor was a kind, sincere gentleman. He spoke to us for over an hour discussing all aspects of our relationship. He didn't rush into the ceremony. It was lovely and inspirational. Jennie was our flower girl; she carried a bouquet almost as big as herself. The ceremony was over in a few minutes, and we're both happier than you can imagine."

Lara interjected,

"Folks, we decided to go through with this before leaving for Toronto. We felt more comfortable about having it happen in a cosmopolitan city rather than in a small town. We thought it would make less waves. Please don't be upset. We opted for something private. Considering the circumstances, we agreed it was the right decision. Look at our marriage bands; aren't they gorgeous? Can you believe we bought them at Walmart?"

The room burst into laughter.

Mavis got up from her chair and embraced the newlyweds.

"Girls, we're so happy for you. You're a great couple, and even more important, you'll be wonderful parents.

God bless you both. Now Lara, let me hold that gorgeous son of yours."

Jim went over and hugged the girls.

"How can anyone question your decision when we see the look of joy on your faces? You know, Mavis and I are equally happy, and for the same reason. We were married by Father McCrory a couple of days after you."

Lara jumped up and embraced her father, her head buried snugly in his neck.

"Oh Dad, finally, finally, thank God!" She turned her attention to Mavis.

"I've always loved you, but I love you now more than ever. You've made my dad so happy."

Hilda hadn't uttered a word. She was in shock. She sobbed and pressed her face against her mother's, tears of joy running down her cheeks.

"Girls, you know we've been living in the new home for a couple of days. Dad hasn't stopped doing odd jobs around the place. Danny's so excited, and he's been a great help. The place already looks nicer than before."

Jim observed, "it's even better built than I first thought. It's in great shape for an old home. And by the way, we're planning a small housewarming party."

"Dad, we're having the baptism next week. Let's have your party immediately after. I'm finalizing arrangements at the church tomorrow."

That evening, they visited their parents in their new home. Lara called her father aside.

"Dad, I need your opinion, your advice and perhaps your permission."

"That's quite an order. So how can I help?"

"I'm naming my son after you. He'll be James Cabot the Second. I hope you approve?"

"Lara, it's indeed an honor, and I thank you."

"Now dad, there's something else. I want the boy to have a middle name. Can you think of one?"

"Not off the top of my head, and I'm not sure if my dad's name would be suitable. He died at a young age, and I hardly remember him. For some reason Aunt Cora never wants to talk about him, and to this day, I don't know why. Do you have any names in mind?"

"As a matter of fact I do. Uncle Jake has been a close friend of the family and has helped us over the years. He once jokingly commented he's often been a best man but never a bridegroom. But he also mentioned that fate made him a frequent godfather but never a father. Dad, what do you think of the name Jacob?"

"I remember my Bible pretty well. If I recall, he was an important guy, the last of the three Patriarchs, and the grandson of Abraham. He's revered in all three major faiths."

"Father McCrory asked me about a middle name, and that's what started the discussion. He told me Uncle Jake's full name is Jacob Murray Allen. Another thing that surprised me was that he almost convinced Jake to go into the priesthood. Jake declined at the time. Evidently he was getting over some personal problems but was concerned he could be rebounding off them into a monastery as a form of escape."

"Well, Jake is a kind and sincere person, Lara. I always liked him and never knew anyone who didn't."

***

The next morning, Lara met with Father McCrory.

"Father, I discussed the naming of the baby with Dad. He readily agreed to James Jacob Cabot. I haven't told Jake yet because I want to surprise him."

"That's quite an honor you're bestowing on him. I'm sure he'll be pleased."

She approached the priest and took a firm grip of both his hands. She stared at him for a long moment and then in a soft, clear voice, said,

"Father, I want to share something with you. Celia was not only my mother, she was my friend and confidante. We never kept secrets from each other. I'm certain both she and Jake would appreciate the naming. Father McCrory, do you realize that both my son and I are in this world because of you?"

The priest was momentarily taken aback. He offered a smile and a knowing nod; it was a moment of remembrance. He wrapped his hands firmly around Lara's and raised them to his lips, kissing them gently.

"Yes, my dear, and perhaps that's why I'm known as 'Father' McCrory." He embraced her and looked into her eyes for a long moment.

"Lara, you're a carbon copy of your mother. God bless you. I know for certain that Celia is looking down at you and smiling."

***

When Bill Gallant returned from Boston, he went directly to his wife's bedside, leaned over and kissed her expressionless face. He sat by her and described how their beautiful granddaughters had grown and how their daughter and son-in-law were in good health, living comfortably and inquired frequently about her wellbeing. The housekeeper summoned him to a sumptuous welcome-home meal.

"Inspector, your office sent in a pile of mail. I put it all on your desk."

After supper, he began opening the letters. A particular one caught his eye. Unlike the others, it was pink and shaped like a greeting card envelope. Gallant's name and address were typed on it, but the envelope bore no return address. He opened it and removed a plain pink card. It was a three-word message in a woman's handwriting,

God Bless You

Gallant pondered the card's origin as he replaced it in its envelope. He then caught sight of the postmark.

CHARLOTTETOWN, P.E.I.

The End

A GLOSSARY OF NAUTICAL
& OTHER TERMS

AGE OF CONSENT: Until 2008, the age of consent in Canada was fourteen. It became sixteen thereafter.

ANCHOR RODE: The line attaching the anchor to the vessel. It can be made of virtually any material: rope or chain or a mixture thereof.

AUTOPILOT: A device which, when pre-set to a particular direction, will steer the vessel without the need of a person at the helm.

BALLISTICS: The science of matching a spent bullet to the gun from which it was fired.

BEARING OFF: A term used when a vessel under sail turns away from the wind.

BELOW OR ABOVE: Refers to below deck or on deck. Another meaning refers to the course one sails when meeting an obstruction, be it a mark or another boat. Above would signify toward the prevalent wind and below away from the wind.

BENDING ON THE SAILS: An old nautical term that means attaching the sails to the halyards and hauling them up in preparation for sailing.

BILGE BOARDS: The floors of cabins in smaller vessels often consist of tight-fitting rectangular wooden panels. Usually, when one or more are lifted, the mechanical and electrical components of the boat are revealed, i.e., batteries, compressors, bilge and water pumps, etc.

BLUENOSE: Was the name of a Canadian fishing and racing schooner built in Lunenburg, Nova Scotia in 1921. For seventeen consecutive years, it won international fame as one of the fastest sailboats of its size in the world, The name originated from a term used to describe New England planters who moved into Nova Scotia in the late eighteenth century. To this day, Nova Scotians refer to themselves as Bluenosers. The vessel's image first appeared on the Canadian fifty-cent stamp in 1929 and on the Canadian dime in 1937. The original boat was lost on a reef near Haiti in the Caribbean in January of 1946. A replica was built in Lunenburg in 1963. In the year 2010, it was dismantled, rebuilt and relaunched in 2013. Thousands of tourists the world over visit the vessel each year at its anchorage in Lunenburg, N.S.

BOOM: A support that is anchored to the mast and extends parallel to the deck and toward the stern of the vessel. The horizontal bottom (foot) of the mainsail is attached to it. The boom is usually made of the same material as the mast, i.e., aluminum, wood or carbon fibre.

CABOT TRAIL: A picturesque and mostly coastal road that encircles Cape Breton Island; the island is situated off the northern coast of Nova Scotia.

DUI: Driving a vehicle while under the influence of alcohol or drugs.

EASING OFF SHEETS*: Releasing the lines attached to the sails in a controlled fashion, usually when turning away from the wind.

FURLING GEAR: Devices that are attached to the sails that allow easy reduction and storage of a sail.

FORESTAY: See STAYS.

GALLEY: The kitchen on a sailing vessel.

HALIGONIAN: A native of Halifax.

HALYARD: A rope or line that hauls up or lowers a sail. If the sail is too heavy to handle, the halyard can be attached to a winch* on the deck.

HAULING IN SHEETS: Tightening the lines connecting the sails. This can be done by hand or with the assistance of a winch.

HEEL: The degree to which a boat will lean away from the wind; it may depend on the force of the wind, the set of the sails, the design of the hull or the manner in which the helm* is being handled.

HELM: The steering wheel on the vessel that controls the rudder and direction of movement. The terms "easy" or "light" helm indicate that the vessel's intrinsic design allows steering with minimal effort.

JIB: A triangular sail attached to the forestay that helps provide wind power for forward movement of the vessel.

JIB SHEET: The line that controls the shape of the jib. It's attached to the free end of the jib near the deck and is controlled from the cockpit.

JIB HALYARD: A rope or thin steel cable attached to the top of the jib; it serves to haul it up to it's proper height adjacent to the mast.

MAINSAIL: A sail attached to the back of the mast and to both ends of the boom. It's controlled by the mainsheet.

MAINSHEET: The line that runs from the boom into the cockpit. It controls the angle at which the mainsail meets the wind by adjusting the position of the boom.

MARINE LIFT: A large, four-wheeled vehicle shaped like an inverted U. It backs into a position that envelops a boat. Two or more canvas straps are placed beneath the hull, and the boat is lifted by hydraulic forces or electric power. The marine lift is backed up over an appropriate pier, and the boat is lowered into the water.

MARKS: (Racing) Temporary buoys, usually brightly colored, used for delineating a course for the racing vessels to follow.

MEMORIAL: The term used by locals to describe Memorial University and/or the hospital in St. John's, NFLD., an educational institute and teaching hospital of high academic standing.

MOOSEHEAD: A popular brand of beer in the Maritime provinces.

MOUNTIE: An abbreviated term for a Royal Canadian Mounted Police (RCMP) officer.

NEWFIE: A person who was born and raised in Newfoundland. It became Canada's tenth province in 1949. Their history goes back almost 200 hundred years to the Irish Potato Famine of the 19th century. These hardy folks became fisherman on the Grands

Banks off the coast. They are a kind, brave and generous people who have erroneously been categorized as naive, being the butt of jokes over the years. Newfoundland's Grand Banks were known as Canada's fishing grounds for centuries. It has, in recent years, evolved into a high tech province and its Memorial University houses an outstanding faculty of medicine.

PEGGY'S COVE: A picture-perfect area about twenty-five miles southwest of Halifax on the eastern tip of St. Margaret's Bay. Peggy Point Lighthouse (1914) is a fifty-foot-high structure, recognized world-wide, and that attracts thousands of tourists annually. Its image appears at the beginning of each chapter of this book and at the top of the front cover.

P.E.I.: Prince Edward Island, one of the Maritime provinces. The capital, Charlottetown, was the venue for the signing of Confederation, the document that created Canada, in 1867.

PORT AND STARBOARD: Left and right. If another vessel is to the port or starboard bow, it is to the left or right and ahead; if it's on the port or starboard quarter, it is to the left or right and behind.

RCMP: The Royal Canadian Mounted Police, whom Canadians refer to as the Mounties.

SHEETS: A nautical term for the ropes or lines that control the shape of sails.

SHOTGUN or HORN: During sailboat racing, refers to the three shotgun blasts signaling the raising of a different colored flag: a preparation shot, a warning shot and a shot signaling the start. These are followed by another blast announcing the first boat to cross the finish line.

SPINNAKER: A large, colorful sail flown from the bow of a sailboat to capture the wind coming generally from the side to the rear area of the boat.

SQUALL: A line squall is a rapidly moving but usually short-lasting storm of heavy wind, rain and limited visibility.

STAYS: Lengths of stainless steel cabling attached from the top or sides of the mast to the hull of the boat in order to support the mast. When attached to the bow (front) of the boat, it is known as the forestay. When attached to the stern (back) of the boat, it is known as the backstay. The steel cables joining the mast to the either side of the vessel are known as side-stays or shrouds.

ST. JOHN'S: Newfoundland's largest city and its capital

ST. JOHN: New Brunswick's most populous city, however Fredericton is the capital.

STEPPING THE MAST: Placing the mast of a sailing vessel upright into its proper position on the deck of the vessel.